WITHER

Book I

D1520197

The Withered Series

DISCARD

Also by Amy Miles

THE AROTAS SERIES

Forbidden
Reckoning
Redemption
Evermore

IMMORTAL ROSE TRILOGY

Desolate

THE RISING TRILOGY

Defiance Rising
Relinquish
Vengeance

Captivate

In Your Embrace

WITHER

Book I

AMY MILES

The Withered Series

Copyright ©2014 by Amy Miles Books, LLC.
All rights reserved, including the right of reproduction
in whole or in part in any form.
Also available in eBook format.
First paperback edition 2014
ISBN-13:978-1502915757
ISBN 9781310018978

ONE

The lights flicker overhead.

I stare up at them, listening to the intermittent hum of the dying fluorescent bulbs. The dim lighting provided by the backup generator casts an eerie glow on the room. Shadows multiply in the corners. My head twitches at every sound, sure that I hear someone creeping down the hall.

A chill has fallen on the room. The fever that arrived earlier this morning has left me flushed and weakened. I didn't tell the nurses. Part of me didn't want to bother them. Another feared that they might throw me out onto the streets like the rest of *them*.

Condensation from my breath hangs before my mouth and a slight tremor has begun in my lips. My fingers cramp as I tighten my grip on the pistol in my lap and try to ignore the aches in my legs.

The gun, though small and easily managed, feels foreign in my grasp. It's not mine. I took it off a man on the street early this morning. He had four rounds in his pocket and several lay scattered around his body in the gutter. A single hole in his right temple, and the splatter of crimson on the brick behind, told me that it wasn't stealing. Not really.

Halos of light dot the window before me, fires set long before the sun fell behind a blanket of heavy cloud. Intermittent gunfire to the east sounds muffled through the panes of glass. That is the direction I saw the men coming from.

Dark shapes converged on the frozen hospital lawn less than half an hour ago. Twenty of them in total. Some appeared slighter in stature. Others large enough to wrestle with a grizzly. All seemed focused on the fortified front doors of the building.

It was only a matter of time before the survivors came for us.

Unease settles heavily in the pit of my stomach as I glance toward my mother lying in the bed beside me. No expression. No movement, apart from the slow rise of her chest. Her lips hold a tint of blue, but that is nothing unusual.

I draw my legs up into the chair, crossing them before me. *What are they waiting for?* They must have found a way inside by now.

The scraping of chairs and rapid staccato of voices from down the hall faded away a few minutes ago. I watched from the door of my mother's room as those few remaining nurses and doctors emptied the waiting room in an attempt to barricade the doors. It won't last long, but maybe someone can get away.

I should have left the city when the turmoil first began. The news anchors tried to spin their pretty little lies about how the military had everything under control, but all you have to do is look out a window to know that things are falling apart faster than anyone could have predicted. Anarchy rules the streets.

Little more than a week ago, the world sank right into hell. I just stood by and watched it. What else could I do?

People started disappearing. Tanks and armored military trucks rumbled through the streets at all hours of the night. Quarantines were established and martial law was enforced for a time.

I could have escaped before the rioting really began, before the gangs formed and innocent blood painted the streets of St. Louis. It would have been easy to slip by unnoticed, clinging to the shadows. One person can hide well enough. But I didn't leave; I stayed...because of her.

I remember the last words my mother ever said to me: "I love you." But it didn't matter. Those words could never be enough to wipe away years of bitterness and resentment, to heal neglected wounds left to fester, to right a thousand wrongs. Too little. Too late.

A part of me will always wish that I could have said *I love you* back to her just that once and actually meant it. That my final words were not spoken with animosity. We never had that sort of relationship though. Never hugged. Never flopped down on the couch just to chat. We were co-habitants in an empty home, and even then I hardly ever saw her. Not until the accident that left her void of speech, thought or any other basic human activity.

I don't really know why I came each day to visit or even why I stayed. It's certainly not out of loyalty. Maybe some twisted part of me just wanted her to wake up so I could get some closure. Maybe I'm just that messed up. Or maybe I was scared. Scared of being truly alone for the first time in my life.

A loud crash from beyond the door wrenches me from my thoughts. My messy curls tumble from their ponytail as I whip around. Several more crashes follow in rapid succession, each one making me jump.

"We need to turn out the lights," a nurse says from down the hall.

"No." Another speaks up. Her words pinch with fear. "They already know we're here."

The sound of shoes pounding against the floor reaches me as someone hurries past my room. I hear the stairwell door burst open.

"Wait! What about the patients?" A lengthy pause, interspersed with loud bangs against the double glass doors that have sealed us in, makes my pulse race. I cling to my gun as I wait for the answer.

"It's too late for them."

I close my eyes as a single tear curls down my cheek. *I don't want to die. Not like this.*

A scream echoes down the darkened corridor as a rain of glass pings against the tile floor. My palms feel sweaty. I draw the gun into my chest and lift prayers heavenward, though I find myself unsure of how any god could allow such horrors to happen.

Pushing up from my chair, I cast a glance back at my prostrate mother and then slowly draw open the door to her private room. Through the narrow crack I spy men scrambling to climb over a pile of chairs, tables and couches stacked chest high at the far end of the hall. Their clothing is wrinkled and smeared with dirt. Their beards and hair unkempt.

Blood slickens the floor as the men rise to their feet among the shards. The large glass doors behind them stand open with a gaping hole smashed through. A chained padlock swings useless near the floor.

I shudder as the men survey the hall. Dark circles shadow their eyes. Their gaze is wide, crazed. I know that look. The look of desperation.

My heart hammers against my ribs as two men break off from the pack and leap onto a middle-aged nurse fleeing into a patient's room. Her scream is shrill as she slams against the wall. Fragments of drywall fall to the ground as the unconscious nurse slumps toward the floor.

The men begin tearing at her. I'm paralyzed with fright as I watch them raise bloodied hands to their lips. They lick their fingers, ingesting the warm, sticky fluid. Its bright red stains their beards.

They have gone mad!

Closing the door, I lean against it and cover my ears as new screams replace the nurse's. A fog settles over my mind, combating the adrenaline pumping through my veins. I shake my head, fighting to remain focused.

Sweat clings to my brow and upper lip. My head feels light and airy as I scold myself. *Keep it together!*

Two doctors remained behind to care for the patients too ill to evacuate or those left behind by family members too afraid to enter the city to collect them. Four nurses stayed as well, though I'm sure more than one has fled.

The screams grow louder. I hear grunting down the hall as men try to break through a door. The wood creaks and groans, finally giving way.

"Grab the supplies," a man yells. The sound of hurried footsteps quickly follows. By pressing my ear against the door I can tell they are getting closer.

Doors bang open and patients' rasping pleas echo in my ears. A tremor works its way through me as I scan the room. My mother lies on the bed before me in a catatonic state. The bathroom is to my left, but it's too small to hide in. The window to my mother's right is made of thick glass. Even if I could break through it, I would never survive the five-story fall.

I rush toward a supply cabinet and tear open the doors, rummaging through bandages, cleaning supplies and bedding. The handful of bullets I scavenged this morning won't last long. I will need a backup weapon if I have any chance of surviving the night.

Nothing! I bite my lower lip as I realize there is nothing of use. Not a scalpel. Not a pair of scissors. Not even a needle.

The lights flicker again overhead and then fade for the last time, plunging the room into darkness. I clasp my hands over my mouth to suppress my scream as something large slams into the door of the room. I hold my breath and wait for someone to enter, but the door remains closed. I clutch my gun to my chest.

Think, Avery! I pound my fist against my head. *I can't shoot them all.*

My lips quake as I sink down the wall, covering my ears to muffle the horrific clamor of death that fill the once peaceful ward. The sounds of butchering diminish, but the hammering of my heart in my ears only increases.

Another loud bang against the door sends me scuttling on my hands and feet toward my mother's bed. The steady droning hiss of her breathing machine catches my attention. The battery pack must have kicked in when the generator failed. They will hear it!

It is inevitable. This hospital wing is easy pickings.

The fifth floor is for long term care patients like my mother. Some are recovering from strokes or heart attacks. Others, like my mother, are trapped in a coma with a slim chance of ever waking again. None will put up much of a fight.

I should have left when I had the chance.

"Check that one," a man commands. It sounds as if he's only a couple of feet from my door. I stifle a squeal and dive head first under my mother's bed. The mechanics of the lift tear at my sweater. I suck in and squeeze. Sharp metal jabs at my back, nicking my flesh.

"You been in here yet?"

My breath catches at the nearness of a feminine voice. *Please don't come in here. There's nothing for you.*

"What are you waiting for? Check it out!" the man yells back.

The back of my jeans rips as I thrust my leg under the bed just before the door swings open, spilling the dim glow of a dying flashlight through the entrance of the room. The feet that approach are small, definitely those of a woman. She walks with a hint of a limp as she approaches the bed.

I bury my face in my arms, focusing on small half breaths. *They will see me. They'll know I'm here!*

"I found another live one!" she shouts. I can tell by the way her soles screech on the tile that she calls over her shoulder.

I stare through thick strands of ginger hair as two people arrive in the doorway. The sounds of screaming have died off, replaced by an eerie silence.

"She one of them?" The work boots on the right pause as they reach the end of the bed.

I don't want to die, shuffles on repeat like a skipping song in my mind. I reaffirm my grip on the gun, pointing it at the feet before me, but I don't pull the trigger. Not yet. I wait for a good shot.

"Does it matter? She's still breathing," the woman responds.

"Ignorant cow!" A wad of phlegm lands on the floor near her feet. "You put any of *their* blood in you and you're as good as gone too. Ain't you learned nothin' yet?"

The woman pauses less than six inches from my head. The tips of her shoes tread on the hem of my sweater. "Fine. Then who's gonna check her?"

A gravelly laugh from the doorway sends chills down my spine. "Why do you think I sent you in here?"

"Aw, come on Rhett. You know I had to check the last one. I still have nightmares over that. I swear that thing looked at me!"

The man at the end of the bed steps forward. I hear gargled cries as the woman's heels lift off the floor. "You know the rules. Bring back the goods or don't come back. If I tell 'em you ain't done your part, whatcha think they're gonna do to ya? Hmm?"

I hold my breath as she drops to the ground and stumbles back a few paces. I imagine her rubbing her throat as she takes several rasping breaths. "Haven't we got enough yet?"

I long to reach out and draw my sweater back but I dare not move. Even in the dim glow of the flashlight they might see my hand.

"No." The clipped response from the doorway sends my heart plummeting into my stomach. "There ain't never gonna be enough."

Enough of what? What is it they want?

"Get it done," Rhett commands and turns. "And don't ya forget that tubing when you're done."

The door swings closed, leaving me trapped with the remaining man and the shaken woman.

"I can't do it, Pete. I don't have it in me tonight." There's a few seconds of silence then a grunt of displeasure. "If you don't do it, it'll be both our hides on the line. You heard what Rhett said. I'm not sleeping outside camp again. No way. The streets are no place to be after dark," the woman says, inching backward.

The waiver in her voice doesn't surprise me. I've seen what's on those streets. Murderers, rapists, and things far worse...the Withered Ones are out there.

"I know how you like it," she lowers her voice as she coaxes him. Sounds to me like she's done this before. "That feeling of power you get. I've seen it in your eyes."

I hear the sound of scratching from above and wonder if this man has a beard as well. "Yup."

"So you'll do it for me?" The man approaches the bed. His silence unnerves me. Why doesn't he answer? "Take her out, Pete."

For as long as I live, I will remember those words and the sounds that follow. Pete moves faster than I could have imagined. He plants his feet and lunges forward. I hear a deep thud, followed by tearing.

I cover my mouth and clamp my eyes closed as the man growls overhead, pounding his fists. Bile rises in my throat as a sharp metallic scent fills the air. Tears roll involuntarily down my cheeks. *I'm sorry!*

There is nothing I can do to stop my mother's brutal slaughter. We may not have seen eye to eye, but no one deserves this.

Pete shakes out his hands at his sides, sending blood splattering against his pant leg and floor. Moist warmth flicks against my arm and I bite down hard enough on my lip to draw blood of my own.

My silent scream is guttural, soul shaking at the sound of splintering bone. It echoes off the walls, ringing in my ears. I feel faint as I imagine Pete snapping my mother as easily as a child cracking a dried twig.

I wait for the blood to begin pouring down from the bed above but it never comes. The man and woman fall still on either side of me. I hear the sound of pattering, like water against a bathroom sink.

What is happening? What are they doing to her?

Though a tremor seizes me, I clamp down and force myself not to move, terrified of making a sound. Of being discovered. Of listening to my mother's heinous death.

Do something!

Summoning a courage that I don't feel, I kick out at my mother's IV pole. It crashes to the ground, making the skittish woman jump back. Her flashlight clatters to the ground. "What was that?"

"Ain't nothin' but you, woman."

One glance at the far wall reveals my illuminated shadow.

Shit!

I grab the man by the ankle and yank with all my might. He cries out as his footing shifts and topples to the ground. A waterfall of blood rains against the white tile floor and splatters my face. I gag at the feel of its warmth trailing down the ridge of my nose. I crawl out from under the opposite side of bed, spitting my mother's blood to the side as I head for the woman.

The walls look like a scene from a horror movie. Blood splatters trail down the once cheerful yellow walls. The floor is slick as I rise. The back of my sweater dampens with blood as I press back against the bed.

My hand shakes as I lift my pistol. The woman glances toward the door, her frizzy auburn hair a sweaty web around her forehead. I tighten my grip on the trigger and aim, noticing a split second before I pull the trigger that there is an angry rash on her left cheek that trails into the neckline of her coat.

The shot is deafening. My hand recoils and I almost lose my grip on the gun. The woman's eyes widen with disbelief as she slides down the wall, clutching the crimson stain blooming along her abdomen.

A swell of pride floods through me but is lost as I am slammed from behind. I watch the tile rise up to meet me in slow motion as a crushing weight settles over me. I turn my head, narrowly avoiding crushing my skull against the floor. My gun clatters out of my hand as my breath is stolen away. Dark spots encroach the perimeter of my vision as pain nestles into my ribs.

The man's breath is hot and rancid, puffing against my ear. His long, beefy fingers curl around my arm, pinning me to the floor. "Get Rhett," he yells toward the woman. "This one's coming with us."

I listen to her moan behind me but don't hear any footsteps of retreat. My cheek mashes into the cold porcelain, grinding bone and flesh. I kick and flail, useless against his weight.

"Get off me!" I screech, trying to claw free, but the blood coating his arms makes it impossible to get a firm grip.

Panic floods through me as I'm reminded that I'm not some super badass chick with ninja skills. I'm just a girl from the wrong side of the tracks who wishes she could be.

"I'm gonna cut you nice and slow," he breathes into my face. The scent of cheap alcohol on his breath is nauseating. From the corner of my eye I notice black spots dotting his lips. "Gonna make you beg as I gut you."

I fall still, terrified of the glee I hear in his voice.

The sound of gunfire from down the hall startles both of us. I take my one shot and slam my head back, grateful to hear a sickening crunch. His grip eases slightly.

"Bitch!"

An elbow to his side and a swift kick once I wriggle forward leaves the man enraged. He cups his nose as blood pours from it, trailing into his matted beard. My nails crack and splinter as I claw along the slick floor, fighting to dig into the grout lines for leverage.

The door stands open wide before me. The wounded girl must have escaped. A blood trail leads into the hall, illuminated by the fallen flashlight. I look around in search of my gun, but it is lost to shadow. Clambering to my feet, I use the sheets on my mother's bed to rise.

My stomach falls away when I find my feet and discover the horror this man bestowed on her. Blood no longer pumps through the wide gash in her neck. It pools in the dip of her collarbone. Streams of crimson trail down what little is left of her arm to soak into the sheets. Her chest is concaved, shredded as if by a rabid animal instead of a human. Much of her flesh lies in ribbons. The muscles in her neck have been flayed open by a knife. Her eyes are open, unseeing but looking right at me.

"Oh, God!" I press my hand to her neck. The warmth of her blood between my fingers and the reality of her brutal end makes the room spin.

One thought slowly surfaces as Pete lumbers to his feet behind me. *He has a knife.*

Looking back over my shoulder in the fading light, I see him wavering on his feet, searching the floor. A glint of silver near his feet makes my heart stop. *Please don't see it.*

He raises his gaze toward me as he grabs his nose and realigns it. A look of unadulterated fury stares back at me and I realize he won't need the knife to hurt me.

I leap to the side a second before he strikes, pushing off from the wall and spinning just out of reach. My cheek smacks into the supply cabinet when I misjudge my escape. I steady myself and fling open the doors, desperately tossing the contents at the man as he turns on me.

Pete bats them away and closes the gap between us. I bring a bed pan down over his head when he takes a swipe at me, but it doesn't faze him. "Got you, girlie!"

His hand wraps around my arms as I try to run and yanks me toward him. I shriek and rake my hands down his arms, feeling his flesh curl under my nails. His arm snakes around my neck, choking off my air.

Gunfire pings against tile and metal in the hall but my attacker is lost to the disturbance. I hear screams in the distance as I fight against his grip, kicking and landing punches that seem useless. *I'm going to die! Oh God, please don't let this happen!*

My screams become strangled gasps as he shoves me to the ground. His legs wind around my waist, stilling my fight. He slams my temple against the floor and stars light up the room. Blood trails down from my eyebrow, stinging my eyes. I feel the impact again and again but am helpless to stop him.

"Pretty girl gonna die," he crows in my ear as he reaches over my head. My eyes bulge as the cold steel of his blade presses to my cheek. His free hand squeezes my throat.

The light in the room fades and lethargy seeps through my body as oxygen is withheld. My hands fall to my sides. I can feel myself slipping away.

"Please." I stretch out my hand for help as a pair of boots pauses in the doorway and turns toward me.

A gunshot at close range makes my ears ring. The grip on my neck releases. Warm matter sprays my face. A foul sludge slips between my lips as I fight for breath. The approach of footsteps sounds like the march of a giant in my wounded ear drums.

Large hands roll me onto my side, pushed away from my motionless attacker. I claw at the floor as my lungs expand, gasping in air. A distorted voice calls to me but I can't make out the muffled words. The only thing I can think of as I stare bleary eyed up at my savior is that their face looks wrong, elongated and grotesque. Then the darkness takes me.

TWO

A fever consumed me sometime during the night. Frequent delirium makes me hear voices that do not exist. They come and go. Sometimes they are nothing more than a whisper. A part of me almost wishes they are real. Then I wouldn't feel so blasted insane!

Nausea impairs my every thought as I roll my head to the side to vomit. I hear it splatter against the floor, but I don't open my eyes. The retching will only grow worse if I do.

There is nothing left in me now. What little food I scavenged from the hospital vending machine is long gone. My stomach twists in knots, spoiled with acid. Every inch of my body aches, though it is not the pain that makes me ill, but the scent of rot that hovers around me.

I feel as if a steel wool pad scratches against my throat when I swallow between heaves. Warm blood seeps from newly opened wounds along my eyebrow and hairline. With each retch, pain lances through my eye.

"Easy," a voice soothes. Large hands wrap around my arm, supporting me until my stomach empties.

I'm delirious again. Now there's a body to go with the voice. I spit and wipe at my mouth, disgusted by the foul aftertaste, then fall back against the sweaty cushion beneath my head.

Pressing my stomach, I will the cramping to ease. Slowly it does, though I have no real sense of passage of time. Only misery and darkness. No light brightens the back of my eyelids. No sound reaches me as I slip in and out of a restless sleep.

Sometime later, a damp cloth presses against my temple and I lean into the coolness. My fever has begun to ease. The aches are not nearly so pronounced. The relief I feel subsides when the cloth is removed. I hear splashing water and covet the refreshing chill until the cloth returns a moment later, only to find a sense of clarity beginning to return. I become aware of my surroundings. The scent of musk and disuse. Sounds of gunfire in the distance. Muffled shouting. The tremor that rises from the floor with each explosion in the distance.

When I hear the steady inhale and exhale of breath nearby, I tense. Fingers press against the inner flesh of my wrist and I bolt upright, suddenly convinced of the fact that I am truly not alone.

"Stop." The grip on my wrist tightens as I buck against the stranger. "I'm not going to hurt you."

"Get off me! Someone help me!"

A bright light flares beside me, shining up to the ceiling. I blink several times to adjust to the light as the man grabs my chin and forces me to come eye to eye with him.

"I'm not going to hurt you," he repeats with emphasis, his gaze never wavering from mine.

My hair falls in sweaty clumps over my face but fails to hide the man before me. His face is angular and his jaw strong. His dark eyes are narrowed with concern. A heavy growth of stubble lines his face, revealing a hint of sandy blond amongst the darker brown of his facial hair. He doesn't look much older than me. Maybe twenty-two or twenty-three at the most.

His grip eases on my arm but he does not pull away. I can tell he is waiting, but for what I'm not sure. Maybe for me to freak out and start wailing like a banshee in fright, or to attack and attempt to flee. As the room begins to spin around me, I realize I'm in no condition to do either.

"How are you feeling now?"

I ignore his question. "Where am I?"

"You're safe."

"Is anywhere safe now?" I croak, rubbing at my throat. The flesh is tender, bruised. I wince, remembering the hands that sought to end my life only a short time ago.

"This place is, for now." I watch his eyes shift, rising to survey the damage I did to my eyebrow. Judging by the burning sting, I have reopened several new wounds. "Are you done fighting me?"

I can tell that he knows I'm barely staying upright. I am weak, far too weak.

"Don't really have much choice," I grumble. My shoulders ache as I hold myself aloft on the edge of a futon, sitting only two feet above a small, matted shag rug that may have once been a neon green. Now it is splattered with drying remnants of my earlier bouts with nausea. Heat floods my cheeks as I look away.

"I tried to clean you up the best I could. You had me worried for a while. I didn't think your fever was going to break."

At the mention of my fever, a chill sprints down my spine. Am I infected too? Am I going to turn into one of the Withered?

Determined not to think about it, I notice for the first time that he is concealed in fatigues. There is a Marine emblem on his chest. "Are you a soldier?"

"Yes, Ma'am. Stationed out of MCRD PI. " I stare up at him. That term means nothing to me. "It's a Marine base located in Parris Island, SC. A recruitment training facility."

"South Carolina?" I rub my forehead. My headache is getting worse and my head feels too heavy for my neck to support, but I fight against my weariness. I try to focus, to keep him talking until I can determine his motives. "How did you end up here in St. Louis?"

His expression darkens. "We were reassigned a couple weeks back."

He says nothing more, but he doesn't have to. Everyone knows the government screwed up. This man, and countless others, were sent in to clean up its mess. What the government actually did was cause a shit storm that no one was prepared for.

"How bad is it out there?" I turned off the TV long before the rioting took out the power plants. I didn't want to know. Didn't want to hear their version of the truth. The problem is no one really knows what the truth is any more. Guesses, opinions, and speculation are all there is now. I guess in the end it doesn't really matter.

He looks away from me. His adam's apple bobs once and then again before he speaks. "It's not good. We've lost New York, Chicago, LA and countless other cities."

"To *them?*"

"The Withered Ones?" I nod, not liking the way the term rolls off his tongue with hardly any emotion. "No. They are the least of our worries."

I'm not sure I agree with that.

I always prided myself in being prepared for anything. Self-defense classes at the Y and a few street brawls have helped me to survive on my own, but nothing could have prepared me for this. The term 'zombie apocalypse' has been thrown around. It's sure as heck not like what I was expecting!

I spent hours at the hospital window watching the Withered Ones shuffling along the streets, waiting for the gruesome deaths to begin, but they never did. They show no signs of hunger, or anger or fear, but I stay clear of them. I keep waiting for this to all be some sick joke, and one of them will finally decide I look tasty and take a chunk out of my arm.

Glancing toward the window, I strain to hear the moans on the street below. They are out there. The Withered Ones, or Moaners, as some people like to call them now. A fitting name I guess.

"You thought I was becoming one of *them*, didn't you?" I ask after a moment of silence.

"Of course you did," I answer for him to fill his continued silence. How could he not? Fever is the first symptom. Anxiety. Unexplained pain. Rashes. Delirium. Sudden lowering of temperature to abnormal levels. Tremors. Loss of memory and a dozen other symptoms that pop up randomly. The end result is always the same...an all-consuming nothingness left in this disease's wake.

I saw it at the hospital. Watched the woman in the room across the hall from my mother slip into an eerie void. She was among the first, the doctors said.

I don't know what they did with her. She just disappeared from the ward. Maybe the military disposed of her. Maybe the doctors did. After more people started turning I stopped asking questions.

He slowly nods and lowers his gaze so that his face is shielded by the brim of his camouflage hat. "Then why did you stay?"

"I had to know for sure. Turns out it looks like you just have a common flu bug, mixed with a heavy dose of shock."

What would he have done with me if my fever hadn't broken? Would he have left me here, locked in this tiny apartment to slowly starve to death? To beat endlessly against the door in a futile attempt to escape?

"Would you have put a bullet between my eyes?" I ask. He clears his throat and turns his face away. His posture grows rigid and I have my answer. "Nice to know."

I look at the room around me and notice black garbage bags duct taped over the windows. Peering around the flashlight beam beside him, I spy used candles on the tabletop, their wicks long since spent. The furniture in the studio apartment is a hodge podge of garage sale finds. Nothing matches. Nothing smells good.

Glancing at the ceiling, I discover that all of the air vents are covered. Torn drapes are shoved into cracks around the window sills. "You think it's in the air, don't you?"

When he glances back at me, I notice something akin to appreciation in his gaze. "We don't really know what caused the mutations."

"You don't know or you don't want to say?"

His gaze narrows. "I don't know."

I nod slowly. "Someone does."

"Perhaps."

"Still. Better to be safe than sorry, huh?" I spy an upturned gas mask on the floor and realize the distorted face I saw before passing out was this mask, not a person's face. I wonder why he has it. I've seen a few people darting around the streets with clothes tied around their faces. Maybe the military knows something they don't deem important enough to share with the general public?

Growing up on the streets, I've learned a thing or two about reading people. You have to when you don't have anyone to watch your back. I can't get a firm read on this guy. He stays near enough to express concern for my well-being but not so close that it alarms me. He is cautious in how he moves, always slow and deliberate when he shifts, and always watching me.

Trying to appear as if I have a choice in the matter, I lower myself onto my elbows. The trembling in my arms eases minimally. It is only a matter of time before I'm forced to lie down completely.

I glance at the array of pill bottles, wet cloths and cleaning supplies accumulated on the floor nearby. "I guess this means you don't intend to hurt me."

I watch his face for any hint of deceit but see none as he shakes his head. "No, Ma'am. That's not my way."

He backs farther away, but remains in a crouch not far from my feet.

"What's your name?" I ask. Reaching near to the point of exhaustion, I push up on the cushion and struggle into a fully seated position. I feel better upright, more in control, though the tilt of the room reminds me that I'm far from well.

"Cable."

I wait for him to continue but he doesn't. Instead, he falls silent. "You got a last name to go with that?"

"Cable is just fine, Ma'am."

"I'm no Ma'am." I brush the hair back out of my face. My cheeks still feel warm and my skin is sensitive to the touch. "You can call me Avery."

When he cracks a small smile, his closed off expression softens. "I knew an Avery once. Had a mean streak to go with that flaming hair of hers."

The wistful tone in his voice makes me wonder. "She steal your heart?"

He laughs, lowering his head as the memory grips him. "Nope, but she managed to swindle me out of a few days' worth of lunch money, though."

"You got taken by a girl?"

It's hard to imagine a man of his build being fooled by a girl, no matter his age. "Nah. She was a pretty little thing. I practically offered it up to her."

I cross my legs before me, enduring a moment of lightheadedness. I clamp my fingers around my knees and focus on breathing until it passes. When I open my eyes I see that he's watching me again. "How long have I been here?"

"Four days."

"Four days!" My voice cracks with surprise as I jerk upright. "How did I...what did you...what the heck?"

Cable pushes back into a seated position, drawing his legs inward to balance on his tailbone. Reaching over, he grabs a wet cloth from a bowl sitting beneath a cluttered end table and hands it to me. I press it to my forehead, grateful for the refreshing coolness. "That guy back at the hospital messed you up pretty bad. You were in a lot of pain when I first brought you here so I gave you something to help you rest. You needed it."

"I wasn't sure I was going to be able to carry you out of there." He pauses to swallow as his gaze grows unfocused. His lip curls with disgust. "I've seen my fair share of death in the past, but never anything like that. That was twisted stuff."

I curl inward, crossing my arms over my stomach in a protective huddle at the memory of my mother lying in a pool of blood, open and exposed like a carcass left on the side of a road. Nothing can erase that memory from me. Nor the sounds, smells, or fear that I experienced trapped beneath her bed.

I won't miss my mother. Not in the normal sense of the word, at least. She was familiar, even if she wasn't always wanted. Still, she deserved better. "The blood wasn't all mine."

He nods and takes the cloth as I offer it back to him. He dips it several times in the water and then hangs it over the side. "I figured that out once I got you back here and cleaned you up."

I run my hand down my bare arms and grow still. I was wearing a sweater at the hospital.

Glancing down at my chest I see that I'm wearing a black tank top that is two sizes too big. My breath catches as I lift the blanket spread across my lap and discover that my legs are bare. "You undressed me!"

He points to his right and I follow the direction of his finger. There, hanging on a makeshift drying line are my sweater and jeans; torn and soiled but far less bloody than they should be. "You went into shock. I had to get you warm."

"So you thought *removing* my clothes was the best option?" Heat races up through my neck and settles into my cheeks as I splutter.

His expression is impossible to decipher but I would bet money that there's a hint of humor buried within his dark eyes before he looks away. "You were wounded and covered in blood. I had to know the extent of your injuries. I'm sorry if this has caused you some discomfort."

"Discomfort?" I run my hands through my hair, wincing at the ratty tangles. On a good day my thick curls are hard to manage. I can only imagine how terrible I look now. "My mother was torn apart while I laid beneath her, listening. I was attacked and bludgeoned nearly to death only to wake to find some complete stranger has been groping me in my sleep. What's to be uncomfortable about?"

He uncrosses his legs, only to cross them once more before pressing back his shoulders and then raising his chin to meet me face to face. No hiding. No backing away. "I told you, that isn't my way."

Tucking the blanket under my arms, I tap my finger against my leg, trying to get a read on him. Nothing about his posture screams guilt. No flush in his cheeks. He doesn't look away, as if embarrassed by his actions. In fact, he seems rather confident that he did the right thing, despite my accusing glare.

"Alright. Let's say you are legit." I concede for the moment. "That you only want to help me. Tell me what happened at the hospital? Why were you there?"

There is a clank of metal and notice dog tags hanging from his neck as he stretches out his long legs before him. A ridge of muscles appear in his thighs as he flexes. "The hospital was overrun. My team and I did what we could to neutralize the threat."

"Your team?"

He nods. "I had nine men under my command. We were on patrol in the area when we saw the lights go out. It didn't feel right, so we decided to check it out. Once we saw the front doors busted open we knew it was a raid."

Despite the headache trying to drill a hole through the back of my head, his words bring clarity as I focus on this new information. I always did like trying to solve puzzles.

"Do you know why they were murdering people?" He grasps his dog tags and slides them back and forth across the chain, stalling. "Cable?"

He looks up as I use his name for the first time. His jaw flinches but he quickly averts his gaze. Even from his profile I mark the pinch of his with disgust. "They were on a blood run."

"A blood run?" I lean my head back against the cushion. The muscles in my neck ache from remaining upright for so long. I need at least another's day of rest to recover. "What's that supposed to mean?"

He leans toward me, his lips slightly parted before he speaks. "How much do you know about what's been going on?"

I shrug half-heartedly. "I'm not really the news watching kind of girl."

"But you know about the deaths?"

"Duh." I rub my forehead, wishing I could search the apartment for a bottle of pain meds. This headache is a real bitch. "That one was kinda hard to miss."

I don't know many of the details, only what the news anchors told us before the stations went down. What started out as a few bizarre deaths up north led to a country-wide outbreak.

Death swept across our land like a biblical plague. Entire families wiped out in mere days. The body counts rose faster than could be controlled. Mounds of decaying bodies were tossed in landfills, mass graves set alight to prevent the spread of the disease. Hospitals were overrun. All the while I stayed close to my mother's room. I knew she wouldn't get sick, not with being stuck in a clean room for risk of contracting a normal infection, but what about me? I figured the best place to be was smack dab in the hospital if I started to feel sick.

The government gave us hope a month ago when they released the MONE vaccine. Our cure for an unnamed enemy. Our redemption.

They were wrong.

The injection that was meant to bring us salvation brought us a living hell. The death count may have slowed but the human mutations began within days of the drugs release. The government scrambled to figure out what went wrong with the vaccines but it was too late. Whatever this new pathogen was, it spread quickly through the populace.

The Withered Ones were born. People not alive but not entirely dead either. They walk the streets, unblinking and unaware. The only sound they make is a rasping moan and shuffling footsteps. A zombie, for all intents and purposes, but nothing like we anticipated. I think I could have handled the flesh eaters a bit better.

That was the beginning of the end.

Desperation and the remaining scum of the earth rule the streets now. It was inevitable that gangs would form, prisons would empty, and evil would assume control, but the true fear runs much deeper. In the early hours of the night, you are left to wonder *am I next?*

I suppose that is another reason why I didn't run when things got bad. Where can I hide when our deadliest enemy may already be inside me?

"We think the vaccines triggered some sort of chemical response in those already infected with the pathogen," Cable informs me. His voice is lower now. His grave tone makes me want to hug myself and crawl back under the blankets and ignore everything outside this apartment. I tried to do that at the hospital, but the world came knocking. "I'm not sure anyone left alive really knows how it spread or even why. It hit so fast that there was no way to contain it once it spread."

"But someone must know the true source. I mean, they have a slew of symptoms to pick from, right?"

Cable scratches the back of his neck. "That's the problem. None of the symptoms are completely the same. Some seem pretty constant, like a fever, but it's different for each person. Half the time it's impossible to know if they've just come down with a cold. By then it's too late."

He rubs his hands along his arm, scrunching up the black fabric. He stares beyond me, his expression as blank as those *things* shuffling along the streets below. "There were rumors at my base. People were suspicious of government involvement. Terms like population control and terrorism were thrown around. Other people thought it might have been some crazy Middle Eastern dictator that found a way to use chemical warfare on our food supply. Others thought maybe there was a mole in the CDC that tampered with the MONE drug results."

I'd be lying if I didn't admit that I'd had similar thoughts over the past couple of weeks. I wouldn't put it past the government to be somehow involved. Plausible deniability and all that crap.

"But the Moaners started showing up after we were given the vaccine," I chime in. "Shouldn't that mean that was the cause of the mutations?"

He turns his hands upward and shrugs, shaking his head. "Could be, or maybe it was just bad luck. The CDC was working on this mystery last I heard, but that was over a week ago. It's been mostly radio silence since then. My guess is they ran out of time."

"Or manpower," I mutter, shoving my hair back from my eyes. It clings to my cheeks, plastered to my neck.

"That too." Lifting his hat, Cable rubs his hair. It's sandy blond, like the highlights along his chin, short and probably at one time was spiked but has since been matted down. "About a week ago I heard static on our comm channel. Nothing unusual, especially now, but a faint message came through that I'm not sure I was supposed to hear."

My hand falls away from my forehead. "What was it?"

"The message said 'blood is the key.' That's when the riots really began and we were called in. My guess is someone else was listening in on that same message."

I rest my head back against the futon cushion. "It's not like that message was much to go on. How could someone take those four words and create such chaos?"

"What other source of hope did they have to cling to?"

"Hope?" I snort. "How does 'blood is the key' bring hope to those lunatics out there?"

"It doesn't, but if they want people to follow them they have to pretend that it does."

"So the leaders of these gangs tell people there's something in blood that can save them and their brainless minions will do whatever it takes to get it?"

"Pretty much. That's why they hit the hospital."

I frown, thinking back to the odd sounds I heard at the hospital. "Was my attacker trying to collect my mother's blood as some sort of cure? If so, there's no way gutting her would have worked. I'm no doctor, but I'm pretty sure mixing the wrong blood is a bad thing, not to mention how easily it could be contaminated when collected incorrectly."

"Desperation drives people to crazy things, including what happened to your mother. I don't know what they are doing with the blood, only that they are rounding up survivors for it."

I heard the screams on the street, knew innocent people were being hurt, but I never dreamed they were being rounded up like animals. The idea sickens me, but a sudden idea makes me mouth fall open. "They're making their own blood bank," I whisper.

"It would seem so." Cable's hands drop to his sides, his fingers uncurling against the floor. Color flees from his fingers under the pressure. "They are systematically taking out quadrants of the town at a rate faster than we can keep up. We are low on men. Half of the guys I came here with have turned, others were mowed down. A few are missing and presumed dead."

His jaw clenches. "Before anyone really knew what was happening, they hit every gun, pawn and redneck shop they could find to stock up. They raided grocery stores for food and blew up a shopping center after they depleted its resources. Then the bastards built walls around themselves. They are shut up tight near the center of town. I lost several good men trying to breach their wall."

"How could they build walls so quickly? It's only been a couple of weeks."

An explosion rattles the window. Cable glances toward the window, his expression grim. "Like that. They blew up entire city blocks, downed buildings all around them. They have snipers on the rooftops. We try to get near them and they pick us off."

Wrapping my arms around me, I feel a shiver ripple along my spine. "Why not just drive a tank in here and blow them all to hell? Don't you have jets or something with bombs?"

"Sure." He shoves his hat back on his head. "We could do that, and risk murdering hundreds, if not thousands, of innocent men and women in the process."

I notice that he doesn't mention anything about children and figure he's trying to gloss over that fact. I appreciate that side step. I've never been one of those people who liked seeing kids get killed in movies. It's just sick.

Lowering my head, I fight to ignore the growing ache in my neck. My muscles are taut. My stomach churns as I sink a little lower. I'm tired, more so than I ever remember being. My mother used to brag to her friends that I was the healthiest kid she ever met. I can count the times I had a cold as a child on one hand. The flu hit me once every couple of years. I guess I've hit my quota for a while.

"I used to watch movies about the apocalypse," I say, placing a hand on my stomach. Even though it is empty, I fear another bout of dry heaves may be in my near future. "Thought it was kinda cool, ya know? Even with all of the death and destruction I always saw it as a rebirth, but this isn't life. It's not even surviving."

I fall silent, thinking over the enormity of what has been lost and its only beginning. Things will get worse. They always do.

For the first time since waking I become aware of the chill on the air. Cable's long sleeves are pulled low over his wrists. His pants are tucked into his boots.

"It's cold." He starts forward in response to my statement, as if with the intent of tucking in my blanket but I jerk back and he instantly falls still. "I meant it's cold in general. Not that I'm cold."

He sinks back to the floor. "They took out this section's power station last night. I don't know what they are thinking. Blow that thing up and the rest of city goes off the grid, including them."

I bite my lower lip, thinking over what he'd said about them stocking up. If anyone in this city is prepared to wait out this apocalypse it's them. "Maybe that's the point."

"What is?"

"If I wanted to take control of a city, I'd go after the essentials first: water, food, fuel and weapons. They've already done that. Now if they send people running scared, they have free reign over anything people need to survive. It's the dead of winter. When the survivors begin to starve or the next ice storm blows through, people will be forced to come to them or die."

Cable tilts his head to the side and I spy the hint of a tattoo rising from the back of his collar. "Makes sense, only I don't think there will be any dealing. Those gangs are out for blood. You can't negotiate with madness."

"Don't I know it." I rub the back of my neck to ease the pain. Multiple sites along my body ache. It's hard to tell what pain is from my recent beating or from the fever. "Did you lose any of your men at the hospital?"

"A few."

Silence hangs between us for a time, thick and impregnable. I should say that I'm sorry. Most decent humans would, right?

"Did you kill that guy that attacked me?" His gaze hardens before he nods. "Good."

"Good?" He brings his knees up into his chest and links his hands in front of his laced combat boots. Splatters of dried blood cling to the soles. "You think killing a man is a good thing?"

I shrug, trying to appear indifferent as I tighten my grip on my waist, desperate to ignore the tremble in my fingers. "He would have killed me."

"I reckon he would have. Still doesn't make it right though."

His answer floors me. Glancing toward the door, I see his gun propped against the wall. I don't know what kind it is, but it's big and mean looking. A heck of a lot scarier than that pistol I lost. "Why do you carry one of those if you don't intend to use it?"

Glancing toward his weapon, Cable frowns and looks back at me. "Why do you carry a gun when you have no clue how you use it?"

My mouth drops open. "How do you--"

"I had to put the girl down that you shot. You missed her heart by a good half a foot. Bullet went through the top of her stomach. She was suffering when I found her." He clenches his fists and looks up at me. "My guess is that you got off a lucky shot."

"So?" I bristle at the accusation in his voice. "At least I defended myself."

"Yes, Ma'am. You did, but that isn't good enough."

"I told you, I'm not a Ma'am, so cut that crap." I slant my body away from him and cross my arms over my chest. "I survived. That's all that matters now."

"No." Cable pushes up from the floor in one smooth motion. When I look up at him I'm shocked by the deep slump of his shoulders. His expression is slack, his eyes dull. "This world isn't lost until we give up on it and I'm not about to do that."

I cling to the blanket, feeling exposed and wearied by this stranger's whiplash morals. I should feel more gratitude for his risking his life to rescue me, but I don't. Not right now.

Instead, I decide to divert his attention. "Where is this place?"

"East side of town. Not far from the river." He walks to a window and peels back the curtain of black plastic. Hail pings against the window. An icy mixture streams down the glass panes like tears, cleaning away the filth. "It's not my place. I had a friend who crashed here from time to time."

"Had?"

He lets the plastic fall back into place then turns to look at me. This time it's a hard, piercing look. "Yeah. Had."

I fall silent as he glances toward the empty armchair across from me and quickly looks away. I can tell he's upset. We have all lost someone. None of us are immune to mourning, though I'll admit I'm better off than most. There's no one in my life that I care enough about to shed a tear for.

"You'll be safe here." He says after a moment, visibly shaking himself. "You need to rest up a bit before you're ready to move."

"Move?" I ask, feeling a little stupid for acting like a parrot repeating everything he says but my head still feels too light. Too unsettled. The quiver in my fingers has yet to fade and my stomach doesn't seem ready to settle any time soon. I glance down the hall and pray that I can make it to the toilet in time if I have to.

"We can't stay here. The gangs are on the move, trying to expand their territory. My orders were to secure the quadrant near the hospital and return to base. It's only a matter of time before this area is lost."

I drop my legs over the side and tuck the blanket around me. The dark blue fabric of the futon is faded and tatty, the stuffing beginning to migrate toward the floor as I shift. "What about your team, squadron, or whatever you call it? Don't you have others like you that you're supposed to be with? Some commanding officer to report to?"

I get the distinct feeling that he has no desire to speak of such things as he begins to collect his gear. I consider pressing him, almost eager to do so as payback for him getting an eyeful of me while I was passed out, but I let it go.

Pursing my lips, I push up from the futon and rise unsteadily. I almost think that I've managed to pull it off until I topple backward, my head slamming into the cushion. Cable is by my side before I am able to recover.

"I can do it myself," I growl and shove off his hand. "I don't need you."

He backs away but doesn't go far. This annoys me. "What's with you, anyways? You one of those guys with some stupid hero complex? Is that why you joined the military?"

I glimpse a hint of a smile but it fades just as fast as it appears and I realize that this guy is tough, but not as tough as he wants me to believe.

"I'm from the south, where people still have manners."

"And you're implying that I don't?"

He shrugs. "A thank you for saving your life would be the normal response."

"I said thank you." At least I'm pretty sure I did at some point.

"Did you?" The corners of his mouth twitch. "It must have gotten lost in all of that self-righteous independence crap you've been spewing since you woke."

My mouth hangs open in disbelief. Is this guy for real? Now he's going to lecture me on being a feminist? I start to whip out a comeback but he turns his back on me and heads for the door. "Where are you going?"

He pauses at the door to don a jacket. I spy the name *Blackwell* stitched into his chest and wonder if it's his name or if he grabbed the coat from another soldier. Reaching into his pocket he draws out a pistol.

"Hey! That's my gun!"

"Not until you learn to use it." He chambers a round and tucks the gun into his waistband. "I'm going for supplies and to see if any of my men made it out. Stay here and stay down. If you're quiet they won't know you're here. If you get into any trouble, just barricade the door and wait for me to get back. I won't be longer than an hour or two."

He grabs a gas mask from the table beside him and pulls it down over his head. He places the hood over his head and slips into gloves, concealing nearly every inch of bare skin. It's not the cold that he hides from, but from the invisible killer he thinks is out there.

When he opens the door, I consider asking exactly who *they* are, but I don't. I consider lying back down to rest while he is gone, hoping that he will bring water to still the unease in my stomach, but I don't. I even consider barricading the door like he said and hiding in the corner until he returns, but I don't.

I don't do anything that I should.

Later...I will regret that decision.

THREE

I grew up in a sleepy town in northern Kentucky, not too far from the Illinois border. One stop-light. One mom and pop grocery store that still had small glass jars of candy near the register. Old tree-lined streets with a tire swing dangling in nearly every backyard. White picket fences straight out of the Leave It To Beaver era. Everyone knew my name. I could trust people back then.

I miss that place. Especially right now.

Looking out from behind the black trash bag covering the grimy window of Cable's fourth floor hide out, all I hear is chaos in the night. I can almost smell the fear and smoke fumes filtering in through the glass and try to prepare myself to enter a world where people have run amok. I guess in a way I don't blame them, not after what Cable told me.

I never wanted to come to St. Louis. Of course, I never wanted my Dad to bail on us either, but as my mom used to say, "shit happens to the best and worst of us." My older brother Connor made out better than I did. Not long after we moved here he took off to be a groupie for some stupid rock band touring the east coast and I haven't seen him since. He never even knew about mom's accident. Never wasted a single minute at her bedside.

Bastard!

With a pained grunt, I force myself to focus as I slip on a navy blue hoodie I scavenged from the bottom of the closet. It smells of stale man sweat. I pinch my nose and second guess myself for the twentieth time since I stumbled off the futon. Is it really safer out there on the streets than in here? Cable did save my life. That's gotta count for something, right?

I shake my head and wince at the throbbing in my neck. It coils down into my shoulder and makes my fingers tingle.

I've always done best on my own. I'm not about to start needing people now.

Discovering a pair of jeans on the floor, I slip them on. They are loose at the waist, tight around my hips and nearly three inches too long. I sink onto the bed to roll large cuffs then pad across the hall to the bathroom.

After relieving my swollen bladder, I lean against the sink. Judging by the ring of yellow staining the porcelain bowl and the thick coating of lime scale residue on the faucet, this apartment definitely used to belong to a single guy. A very disgusting guy.

I glance at my reflection in the mirror. The skin around my right eye is puffy and angry looking, the bruising dark and extensive. I have several small bandages patching my chin and cheek, hiding some of my freckles. Dark ginger hair lies in tangles about my face, the fringe around my forehead still matted from fever sweats. My lower lip is a deep shade of purple and split down the middle. My hazel eyes are lifeless, dull. Dried blood trails the curve of my cheek. I knew I looked bad but I had no idea it was *this* bad!

"Maybe I'll look roughed up enough that no one will want to mess with me when I leave." Wishful thinking, but it's all I've got.

After digging through the contents of the medicine cabinet, I down a couple pain pills then stuff the bottle in my pocket. I grab some stomach pills for good measure then turn away from my image and limp back across the living room, feeling a sense of urgency to escape before Cable returns. He would try to stop me. I can't let that happen. Gun or no gun, I'm not waiting around.

I feel out of place in a strange man's clothes as I grab a plastic bag to stuff my jeans in. My sweater is still too damp to defend against the frigid night air. My red Chucks bear a hint of moisture but they will have to do. Even with Cable's scrubbing, blood still stains the white soles.

I pass by a stack of plates piled haphazardly with molding food on a small two-seater table and chair setup in front of a lifeless TV. Stacks of credit card bills teeter on the edge, unopened and long forgotten. I tread as lightly as possible on the wooden floor as I press my ear to the front door. The peeling paint scratches my cheek as I listen for sounds. I hear nothing beyond my own labored breathing.

Brushing my hair back out of my eyes, I take a deep breath and draw the hood up over my head. "You can do this. Hit the stairs and don't look back. Don't slow down. Just move."

I glance back at the gas mask lying on the floor. Indecision hits me. What if Cable is right to be cautious? What if I can get sick just by breathing?

My pulse dances in my throat as I make my decision and turn away from the mask. I unbolt the lock and grasp the knob, slowly opening the door to peer out. The hinges squeak loudly. A gust of frosty wind seizes me from the right and I realize the window at the end of the hall is blown out.

Gathering my courage, I release the door and hobble for the stairs. The door slams behind me with enough force to vibrate the bannister beneath my palm. I wind down a stairwell that has an overwhelming stench of mold and body odor. It seems to leach from the walls.

In the flickering of light entering through the window before me, I notice that the wallpaper to my left is yellowed and peeling. At one time it appears to have been a pale pink but it's hard to tell under the water stains that trail from the walls above. The floor is old wood, knotted and gouged over the years.

"And I thought my place was rough," I mutter under my breath as I pause on the bottom floor, breathing hard. I stifle a cry and duck low as a car alarm bursts to life. Headlights spill through the windows then disappear again, leaving me in near darkness.

Leaning forward, I wipe the window with my sleeve and peer out. Flames pour through a shop down the street. Maybe at one time it was a small pharmacy or liquor store. The fire rises high into the night, flickering against towering brick and wood sided buildings. In the light I spy four men jumping and shouting, glass bottles illuminated in their hands.

I'm trapped.

Despite the cold flowing under the wide crack at the bottom of the door, a bead of sweat trails down my brow. My head feels weightless as I pause to focus on my breathing. It won't do me any good to step out there if I'm just going to pass out.

I glance to my right and spy several cars weaving down the streets. There is debris in their way, making the path treacherous in the dark. The men celebrating down the road turn to inspect the new arrivals.

Shouts are quickly followed by gunfire. I watch in horror as a man slams his elbow into the rear window and drags a woman out by her hair, kicking and screaming. Seizing my chance, I decide to make a run for it, ignoring the shrieks of fear. The instant I open the front door I am assailed by the scent of garbage left out to rot. Cat urine is nearly as potent. I press my sleeve to my mouth and take a shallow breath as I keep to the shadows and move away from the fight, wishing that I could plug my ears against the screams and laughter.

My hoodie catches on the brick as I weave around overturned garbage bins and discarded bicycles. Suitcases spill from forgotten vehicles, their engines dead and cold. Car doors stand open like empty tombs as I pass. Apartment windows remain dark, blinds pulled and curtains drawn. I wonder if anyone has remained in this part of the town.

Gunfire up ahead makes me eat pavement. It chews at the skin of my palms and knees but I choke down my cry. That was close.

At the ping of bullets hitting metal and brick, I belly crawl toward an abandoned car. Crouching in the space of an opened passenger side door, I peek into the back seat to make sure nothing is going to leap out at me. A vacant child's car seat sits behind the driver's seat. Its pink material is splattered with flaking blood. I shiver and draw my gaze away, checking under the car to be sure I'm safe.

Screams spill out into the night, shrill and filled with terror. A man's bellow cuts off suddenly. An eerie silence follows. I clutch the seat belt for support, feeling the fibers dig into my bloody palms as I frantically look all around. Which direction did that come from?

The narrow streets and tall buildings make it nearly impossible to determine the location of the screams. A loud explosion comes at me like a rolling echo and rumbles in my chest as a fireball rises into the sky from two or three blocks away.

I trip over my laces as I get to my feet, using the car to steady me. Staggering back toward the edge of the building, I slip down the darkened alley. The sound of my shoes slapping the ground is covered by more gunfire. This time it sounds closer.

Headlights pass by, zipping erratically. A crunch of metal is followed by a steady honk of the horn. They will hear the sound. They will come.

I know who *they* are now. Cable tried to warn me about the rioters but I didn't listen. He said they were in another part of town, over by the hospital. That's at least ten miles to the west by my best guess. Have they moved into this area so quickly? Has the entire city already been lost?

I look around to get my bearings. I'm not overly familiar with this part of the city. I lived further west, towards the outskirts of town. I used to take the Metro each morning to see my mother and return long after dark. That was before the Moaners arrived.

Reaching the end of the alley, I hug the wall and peer around. This street is not as well lit and that scares me. Shadows mean plenty of hiding places for things lurking in the dark.

As I step forward, glass crunches beneath my sneakers. I look up to see that the streetlight overhead has been knocked out. My hands seek purchase on the building for support as I gulp in air. Darkness encroaches along the edge of my vision.

"Don't pass out. Don't pass out." I chant to myself for a minute until the dizziness passes. I clutch my stomach with my free hand and double over, desperate not to be sick. Grabbing the stomach meds, I fight with the plastic cap then toss back a couple of pills without looking at the dosage. I hold my breath and count. After a minute I feel better and rise.

As I push off the wall my fingers sink into a hole. I turn and trace the indentation. Six more span a two foot radius. Bullet holes.

I search the fire lit street behind me. My mind imagines all sorts of foul things crawling toward me in the dark. Evil men with lurid thoughts. Faceless people endlessly walking the streets. I listen for the tell-tale moan of the Withered Ones but hear nothing.

I look to the darkened windows all around and wonder who lived in these homes. Did they make it out alive? Did they become Moaners?

The florist at the end of my street back home was among the first to go missing near me. She used to set up her wares each afternoon and sell to the businessmen as they returned home to their wives or rushed to rendezvous with a weekend lover. Next, it was the mailman. An entire week went by without a single delivery. At first I thought it was a little odd. Then it became downright worrying. The post office never bothered to send anyone else. I haven't seen either of them in two weeks. I'd like to say that I believe they caught wind of the coming panic and skipped town, but I don't.

The kids that used to hang out on my street corner, playing chicken with taxis or dodging in and out of stores in small groups vanished not long after. Poof. Gone.

Ten days ago, during those hours in the night when I was halfway between sleep and dreamsville, I heard shouting and the rumbling of engines. Men on loud speakers directed soldiers who scurried out of open bed trucks and Humvees. They broke down doors and ransacked homes. I curled my pillow around my head and hummed as loud as I could to cover the shouting till the sun rose. When I awoke, silence had fallen over my street.

That was the last night I slept in my house alone. After that I stayed at the hospital.

The sound of glass crunching underfoot behind me makes me freeze. I strain to listen, praying that I'm mistaken. Maybe it was a cat. Judging by the smell there are plenty of those still around.

Another crunch. And another. The shuffling gait makes my pulse thump in my ears. I hear heavy breathing now, a rasping that sounds like wind funneling through a moist cloth.

"Oh God, no!"

If it were day, I would easily be able to see vacant, glassy eyes. Pallid skin. Oily, unkempt hair falling over her face. It is a her. I can sense that. Maybe it's her body odor that alerts me, or the small catch in her breathing.

The thing walking toward me doesn't move fast, doesn't show any sign of hesitation at the sound of nearby gunfire. It just keeps coming.

I back toward the light, terrified of being seen but there is no way I'm staying in this alley with her. At the exit, I pause and glance around. I'll be exposed when I step out but it's a risk I have to take.

I take three steps backward and hit something cold and solid. A scream erupts from my throat as I turn to see a man standing behind me. His cheek-length blond hair is matted with filth. A deep gash has peeled back the skin over his right eye. Flesh is torn from his jaw, revealing six teeth buried in his gum. There is no recognition of pain. No attempt to stunt the blood seeping down his face. He does not look at me, but beyond me.

His right foot is turned inward. He steps toward me and I panic. I trip over the gutter and land hard on my back side. Still he comes. Unseeing.

I have never been so close to one of them. Judging by the foul scent clinging to his clothes, he turned a while back. Perhaps as much as two weeks ago when people first started disappearing.

Over my shoulder I see the woman behind me. She can't be more than five steps away now. The stench of feces emanating from these two makes my eyes water.

Scrambling to my feet, I ignore the pain in my palms and knees as I narrowly miss the man's step. He jerks as his broken foot lands unevenly in the storm drain. His hoarse moan grows deeper as he twitches, trying to yank his foot free. I cower against the wall, watching in wide eyed disbelief as the woman emerges from the alley and walks straight into the man.

Turning to the side, my stomach heaves in response to the sickening snap of bone. The woman barrels over him. Together they fall toward the street, the man's foot now attached only by a stretched bit of skin.

I can't look. I hear the sounds of their struggle but I can't bear to see it.

A hand falls over my mouth and I rear back. "Don't make a sound."

I buck against the stranger's grasp but he holds me tight, pressed against the length of his body. He is taller than me and much broader. His hand across my mouth muffles my screams.

He pulls me backward down the street, forcing me to stumble to keep up. After dragging me a full city block, he pauses at an intersection. I can feel his torso shifting to look behind. "We're almost there."

I fight against him, digging in my heels to slow us down but he doesn't relent. His grip on my mouth shifts so that I'm incapable of biting him. His arms tighten across my shoulders, leaving me with little option to fight back.

In the distance, the Withered Ones continue to struggle against each other in the street. They don't stand up. They don't roll off each other. Instead they lay, one on top of the other and flail, like a fallen infant.

"In here."

The grip on my mouth falls away and the hand across my chest releases me. In the split second that I consider screaming for help, I am thrust into a darkened doorway and fall into darkness.

FOUR

Pain ripples through my palms and knees when I hit the floor. Dust rises up around me, choking out the clean air. I pound on my chest and roll onto my side.

"You'll get used to it," a masculine voice says from behind me. The metallic ring of the lock sliding into place feels foreboding as he steps around me. "Follow me."

"I'm not going anywhere with you," I wheeze, gripped with a dizziness that leaves me temporarily immobile. My arms quiver as I try to push off the ground but they give out on me.

"That's not the right answer, missy." An arm wraps around my waist and hauls me to my feet. I beat against his grip but my escape into the streets has left me weakened. The man chuckles and hoists me easily into his arms, ignoring my pathetic rebuff.

I feel suffocated in his embrace, though I'm not sure if the blinding heat is coming from him or me. I stare blurry-eyed at a row of tall grimy windows as we pass. The light is a stark contrast to the darkness surrounding us. I stop counting after we pass the tenth window and realize somehow I have made my way down toward the river where the old warehouses stand.

The sound of my captor's footsteps echo around me as we burrow deep into the building. It feels hollow, enormous in size. Hulking shadows fill the room. The man weaves effortlessly around them, as if he has the eyes of a nocturnal feline or a really great memory. I'd bank on the latter.

My head bounces against his chest as he ascends a set of stairs. My eyes droop with heaviness. "You are safe," are the final words that I hear as my body betrays me and my eyes fall closed.

From time to time I think I hear whispers in the dark. Voices hushed and muffled, but I can't place them. My forehead feels damp, cooler than the rest of my body. I try to turn my head but am held still.

"Don't move. Not yet."

"Who are you?" I taste blood as I swallow. My lower lip splits down the middle and I almost welcome the blood over the cottonmouth taste lingering.

"A friend."

"Yeah? I had a guy tell me that earlier today. Didn't believe him either." My lungs feel on fire as I turn toward a light glowing bright a few feet away. As my nostrils flare I detect the scent of gas.

A delicate hand presses against my cheek. "You've been ill for several days. It's lucky that Alex found you when he did."

"He didn't find me," I grunt, shoving the girl's hand away from my face. I try to peer through the light to match a face with her voice but it is too brilliant and my eyes are sensitive. "He kidnapped me."

I spy a pursing of her lips just beneath the glow of lamplight. Water splashes nearby as she wrings the cloth out that was on my forehead. "He wouldn't do that. Alex is a decent man."

"Sure. Any girl would be lucky to be snatched off the street by a complete stranger." My side feels unnaturally tight. I place a hand on my right side and feel bandages wrapping my bruised ribs. Thoughts of another healer strike me as I try to steady my breathing. *Cable.*

I'm not well, but I'm a far sight better than I was when he found me. I guess I have that to be thankful for. "Where am I?"

"Our Haven. At least that's what I like to call it." I can almost see the girl smile as she turns away. The wistfulness in her tone surprises me though. She sounds young, naïve. "Alex went to fetch you another blanket. I think your fever is starting to break finally. You should have heard Sal and Devon getting into it with Alex over you."

"Why?" I cough and wince as I grip my side.

The girl grabs the gas lantern and moves it away. I blink several times to clear away the lingering effects and finally spy the girl beside me. She is young, perhaps no older than sixteen or seventeen. Her eyes seem kind. I noticed that her fingers are slender as she presses the back of her palm to my forehead.

I raise a hand to push her away and realize the tip of my finger is sore. "I don't remember hurting myself," I mutter as I inspect the slit.

The girl's lips purse as she looks away from me. Her hair falls in greasy white blond strands over her face, hiding light dots of freckles along her nose, a much smaller patch than my own. I notice that she sits sideways beside me and roll my head to see a swollen belly pressing against her tight shirt.

"You're pregnant."

She laughs and nods. "And you're observant."

I smirk at her whiplash response. I roll my head away to look up at the ceiling, noticing uneven ceiling tiles held aloft by silver strips. I must be in some sort of office. Surely the ceiling of a factory would be far more vast and littered with exposed piping or sheets of metal roofing. Rain pings off of it from the space beyond the closed door to my right. One glance at it tells me that the door is locked. Figures.

The room I lie in is small, not much larger than the studio apartment I shared with my mother. A couch lines the far wall. Something lumpy and decidedly human in shape is curled up on the cushion. Soft snores rise and fall from the shape.

A darkened window looks out of the room. I can just make out a hint of light and remember being lifted up a flight of metal steps. I've been brought to a room that overlooks the factory below. The fluorescent lights overhead are dead. The only heat in the room comes from a small metal canister with plumes of smoke rising from within.

"Is this your home?" I shift, trying to roll onto my side but the girl holds me down. She places a pillow beneath my head and lowers a cup of water to my lips. I drink greedily. The cold fluid spills over my lips and down my chin but I don't care. I feel as if it's the first drink I've had in weeks.

"For now. Alex and Devon have been talking about moving across the river, away from the city. I overheard them talking about the dangers if we stay, but they never say anything openly to me. They all think I'm too young."

Her lips tug into a pout. I start to speak but a door across the room opens and a man steps through. Even though it was dark when the stranger snatched me off the street, I recognize him from right before I passed out.

"Well," his smile is oddly genuine for a kidnapper, "look who's decided to rejoin the land of the living."

A woman follows behind him. She turns just this side of the door and closes it. "She's awake?"

Her voice sounds clipped and breathy. I shield my eyes from the lantern light to make her out. She stands off to the man's side, her arms wrapped tightly around her ample bosom. Wavy hair sits on top of her head in a bun, curling at her temples. Large red-rimmed glasses sit askew on her nose, magnifying the crow's feet around her aged eyes.

"Finally." The girl offers me a small smile, grabs her cloth and bowl and rises unsteadily to her feet. My captor rushes forward and grabs her arm.

"I'm fine." She reassures him with a smile. He steadies her a moment longer then releases her arm. When she walks toward a cherry wood desk I notice that she waddles.

The older woman squints at me from behind her bottle cap lenses. "I still don't like it. It's not safe to invite strangers." The woman's chiding voice is one of those nasally tones that remind you of nails on a chalkboard, but a smidgen less annoying. Only just.

"Invite?" My snort turns into a hacking cough that leaves me with a splitting pain in my side. I grimace and hold my bruised ribs. "You're off your rocker if you think I want to be here, lady."

"Lady?" She bristles and adjusts her glasses upon her nose. A chain dangles down from either ear piece. I wouldn't be the least bit surprised to spy a hearing aid or two as well. "My name is Victoria, and I'll thank you kindly if you will address me as such from now on."

My captor dips down before me and smiles. "Don't mind Vicky. She's a prickly one, even on a good day." He offers me his hand in formal greeting but I don't accept. Finally he lets it drop. "The name's Alex Thornton. Pilot extraordinaire...well, at least I was until all of this crap hit the fan!"

I stare at him. He stares back, appearing unfazed by my obvious lack of caring. "Why did you bring me here?"

"You're sick." I turn to look at the pregnant girl as she lowers herself onto a chair against the wall. As she sinks back I can't help but notice she looks as if she's about to pop.

"So?"

She refocuses on her stomach. "So you needed help. We all need a little help at times."

"I didn't ask for help. I'm just fine on my own." I press on the ground in an attempt to rise. My arms quake and give out on me a second time, spilling me back onto the thin mattress I'm laid out on.

"You were saying?" Alex helps me rise to a seated position against the wall. He presses the back of his hand against my forehead and his smile fades away. "She's still a bit feverish."

"It's better than it was though," the girl speaks up. At a vicious glare from Victoria, she draws inward and falls silent. I stare at her. No girl this timid will survive in this fallen world. She needs someone to protect her from people far worse than the likes of this old bat.

"I told you time and again that she shouldn't be here." A cold voice calls from the couch. I glance over to spy a man in his mid-forties emerging from the blankets. His hair is receded at the temples and splattered with gray. "She's turning into one of *them.*"

Victoria paces back and forth in a stunted line. Two steps left then shuffles back again. She fumbles with her hands before her, almost like she longs for knitting needles to busy her hands. "I knew this was bad," she moans and pats at the wild strands falling from her poorly constructed bun. "Bad, bad, bad."

"Quiet," Alex commands. He places his hand upon my chest and I smack at him. He ignores me as he presses against my side, splaying his fingers over my bandaged ribs. When he lowers his head to press it against my breast, I whack him hard enough to get his attention.

"I am not one of them."

Alex's shrugs and draws back, leaving me in peace. "I think she's right."

"How can you be sure?" the surly man over his shoulder presses. I don't like the look of him. He seems shifty. A real loser that would give me the creeps any day of the week. I glower back at him as he gives me a once over. "Then again, she could be good for something."

"She's not coughing," Alex interrupts as I ball my fists against my lap. "No phlegm in her throat. I don't see any rash or blisters, and she's obviously aware enough to be preparing to smash your nose in, Sal. And for good reason."

He turns to look at me. "We aren't like that."

"Sure you're not." I scowl as Sal rolls his eyes. "You're just a bunch of good Christian men looking out for an old lady and a teenage girl. Nothing wrong with that."

Color seeps from Alex's face. His gaze narrows but he says nothing in response to my biting remark.

"The signs could be hidden," Victoria speaks up as I start to slide to my right. I notice she has inched closer, her fretting mounting with each step. She reminds me of a squirrel, pulsing her bushy tail to show her nervousness. Her beady little eyes don't help her case any.

I push against the floor and right myself fully. "If you think I'm going to sit here and let you people strip search me, you're nuts! Toss me back out on the street if you want. That's where I'd rather be anyways."

"It's too late for that." I turn to see a man enter the room from the door Alex and Victoria emerged from a few moments before. I try to see beyond him, to make a mental map of my location. When the opportune moment strikes I am out of here and I need to make sure I run in the right direction.

At best guess I would say the new guy is probably hanging out around his mid-thirties. His skin is dark as night and the top of his head gives evidence to recent hair growth on what I assume was once a shaved scalp. Two rolls of fat appear along the back of his head when he sinks down beside Alex to look at me. "Too much risk now that you know where we are."

"You're worried that I'm going to tell...who, exactly? My best friends out there blowing shit up?" I laugh and shake my head. "I've got no one left to tell, dude."

The young pregnant girl in the corner finds my gaze. "Don't you have anyone out there worried about you?"

"Do you?" I counter.

She looks stricken and for a moment I almost feel sorry for my jab, but the moment passes as she turns inward again. I meet the new guy's direct gaze. "Look, I didn't ask to come here. Your boy over there dragged me down the street against my will. All I'm trying to do is get a ride out of here."

"A ride to where?" I turn to look at Alex. I can almost picture him as a pilot, sitting behind the wheel in some jumbo plane, jetting off to Hong Kong or Australia. He has the look and the swagger. Albeit probably a lot less pronounced now. I bet he even rocked the aviators every chance he got. "Anywhere but here."

Alex shakes his head and pushes up to his feet. He runs his hands through his hair and blows out a deep sigh. "There's nothing out there anymore. Trust me, I've seen it."

"You don't know that. There will always be pockets of survivors."

"That's a kid talking for you." The man before me laughs. The whites of his eyes seem brilliant against his dark skin. "This isn't a movie, girl. This is real life and contrary to what you might like to think, this shit is real. People are dying beyond these walls. Some in ways I don't even want to speak about. You hit the road in your condition and you won't last the night."

"And I will here?"

He smiles. "There's a better chance of it."

"Wow." I turn my head to spit to the side. Blood tints the glob of saliva that lands a few inches from Alex's shoe. "That's real reassuring."

The man rises and walks away, heading toward the door. With his hand upon the handle he turns back. "You're gonna have to grow up fast, kid. This world is no place for fairy dust and happy thoughts."

When the door closes behind him I bark out a laugh. Alex glances down at me. "Sorry," I smother my laugh as I rely on the wall to hold me upright. "I just think it's funny that he totally referenced Peter Pan when he was trying to be all macho."

There is a twinkle in Alex's eye. "Devon has his moments. They are few and far between, mind you. You just gotta learn how to roll with his moods."

"Is that what you do?"

He grins and dips low, grabbing my arm to help me stand. I follow his lead, only because I don't have the energy left to fight. "All I can promise you for tonight is a place to sleep and a little food in your belly. Tomorrow everyone will decide if you can stay."

"And if I don't want to?"

He eases me down onto a thin sheetless mattress spread out on the floor not too far from the pregnant girl. She casts a furtive glance in my direction but says nothing as I lay my head back. Alex bends low over me. His hair looks wind tousled and I wonder if he's been outside again. Maybe to round up his next victim. "You sure you don't have someone out there looking for you, missy?"

I start to speak, to give him a definitive *mind you own business* response but I pause. Cable is out there. Will he come looking for me? Has he already given up and skipped town with his team?

Alex chuckles. "I thought so. Pretty girl like you must have someone that still cares."

I roll my head to the side to watch him walk away, knowing that my hesitation just gave him the upper hand: knowledge.

Annoyed with myself, I roll onto my side and stare at the wall. I hear footsteps from time to time, whispers in a distant space. At one point I'm sure I hear a cry of pain, but it vanishes the instant it arrives.

Victoria's mutterings drive me up the wall but no one else seems to pay her any mind. They must be used to it. After an hour I begin to wonder if she's a little bit off. Maybe her dementia is legit or maybe she's starting to change.

At some point I doze off, despite my efforts to remain alert. I don't trust Devon or Sal. I'm still on the fence about Alex and Victoria. The only one who seems halfway normal is the teenage girl nearby, but she isn't saying anything. Doesn't make a sound. Her silence is a bit unnerving since she was so chatty before. Maybe I really did hurt her feelings.

Remorse floods in as I watch her smooth her hand over her belly. Her smile is filled with expectant love and it makes me ache for that connection. I don't think my mother ever looked at me like that.

"I had a kid once," I say to the ceiling. Startled, she turns to look at me. When she doesn't say anything, I breathe out a sigh and roll onto my side to meet her expectant gaze. "The guy was a real loser, but for a while he made me feel special. Took me to a movie. Bought me ice cream. Won this ridiculously large teddy bear when the fair came to town. Small stuff that no other guy had done for me before. Guess you could say I fell pretty hard. Stupid really, but it happened."

She shifts to cross her legs before her, draping a blanket over her to ward off the chill on the air. The fire has died down with no one to tend to it. Sal fell back asleep a while ago on the couch, ignoring his fire tending duties. His snores were a welcome change only so that I didn't have to listen to Victoria's rambling.

"His name was Tommy Wainright. Had a mop of the blondest hair you've ever seen and more freckles than a spotted owl." I smile at the moment. "My little boy had his coloring but he had my eyes and nose."

The girl leans forward and props her elbows on her knees. "What happened to him?"

My smile falters and I glance down at the floor, wondering why I allowed myself to open that door again after so many years. "Found a better home and never looked back."

Her eyes widen. "You gave him up?"

I snort and shake my head, curling my knees in toward my chest. My back curves, allowing me to hug myself into a ball. The stretch in my muscles feels good now that my fever broke. "I didn't give anything up. My mother stepped in and took him from me."

"How could she do that?"

Anger, set on a low simmering these past few years, begins to bubble up within me. "I was fourteen. An unwed and unfit mother. My own mother said she wouldn't lift a finger to take care of someone else's offspring. Can you believe that? She couldn't even call him a child."

My back teeth grind. I take three slow breaths, as familiar as they are necessary. A trick I've learned over the years of living with my mother. "I only got to hold him for a moment," I glance over at her and smile, "but it was the best moment of my life."

She looks sad as she places a protective hand over her belly. "Did you ever look for him?"

"No. I never did. I couldn't. What sort of mother doesn't fight for her child?" The words catch in my throat as I shake my head. "Maybe I was too young. Maybe I would have done a crap job of taking care of him, but I deserved the chance to find out. I deserved a mother who would at least have a little faith in me."

She lowers her head. Her eyes cast downward, her lips purse. I can tell that I've made her sad.

"You never told me your name." I draw her back.

"Oh! How silly of me. I'm Evangeline." Her smile pushes aside her sorrow. This sweet girl's sympathy touches me and I'm reminded of the girl I once was, before life became a battleground. Maybe she and I share more in common than I first thought. A snap judgment gone awry. "My friends called me Eva for short."

"Nice name. I'm Avery." My returning smile is tentative but genuine enough. I wish that I could offer more. She seems like a nice girl, but nice girls always end up getting hurt. For her sake, I hope I'm not the one who does it. "When are you due?"

"I don't really know any more. I've lost count of the days."

"Are you excited?"

She falls silent for several moments, long enough to make me think that she will refuse to answer, but finally she responds. "I've always wanted a boy. Ever since I was a little girl and the neighborhood girls would torment me. They would dip my hair in honey and laugh when the bees would come for me. Boys aren't cruel like girls are..." she trails off and places her hand over her swollen belly button, "but I know they will come take him away from me."

"Who will come?" I push upright and draw my legs under me. I have no way of knowing what time it is or even if it is still night. I feel stronger than I did before, but not by much.

"The soldiers."

I blink, sure that I've heard her wrong. "Why would soldiers take your baby?"

"Experiments, of course. Haven't you heard what's going on?"

Brushing my hair back out of my face, I press my hand to my neck. Still warm but not as bad. "No," I shake my head, feeling the ache that's settled deep into my neck muscles. What I wouldn't do for a good dose of pain meds right about now I looked for my pill bottle when I awoke earlier but they were gone. No doubt Alex confiscated them after I arrived. "I've been out of the loop."

The soiled layers of her skirt brush against the floor as she moves toward me. She glances over at Victoria and waits until the older woman's snores begin again. Between the old bat's whistle snores and Sal's foghorn there's no way I'll get anymore sleep tonight.

When Eva is within a couple feet of me she pauses and tucks her skirt under her legs to seal out the cold rising from the concrete. Even at this height the cold feels inescapable. "I had a younger sister before I ended up here. Her name was Claire. Sweetest little face you ever saw." Her smile wanes. She clasps her hands in her lap. Strands of hair fall about her face, concealing her from sight. I get the feeling that's exactly what she needs at the moment.

"Mom and dad never planned to have a second child. They called it a miracle, but I think it was an accident. I never really minded that Claire was doted on. I guess a part of me was excited about the idea of my son having someone close to his age."

Tears swim in her eyes as she looks up. She wipes them away and offers me a sad, pained smile. "Before all of this I used to go pick her up from daycare. I wasn't able to go to school anymore because of my pregnancy, so I offered to be on babysitting duty."

She falls silent for a moment. New tears trail down her cheeks but she doesn't brush these away. "About two weeks ago I went to pick her up and she was gone."

"Gone?"

Pale, thin fingers fumble at the neckline of her dress. I watch as she grasps a thin chain and draws out a small golden cross. She holds it between her fingers and closes her eyes. "I could see blood seeping out from under the front door of the daycare. It stained the concrete of the first step. I didn't know what to do. I was scared but couldn't just walk away. I pounded on the door for a while but there was no answer."

She pauses and stares at her upturned hands, as if the blood was still on them. "Finally someone heard me yelling. A neighbor from down the street, I think. He broke the window and unlocked the door."

Her voice catches. "Mrs. Spurneky, the owner, fell out onto my feet when we opened the door. Her throat had been slit from one side to the other. I still remember her eyes…"

I take a deep breath as I fight not to picture my own mother's death. To remember the fear and the sounds. "Then what happened?"

Her fingers quake as she continues. "We found three other bodies. All women I knew as teachers from my sister's class. Each one had a look of shock on their face. Gun shots to the forehead and chest. That neighbor rushed out of there so fast you'd have thought there was a gunman on his tail. I told myself that he was going for help but no one ever came. He just bailed on me."

"I searched the entire building and couldn't find a single child. I'd guess there were over thirty that went there every day. All gone."

"If no one was there, then how did you know it was soldiers that took your sister?" I ask.

Watery eyes rise to meet mine. Her lower lip trembles. "I found one of their radios. Must have been left behind. I turned it on but all I heard was static. When I found my way back outside I noticed a footprint in the edge of the blood trail. I'm sure it was a combat boot."

When she falls silent this time I let it sink in. I don't want to speak any more. I don't want to hear any more tales of how messed up our world has become. How could a grown man run away and leave a helpless pregnant girl all alone? How could soldiers break into a preschool and steal children? And for what purpose?

"Did that happen around here?"

"No." She wipes at her nose. "I'm from Ohio. After we lost Claire and things started to get weird, my mom sent me to visit my Aunt Edith."

"Did you find her?"

Evangeline shakes her head. "I was on Alex's plane when we were rerouted here. When the stewardesses took off and left me alone, Alex found me. He took me in, kept me safe."

I nod, finally understanding why she is determined to see Alex as a good man. "Well, it looks like he's done right by you so far."

She offers me a tiny smile. "I should probably get some rest."

"Yeah." I lie down as she crawls back to her bed. It seems like the easier option for her rather than standing. I listen as she settles down. It only takes a few moments before her breathing grows slow and steady.

I glance toward the door, the only exit that I've discovered since arriving. Maybe I could pick the lock without anyone hearing, and maybe I could sneak out onto the street and find my bearings, but not yet. As desperate as I am to leave, I also have to be smart about it. The only reason Alex got the better of me was because I was weak and vulnerable from illness. I won't make that same mistake again.

FIVE

I miss the sun. Miss its warmth and false cheer. I miss how it chases away the shadows and almost makes me forget all of the darkness around me.

For three days I have been stuck here. Three long, endless days without any hint from the outside world.

Despite my prolonged captivity, my relationship with Evangeline has bloomed, far more than I should have allowed. Her laughter is soft, her humor sweet and innocent. For a girl who has obviously had a rough go of things recently, her sunny disposition seems like a precious trait. One that I could probably use a bit more of, if I were honest with myself.

As the days passed, I found myself protecting her from Victoria's barbs. Eva would always brush it off, claiming that Victoria didn't really mean it, but I know better. I've met women like her. Women who get their jollies by lording over younger women, pointing out their faults with the express purpose of making themselves feel lofty, still important.

During one of my chats with Eva over a lukewarm pot of bland tasting soup, I discovered that old Vicky is a retired high school science teacher. My initial impression of her was spot on. She is rude, harsh and a no-nonsense sort of person whose greatest weakness is having no clue that no one wants her around. I still haven't figured out how she fits into the group...or even how the group was formed to begin with.

Salvador Jenkins has been unofficially dubbed 'Sleazy Sal' in my books. One of those guys you know are trying to work out a situation to benefit themselves. Eva told me he used to be a used car salesman. I wonder why that doesn't surprise me.

I watch Sal like a hawk when he comes near Eva. I don't like the way he watches her as she moves. It's not an entirely lustful gaze but it's certainly an inappropriate one for a girl her age and in her condition.

Devon is a prick. No way around that fact. He rubbed me the wrong way my first day here and has been grating my nerves ever since. Whenever Alex is around, he manages to tone down Devon's strong personality, but if I stick around long enough we are gonna clash hard.

Alex is a wild card. One that I'm still trying to decipher.

Other than Evangeline, I suppose I trust Alex most. Though he's a bit cocky, he seems decent enough. He cares for Eva. I've watched how he tries to help her whenever he can, bearing her burden of chores without complaint.

A soft moan draws me out of my musings. I turn to look at Eva, rising to go to her side but she motions me back. "I'm fine. Really."

That's the third time she's said those exact words in the last thirty minutes. Each time she does, it doesn't help to convince me. The signs of her progressing labor increase. The pains started nearly three hours ago but she told no one. Only bit her lip and forced a smile. She may be sweet, but that girl's got iron in her too.

I admire her. In spite of her silent throes of agony, she remains a hard worker. Eva sits quietly in the corner of the office, peeling carrots with a glorified butter knife. Victoria sits nearby, plunging her fingernails into a potato to dig out the eyes that have begun to grow. I'm not really sure where the provisions came from, especially ones that are moderately fresh. Alex must have gone on another supply run.

I've learned not to ask questions that I have no hope of getting an answer to. That doesn't mean I'm unobservant though. I watch and wait, learning my companions' intentions.

None of the members are related. None seem to have known each other prior to the week before and yet here they are. Every time I try to speak to Eva about it she goes tight lipped and I'm beginning wonder if she wasn't the only stray Alex picked up at the airport.

Their accents don't seem to fit with the Midwest. Alex's lack of any discernable accent makes sense I guess, because he's a pilot. I'd peg him as a California guy, myself. Eva has a bit of a northern clip to her words that would match up fairly well with her Ohio lineage, but I'd bet tonight's dinner that one of her parents were from Boston. Only Devon Meeder, the Peter Pan quoting, thinks he's in charge of everybody guy who made the mistake of thinking he's the boss, sounds Midwestern. He fits right in.

It's my guess that he's the one who brought everyone here to this factory. He seems to have an understanding of the area. The real question is why he chooses to linger when he should be running. My gut tells me there is something here in the city that calls to him. I'd love to find out what that something is.

Glancing over at Eva, I watch as her fingers curl into her palms. Her breathing hitches, her eyes close as she presses back into the wall. I capture Alex's knowing gaze. He says nothing though he is just as aware of her condition as I am. Why else would he have joined in with the peeling party? That's girls' work, according to Sal.

Casting a cautious glance at the closed door to my left, I hear voices on the other side. Devon and Sal are within. In the three days since I have been here I have hardly glimpsed a sliver of sight into that room. They are hiding something. Of that I am sure.

There was never any official vote for me to join the group. No welcome party or hugs all around. I stayed, biding my time. Sooner or later the men will have to leave. When they do, I've already decided that I'm getting Eva out of here. Victoria is on her own for all I care!

With each day I grow stronger. My ribs ache less. My fever has been gone for three days and my stamina returns. If it comes down to a fight I stand a good chance against Sal and Victoria. Devon, though obviously a once polished businessman, looks like he's spent his fair share of time on the streets. He has the swagger and the large gold nugget bling on his fingers to prove it. The one kicker is Alex. I'm just not sure which way he would sway.

Sooner or later the group will be forced to move on. The food supply must be running thin. The last of the vegetables at Victoria's feet have begun to wilt. Clean water has grown scarce.

We've taken to melting some of the icicles that formed overnight in a pot near the corner.

Burst water pipes have left the drinking water in danger of contamination. I'm not nearly thirsty enough to risk it, but I'd be happy to let Sal test it for me.

A hiss of breath returns my attention to Eva. I tense, poised to rush to her side but she offers me a pained smile, shaking her head again. I ease back and count the seconds in my head. Her contractions are only five minutes apart now.

"Aren't you done yet, girl?"

I glance up to see Victoria hovering over Eva like a mother hen, too dense to see what is right in front of her thick lenses. "You'd think we had plenty of gas to spare for cooking," she clucks, jutting her chin toward the gas lantern sputtering near her feet. A small pot of water struggles to boil.

I rise to go to Eva's side, but Alex beats me to it. "Ease off, Vicky. She's not feeling well."

Victoria pushes her glasses back up her nose and shoves aside the frizzy strands of hair falling into her eyes. Her stern gaze narrows on Eva's quivering lip. "Is she sick? Did that blasted girl give her something?"

"I've got a name, you know?" I toss my peeled onion into the sack at my feet and rise.

Alex raises a hand to motion that I remain back. I begrudgingly stay put, but not without shooting the old bat a lethal glare first. "Why don't I finish up for you, Eva, huh? You need to get some rest."

"Yes." She nods and hands him the bunch of carrots. As he takes it from her grasp I realize blood stains her palms, her nail beds painted crimson. I grit my teeth at the evidence of her torment. She is young, scared, and practically alone, and I won't stand by and watch Victoria poking and prodding her.

"Coddling won't fix a lazy child." Victoria tsks and stirs the soup. "Back in my day—"

"Shut her up, Alex, or I will!" I wrap my arm around Eva, helping her make her way across the room, past the Victoria's pot of murky water soup. A chicken based stock, or so Alex claims. It doesn't smell like any chicken I've ever had before.

Eva's steps are slow and cautious. I glance back at Alex over my shoulder. His posture is rigid, his elbows digging into his thighs as he leans over and steeples his hands before his mouth, whispering to Victoria. He'd better be putting her in her place.

Soon everyone will know that Eva's in labor. Then the screaming will start. I need to know if Alex is with me on this.

What will happen if he's not? Will Devon gag Eva and force her to endure her child's birth in silence? He is already wound tighter than a spring. He paces every time he enters the room, like an animal wild and caged. His own inner demons have begun to eat at him. Sooner or later he will snap. I don't want Eva anywhere near him when that happens.

"Won't be long now," I whisper in her ear as I ease her to the floor. I gave her my thin mattress during the night to try to help ease the ache in her back. It didn't help much, but it's all I could do.

"We should tell Devon," Eva says, her head lolling to the side. I mop her brow with the back of my hand. Sweat clings to her rosy cheeks. Her eyes are glossy, her lips pale.

"No." I shake my head. "Let Alex take care of him while I look after you."

A ghost of a smile touches her lips as she closes her eyes. "I'm glad you're here."

My throat clenches as she closes her eyes. I clasp her hand in mine, allowing her to rest for the remaining two minutes she has left before the pain builds once more.

All too soon her breath hitches and her fingers clamp down on my hand. I ride through the pain with her, drawing inward to ignore the loss of circulation. I vow, no matter what I will stay by her side as my mother never did for me.

"That's it," I whisper as her grip slowly loosens. A breath of pain slips past her lips as her body relaxes once more.

"Laziness, that's what it is." I look up to see Victoria pacing nearby. Her hands flutter before her, as they have been prone to do of late. Her gaze seems unfocused, her recent bout of insomnia starting to take its toll on her.

"Do you ever shut up?" The woman just never stops.

"Nothing wrong with stating a fact, dear," she responds with a syrupy sweet tone that makes me want to throttle her. "The truth never hurt anyone."

"It will when I rearrange your face," I mutter under my breath, eliciting a soft chuckle from Eva. I wink at her and then watch as Alex frowns and crosses to exit through the door. I wait to hear the tell-tale click of the lock but it doesn't come. His preoccupation was the first mistake I've seen him make.

"I'll be right back." I pat Eva's hand and rise, heading straight after him.

"Wait!" Victoria shouts, bustling up behind me. "Where are you going?"

"In there."

"You can't! You're not permitted." Her hand feels cold and wet when it lands upon my arm. The gas burner isn't wasted on scrubbing water for the vegetables.

"Don't touch me." I shove her off and place my hand on the doorknob to open it but jump back when Devon appears in the doorway, his broad frame filling the space.

"What's going on out here?" His gaze falls on me, standing less than a palm's width from his chest. "Well?"

I step back, not the least bit intimidated by him, but his limited bathing opportunities has left him with a funky smell. "Eva is going to need supplies. It's time."

His jaw tightens as he looks beyond me to see Eva curled up in the corner. A soft moan escapes her and another wave of pain has begun to build. "No. We can't risk it. Sal said he saw men on the streets below. Those gangs have moved into the area. If they find out we are here, we're all done for."

From the corner of my eye I see Victoria nodding in agreement. His callous words leave a bitter tang in my mouth as I step forward once more. "Eva is about to have a baby and that means things are going to get pretty nasty around here. Blood. Slime. And God knows what else is going to be coming. I don't have a clue how to deliver a baby, and I'm betting you don't either. The least we can do is to find some clean towels, boil more water, scavenge blankets, diapers, food, and heck, even a doctor if we can find one."

Devon's eyes narrow. "Those are all luxuries that we can no longer afford."

"Luxuries?" My anger tips dangerously close to the edge. My pulse pounds in my ears as I rise up to meet him as close to eye to eye as my shorter height allows. "That baby and Eva may die without them."

When his shoulders begin to rise into a shrug I snap. I slam my fist into his jaw hard enough to crack my knuckle. Pain radiates through my hand.

"You bitch!" He staggers back, his shoulder taking the brunt of the doorframe.

His livid glare doesn't still my anger as I jab him in the chest. "Have you no empathy? No emotion? How can you call yourself any better than the beasts that walk these streets if you feel nothing for that poor girl? A girl who you're supposed to protect!"

"There's no need to overreact—" Victoria says. but cuts off when I turn to glare at her.

"Overreact? You're too blind to even notice that she's been in labor for hours! All you care about are your stupid potatoes." I'm sure that my shouts can be heard to the far reaches of the building but I don't care. Maybe someone with some common sense might hear me and come to our aid.

I round on Sal as he steps into the doorway behind Devon. His frame is smaller, his shoulders not nearly so broad or strong. He stands a couple of inches taller than me, and in the gap I see that he is not alone. Alex follows my gaze as I shift past him to the two people sitting on the floor off to the side.

"Who the hell is that?" I storm forward, brushing Sal aside.

Sal recovers and shoves the paunch of his stomach into me, forcing me to back away. Alex quickly steps up behind him and together they walk me backward so they can close the door. "None of your concern."

"There is a man and woman in there. I saw them." Their faces were pale, their eyes wide with terror. They looked filthy, hair matted, clothes several days worn. I glimpsed enough in that brief moment to know that they are not here by choice.

Devon tugs on his shirt, visibly pulling himself together. His shoulders square as he pushes back off from the wall. Alex gives him a brief nod and I see his countenance change. Gone are the laugh lines I've come to know when Alex tells stories of distant places to Eva late at night. Gone is the friendly smile. He is all business now.

I cross my arms over my chest and scowl, standing my ground. Victoria begins her staccato pacing and I have to force myself not to scream at her. "I want to know what is going on in that room."

Devon exchanges a loaded glance with Alex, who nods and approaches, taking the lead. "Those people in there are no one. Just a couple of stragglers we picked up a couple days before you came. They were sick so we kept them separated. That's all."

"They didn't look sick. They looked terrified," I counter.

"Looks can be deceiving," Devon says in a deep baritone voice. I watch his muscles flex as he crosses his arms over his chest to match my combative stance. He's a heck of a lot more imposing in this position. I was right to not underestimate him.

That's when I notice a dot of blood on the inner flesh of the crook of his arm for the first time. It is barely noticeable against his dark skin but the shine of moisture catches in the light.

"Oh, God." I step back, sickened as the truth sinks in. "You're no better than those people on the streets!"

Alex holds up his hands as I begin to back away. The bruising scattered along his forearm is suddenly a stark contrast from the pale flesh of his inner arm. "Now hold on just a minute. It's not what you think."

"No?" Hysteria rises in my voice. "You gonna stand there and tell me that you're not stealing blood from them? That you haven't created your own mini blood bank? How did you even know to do that? Was it Eva's radio? Were you spying on the military?"

Devon stiffens as Victoria's head snaps around. "You never told me that's why those people were in there."

"Oh, come off it, Victoria." I yank at my hair, feeling as if madness is only a step ahead of me. "Are you really that dense? Did you not hear their screams or did you just not want to?"

She steps back, her face blanching at my attack. Her hand flutters at her throat before she turns and sinks onto a chair, beginning to rock slowly.

"You all act like you have a freakin' clue what is happening out there, but the truth is, you don't. None of us do."

"Isn't that the point?" I turn to look at Alex. "We don't know how this thing spreads. We don't know how to stop it or protect ourselves against it. So we do what we can with the little knowledge we possess."

"That message was cryptic. You don't even know what or if blood has anything to do with a cure or prevention. The message was cut off before they could say why or even how it could be used. How can you allow yourselves to jump to such extremes without the facts to back it up?"

"Because we want to live," Sal says without emotion.

"And what about them?" I point to the closed door. "Don't they have that same right?" I retreat as Devon and Sal approach, shifting backward until my spine is pressed against the door on the opposite side of the room. The one door that leads to the stairs and the factory beyond. The one Victoria came through only a short while ago with her bucket of vegetables. *Please let it still be unlocked. That rotten woman has a terrible memory.*

As Devon and Victoria's voices begin to rise in a dance of angry accusations, I grip the door handle and test it. I nearly cry in relief when it gives way.

"Enough!" Alex's shout echoes off the walls. Eva moans and curls in on herself. My grip on the door wavers at the sound of her pain. *I can't just leave her with these people.*

"Now that I have your attention," Alex says, smoothing his hair back from his face, "I think it's time we all had a chat about reality."

He motions for me to move away from the door and sit down. The urge to throw open the door and bolt is so strong I nearly give in, but another moan rises from Eva. Her back arches and I know that I have no choice. I can't turn my back on her. If I do she's as good as dead.

I sink down beside her, placing a hand on her arm. The muscles in her neck cord, her teeth gritted against the pain. Her screams build deep within in her throat. It's only a matter of time before she lets go.

"I realize this may come as a bit of a shock to you," Alex begins, waiting for me to turn and look at him, "but bad things happen to good people, including those two in that room. Reality tells us that not everyone is going to survive. I, for one, am not willing to just roll over and die. Are you?"

He stares at me long and hard but I fight to show no emotion beyond the flaring of my nostrils in repressed anger. Devon nods in agreement when Alex glances at him and for the first time I realize that I was mistaken. Devon isn't the one in charge. Alex is.

When the pilot turns to look at Victoria I almost feel sorry for the ashen woman. She looks faint and trembly. I can almost see the moral dilemma waging in her eyes but she cowers under Alex's stern gaze and nods.

"What we do is for the good of the group. You all need food and water. A safe place to sleep. How can we provide that for you if we become infected? If Eva needs blood and we can't give it to her, then what? We just let her die because we didn't prepare?"

Bile rises in my throat at the sound of Alex's justification. "You think that makes it ok?"

"Yes." I flinch as Devon closes the gap between us. His button down dress shirt is soiled and the pocket torn away. His pants are filthy, as if he has been rolling in the mud. I can't help but wonder what he's been up to behind that closed door. "You know those gangs are stealing blood. Why? Because it's the only way to survive. If that's what it takes, then so be it. I can sleep at night knowing that I did what it took."

"We aren't stealing their blood, Avery," Alex says in a softer tone. "We're borrowing it."

"Borrow?" I snort and shake my head. "How exactly are you planning on giving back to those people?"

"By allowing them to live."

The cold insensitivity of his statement sends chills down my spine. "And Eva? What if she has complications beyond her need for blood? Will you just let her die for the betterment of everyone?"

Alex's adams apple bobs as Devon looks to him with indecision. "She is part of the group."

"So are they." I point toward the closed door.

"No. They are outsiders."

I am rocked by Alex's blatant callousness. Maybe I didn't know him as well as I thought. I rise to my feet. "So am I."

"Not anymore."

"Why not?" I press, stepping forward. "Isn't that why you brought me here? To use me as a blood donor, too?"

His hesitation doesn't go unnoticed by everyone in the room. Even Eva has rolled onto her side to listen as she pants between contractions. I want to go to her, to ease her fears but this needs to be dealt with.

"I'm right, aren't I? You grabbed me off the street in the hopes that I could be a match for someone here." I whirl around, looking each person in the eye. "Well, who is it then? I must be a match otherwise I wouldn't be here right now."

Alex averts his gaze. Devon remains stony faced. Victoria looks bewildered. A look of hurt betrayal tints her grimace. She may be an idiot but at least of this crime she's innocent.

"You're a universal donor," Sal speaks up from the back of the room where he lounges against the wall.

"I see." Lifting my finger, I run my thumb over the healing slit that I noticed when I first woke. "You tested my blood while I was unconscious. Clever. I'll give you that much."

"It's not like that--" Alex starts but falters under my damning glare.

"Oh, no." I shake my head, my hands quaking at my sides. My pulse beats like a bass drum in my ears as I turn on him. "It's *exactly* like that."

Devon bears his teeth as he towers over me. I don't back down. Alex pushes Devon aside with far more ease than I would have liked and steps between us. "Yes, you're useful, dammit but that's not why I kept you."

"Then why?" I press into his face, forcing him to look at me as he spins his lies. Although I'm several inches shorter than him, he reacts instantly to the animalistic growl that bursts from my throat as he tries to grab my hand. I whip my hand away and crack it across his cheek hard enough to make my palm sting.

A vein pulses down his forehead as he steps back. A red patch grows along his cheek. I wait for the return hit, preparing myself for the pain, but he doesn't move. Doesn't speak. After a moment of tense silence his hardened gaze softens and the lines along his forehead disappear. His shoulders sag as his head dips low. "Because you remind me of someone. Someone I once cared very much for," he whispers.

Devon glances over at him. His displeasure is clearly written in the tensing of his stance. He starts to speak when a terrible howl from behind me makes my heart plummet into my stomach. I whip around to find Eva curled tightly into a ball, her mouth gaped open as tears spill from her eyes.

"What's wrong with her?" Victoria shouts, covering her ears against Eva's shrieks.

Glancing down at the mattress, my throat clenches at the sight of a small trickle of blood seeping out from beneath the folds of her dress. "Oh, god! She's hemorrhaging."

"What do we do, Avery?"

I cast an incredulous look at Alex. "Why the hell are you asking me? I don't have a clue!"

Eva's screams mount as she thrashes, curling inward then arching back. Her stomach heaves and sweat begins to dampen her hair.

"But you've done this before. Eva told me about your kid."

I press my palm to my forehead, trying to think around Eva's screams. "I was in a hospital with people who knew what the hell they were doing!"

From the corner of my eye I see Devon backing away. Sal slouches against the far wall, looking indifferent to the scene before him.

"Victoria?" The older woman glances at me as I shout her name to be heard. "You're the group know-it-all. What do we do?"

She presses a hand to her hair, patting it as if lost in thought. She looks down at Eva but says nothing. Does nothing. She just shakes her head and clams up.

"God!" I yell and rush toward Eva's side. "You are all useless!"

I grab my blanket and roll it up beneath the Eva's head. Her eyes clench tight, lost to the pain. "Someone get me something for her to bite on so she doesn't sever her own tongue."

Alex is the only one to react. He rushes toward a stack of boxes and begins digging, tossing packing peanuts and bits of tape over the side. Victoria watches from a distance as I brush Eva's hair back from her face. She is pale. Blood has begun to slowly stain through the front of her dress.

"That's a lot of blood." Alex says as he drops beside me. He hands over a long thick wooden stick and I realize it's a snapped broom handle.

"Something's wrong." I gently pry open Eva's mouth between screams and place the handle between her teeth. "Bite down on this. It will help."

Her head moves but I'm not sure she's coherent. Grabbing the end of her skirts, I begin tearing them, casting them aside. Blood coats my hands as I ease her legs apart. My stomach lurches at the sight but I force myself to remain focused. Devon backs away, his head shaking rapidly as he fumbles back over a stack of crates that fall far too close to Eva's head for comfort.

"Leave," I shout, pointing a bloody finger back toward the room with the cowering couple. Devon rises and rushes on the door.

"Do you have any needles?" I ask Alex. " Tubing? Something to start an IV so I can transfer blood to her?"

Alex shakes his head. "Nothing. Someone tripped over the one line we had left and snapped the needle. Sal's doing, I'd say. That's why I went in there to check. I knew Eva might need it sooner or later. We've been collecting blood in bowls and trying to cover them with pieces of cardboard but even that's useless now."

My hands clench against Eva's knees as I bite my tongue at their stupidity. They aren't even preserving the blood they are stealing!

Eva moans and rocks to the side, her knees trapping my hand. A steady trickle escapes between her legs. "Someone throw me a towel."

From the corner of my eye I glimpse Sal a moment before the door closes behind him. Victoria begins her frantic pacing, right past a small stack of clean cloths. I watch her, waiting for her to hand them to me but she doesn't. The squeaking of her shoes drives me over the edge.

"Get out!" She jumps at my scream, her eyes wide behind her red-rimmed glasses. "If you aren't going to help then get the hell out of here so I can think."

Victoria sniffs indignantly, hesitates as if she might actually consider helping, then hurries toward the door.

"Coward," Alex mutters under his breath beside me.

As I scoot closer blood soaks into my pant legs, warm and sticky. "She's a science teacher. She must know how to stop this bleeding. She's dissected animals, for pete's sake!"

"She's scared."

"I don't give a shit, Alex. Go in there and force her to focus. Eva's life depends on it."

I wipe my hands on my shirt and prepare to try to search for the baby's head but pause when I feel him staring at me. "What?"

"How are we going to do this?"

I've been asking myself that same thing over and over since I first noticed Eva's contractions. "I don't know, but we are going to. Somehow. I won't let her die."

SIX

Exhaustion weighs down on me as I fight to keep Eva with us. My knees bruise from kneeling on the floor. The sound of her screams makes my ears ring. The worst part is not knowing if it's from labor pains or something worse, something internal. My hands tremble as I sink back, pressing my bloodied hands against my thigh as I use my arm to wipe my brow.

I'm worried about how much blood she has lost. Eva is barely conscious and she hasn't begun to push yet.

The hairs on Alex's arms are matted with blood. The shirt in his hand, pressed against Eva to slow the bleeding has begun to soak through. We ran out of towels fifteen minutes ago and began using clothes. Alex gave the shirt off his own back to help. It's not sterile but if we don't do something she's going to bleed out and it won't matter.

"She's not going to make it, is she?" Alex says beside me. It is not really a question and we both know it. Without help Eva will not last much longer.

The towel I wipe my hands with is soaked through and just as sticky as my hands. Victoria finally got her head out of her backside and managed to scrounge up some minor supplies from the warehouse. A small first aid kit, a couple moving pads that are stained with oil, a mop bucket to hold water to clean our hands in and some unused mop heads to soak up some of the mess on the floor.

As Alex pulls his shirt away, I spread Eva's legs and cry out. The crown of the baby's head is within sight. At least I think that's what it is. The idea of grasping this tiny life makes me nauseous but I'm the only chance Eva's baby has. But what happens after that? What if we can't stop the bleeding? How do we care for the baby if Eva dies? What if…I have a million of those questions going through my mind right now.

Pushing back off my knees I rise. Eva's head has rolled to the side. She stares blankly at the wall. "I'm going for help."

"No." Alex struggles to rise. His own legs must be suffering from the same pain that mine are.

"She's going to die. We both know it, Alex. You have to let me try to find help."

He shakes his head. "Sal could go. Or Devon. I can't let you be the one to go. I have no clue what I'm doing here."

I reach out and grab his arm, digging my cracked nails into his flesh just enough to get his rising panic to subside. "You told me earlier that Eva is part of your group. That she is yours to take care of. I'm asking that you let me help you do that."

He glances back down at Evangeline. "We both know Sal and Devon don't care about her like we do. If you want her to make it you have to let me go."

I realize, staring at him now, just how deep the extent of his feelings of responsibility for her goes. He has proven that he is willing to do whatever it takes to protect his own, even stealing blood from an outsider. Now I need to lean heavily on that need if Eva has any chance.

"She's only sixteen, Alex. Can you really live with yourself if she dies on your watch?"

He closes his eyes and shakes his head. "What is something happens to you? What if someone follows you?"

I bite on my lower lip as I look around for a solution that will placate him. *So close.*

And then I remember Eva's story. "Do you still have the radio Eva brought with her?"

"Sure." He motions toward the closed door. "We've been monitoring the military's movements with it."

"Ok. If anything happens to me, if I don't come back, I will find a way to contact you. Keep it with you, no matter what." The moment his shoulders sag in reluctant defeat, I race for the door, shoving Victoria aside. I barely have time to feel vindicated when I hear her topple to the floor as I race down the metal stairs and through the vast warehouse.

The first time I came through this darkened maze I had no real idea of how large the factory was. Shadows rise up before me just seconds before I slam into a piece of machinery and bounce off. Battered and bruised, but fueled by a new round of screaming from behind me, I rush past the endless row of windows in search of a door.

Years of disuse and grime smudge the glass, affording only a dim light to see by. The sun looks to be on the rise and I'm desperate to feel it's warmth on my skin again.

The blustery cold steals my breath away as I throw open the door. The wind tugs the handle from my hands and it bangs loudly against the brick wall. I squint against the brilliant dawn, shielding my face until my eyes have a chance to adjust. I don't recognize any of my surroundings. In the distance I can see the arch gleaming like glass against the brightening sky. A bank of storm clouds move off to the East leaving the city in temporary sunlight.

Without thinking I sprint down the road, weaving around potholes and abandoned cars. Graffiti decorates the brick walls around me. Some of the roofs have caved in, charred and left to ruin by the fires. Bullet holes scatter the streets, in car doors, through glass windows and mailboxes.

I skirt the opposite sidewalk to avoid a burst fire hydrant that gushes water high into the air. A Jeep is jacked up on the hydrant, its alarm blaring and lights flashing. There is no one inside, but I spy a puddle of blood beneath the open door as I jog past.

Before all of this happened I would never have walked down these streets, even in broad daylight. Every city has its places that you don't go alone. This was one of them. The other lies across the river, my path of escape should I ever make it out of here.

I hold the stitch in my side, counting the slaps of my blood stained chucks against the pavement as I run in spite of the pain in my ribs. I grow warm beneath my scavenged hoodie and pull it over my head, tying it around my waist. The cold air feels amazing against my exposed skin, cooling the heat trapped within the black tank that I wore beneath.

After several minutes the arch begins to rise into the sky and I discern shops dotted along the street, interspersed with offices and entrances to condos. I race around a corner and come up short.

Less than a block away people mill about. The stench wafts my way and I'm forced to double over, clutching my nose and mouth. The scent of rotting flesh, urine and feces hits me like a wrecking ball. Death lives here.

I rise to my full height and then up onto my toes as I spy a familiar sign. Nearly thirty Withered Ones stand between me and a pharmacy on the corner two blocks away. It is small but should have something that I can use to help Eva.

Glancing down the street I look for a way around the Moaners but the path is blocked by a pileup of cars. It's either go straight through or adds a few extra blocks to my journey. Time is not on my side.

"You've got this," I whisper to myself as their raspy moans echo down the alley toward me. "Nothing to it."

I walk cautiously forward, watching those closest to me. A girl wearing a Washington University sweatshirt slams into a wall ten feet in front of me. She stumbles back and slams again, repeating the action with maddening persistence. The flesh of her forehead clings to the trail of blood she has left on the wall. Her shattered nose gushes, the bone and cartilage concaved into her face. The bones of her right cheek splinter, poking through her flesh.

Clutching my stomach, I step past her and try to ignore the squelching sounds each time she hits the wall. I come upon a man of Asian descent wearing a business suit. Shattered metal-framed glasses slide down his nose as he bounces off the trunk of a car and veers into my path. I swallow my scream as I duck to miss his flailing arm. The scent of gasoline is strong on him as he passes.

I clutch my head with trembling hands as I remain crouched. Three more shuffle past me. One has a huge gouge out of her leg. Teeth marks have torn through muscle and scored bone and I wonder if a dog got ahold of her. As soon as my immediate path is clear I rise and come face to face with three men less than eight steps before me. Their eyes are vacant, unseeing. The one on the right is missing an ear. A gaping wound oozes with blood, trailing down his neck and soiling his white suit coat. The nails on his right hand have been torn away, leaving flies to swarm the fleshy beds of his fingers.

The second man's cheeks are shredded. Between strips of flesh, broken teeth jut upright like shark's teeth. His neck looks like ground meat. The stench surrounding him nearly debilitates me. My eyes water as I raise my shirt to cover my mouth and nose, only sucking in tiny, necessary breaths.

The third man is covered in muck, his hair and every inch of his body is coated in bits of old garbage, soot and refuse. His clothes are torn and bloodied. He walks with a pronounced limp but he appears to have fared better than most.

The three Withered Ones seem to keep in pace with each other walking side by side, though they show no conscious thought in doing so. I duck beneath the raised arm of the limping man on the right only to find myself face to face with another small group.

My throat clenches as I realize I've burrowed into the heart of death central. "Just breathe and keep moving," I whisper to myself as I crawl forward on my hands and knees. I stifle my cries as I bounce between legs. Their fingers claw through my hair, tugging me back as they continue on their mindless walk. My shoulders grow slick with gore. I pause and flick a patch of skin off my shoulder and shake out my hair. Bits of fingernails fall from my matted curls.

"Oh shit." I allow only small gulps of breath as I fight to still my rising panic. The air tastes foul on my tongue.

"Almost through," I try to reassure myself as the legs before me begin to dwindle.

I cry out as a piece of glass on the street slices my palm. I falter to the right, slam into the leg of a man, and buckle under the weight of him falling on top of me. I scream and flail, writhing to be free in spite of the shattered glass beneath me.

Blood splatters my face and enters my mouth as I beat against the man. He doesn't fight back, doesn't yell or show any sign of pain from my attack. His arms and legs continue to move, as if he were still walking.

Slowly I crawl out from under him and drag myself up onto the curb and press back against the wall. I stare at the Moaner, horrified to find most of his left side has been torn away.

I roll to my side and hurl as bits of what looks like ground beef slide off my sleeve. I wrench my hand away. As I empty my stomach onto the sidewalk, I realize that the scent is actually an improvement.

Wiping my mouth clean, I'm forced to gasp for breath and my stomach instantly begins to churn anew. I long for a fresh country breeze instead of this vile, stench ridden street. I beat at my arm, removing any signs of that man from me before I pull my legs into my chest.

My fingers tremble as I hold myself, watching the Moaners, walking side by side. I bury my head in my arms and count slowly to 100. I listen to their stunted steps until they move on, like a herd without direction.

Slowly the air begins to clear and I raise my head. I wipe tears from my face and glance toward the pharmacy. It's only a block away. Determined to save Eva, I force myself to my feet and scan the surrounding streets, peering around the corner for any sign of more Withered Ones. I spot two females at the end of the block to my right and four more to my left but the path directly to the pharmacy is clear.

"Eva needs me." I gather what few shreds of courage I have left and sprint toward the glass doors of the shop. I slip several times in dark puddles and pray that it isn't urine. Less than a minute later I hit the front door and bounce off, my footing unsteady in the collection of glass on the doorstep.

I peer into the darkened shop and feel the hairs on the back of my neck rise. There is a moan from within.

I turn and press back against the wall, swearing under my breath. "Really? Does someone have me on their 'let's fuck with Avery' radar today? Scenes like this in horror movies never turn out well."

The sun has risen over the top of the nearest building, the heat helping to ward off some of the biting cold. The wind whips mercilessly down the city streets, chilling me as it seeps through my bloodied clothes. "At least it's not nighttime," I mutter to myself, though walking into a pitch black building makes this fact pretty much irrelevant.

Glass crunches beneath my shoes as I duck and slip through the empty-framed front doors. The open sign jangles against the door as I reach for a shopping basket to carry my items in. I freeze and wait for the metallic clanking to cease, holding my breath. I hear nothing, but the knowledge that I'm not alone makes me cautious. There is at least one of them in here. Most likely more.

After moving only a few feet into the store, the amount of visible light diminishes drastically. I rise onto my toes, squinting against the dark in an attempt to see the aisle signs. "I don't even know what I'm looking for," I mutter under my breath.

The shelves are ransacked, much of their contents either stolen or left scattered on the floor. I force myself to tiptoe past the shampoo and conditioner aisle, though I would dearly love to grab a few bottles for later. I pass a row of sunscreen and cold medicines, canes and those little round pillows people sit on after surgeries. When I hit the vitamin aisle I stare long and hard into the shadows to make sure nothing is moving before darting down to find prenatal vitamins. I snatch boxes of gauze and tape, hydrogen peroxide and pads to help with the clean-up.

I snag a box of gloves and am heading to find baby formula when I hear it. Sluggish footsteps. I press back against the shelf and listen, trying to drown out the sound of my racing heart as I try to decide where the steps are coming from.

My head whips around at the sound of a loud crash, followed by the cascade of cans falling. It must have hit a display. Crouching low, I inch toward the back of the aisle and peer out. The light spilling in from the windows on the far side is blinding, making it hard to see anything in the shadows. Something hits my foot and I clamp my hand over my mouth to still my cries.

I hear thrashing and more cans spiraling across the floor. I reach down and grab the can at my feet and hold it up right. "Of course it would be baby formula!"

If Eva is too weak to push without help during the delivery, there's no way she will be strong enough to feed her baby. I don't have a choice. Tucking the shopping basket beneath my arm, I creep forward in the dark, collecting any cans I find in my path. I reach for one final can, praying that I have collected enough when a hand seizes mine.

It is unnaturally cold, the skin loose and sagging. I scream and buck as fingers curl around my wrist, locking down. The rasping moan grows louder and I feel myself being tugged forward.

"Get off of me!" I beat at the hand, scratching and clawing, yanking with all my might. That's when I smell it: a new scent of sweat over the scent of death.

I hear a footstep behind me a second before a bag is pulled over my head and I'm yanked to my feet. The gruesome grasp releases me. I hear a gunshot nearby as something sharp stabs into my upper arm and my protests grow weak.

"No." My head swims and my eyes flutter closed. "Eva needs me…"

My wrists are pinched together in cuffs as I am hauled to my feet. I see dots of light through the dark hood but trip over my basket and nearly face plant when my legs don't react as fast as I need them to.

"Easy with this one. We need her unharmed." I turn my head at the voice.

"Who are you?" My question goes unanswered. Strong hands grip my arms as I'm lifted off the ground and carried out of the shop. I hear the rumble of a large engine, feel the heat from it as I'm placed on my feet, held aloft by the men beside me. Their grip on my arms is tight, though I can barely keep my head upright as I sag against them.

"Why are you doing this to me?" My words slur as my head falls backward. The muscles in my neck pull taut.

The sound of clanking metal chains sounds distorted in my ears. A tailgate squeals as it lowers before me and I'm hauled inside. Darkness rushes in as my head hits the metal floor; the pain insufficient enough to keep me lucid and I lose consciousness.

SEVEN

My head hurts. Not like a small sinus headache. More like someone using a buzz saw to separate the two hemispheres of my brain.

My body feels weird, heavy and lethargic. Shooting pains rise along my neck. As I try to lift my head, I realize that my wrists and ankles are bound. I am seated upright, my chest and thighs strapped down tight enough to cut off circulation. A blindfold covers my vision, pressing tightly against my closed eyelids.

Dripping, as maddening as it is constant, sounds around me. There is a high pitched beeping coming from somewhere behind my head.

"Hello?" My voice cracks and I clear my throat to try again. "Is anyone there?"

I hear breathing in the dark. Slow and steady. Rhythmic. It scares me. Almost like a prank call gone too far.

"I can hear you." I hate that my voice trembles.

Nothing. No response. I call until my throat is raw but no one answers my pleas.

Slowly my other senses begin to kick back in. I become aware of the beat of my pulse in my neck and realize that it pulses in time with the beeping from behind my head. It must be some sort of heart monitor.

I smell nothing. Literally nothing. It is as if the space has been sanitized and then stripped of all recognizable scent. A clean room. My lips part and I breathe deep, hoping to taste something on the air but even this test fails me.

I am alone in the dark. No. Not alone. Just ignored.

"Let me out of here!" I scream. I listen as my cry echoes around me, twisting against my restraints but manage only to burn my skin.

"Hello?" I listen again, focusing on the echo. I'm in a large room. That much I do know. The sound does not bounce back at me but diminishes as it travels away. I turn my head this way and that, attempting other calls. As best I can tell there is a wall to my left not far away. Nothing before me or to my right.

"Think, Avery. Just focus on what you know."

I'm in a shitful of trouble, that's what I know! My panic begins to rise and I struggle to squash it down.

I freeze at the sound of grinding gears. The sound is distant. I let my head roll back to my shoulder as a door bangs open. Heavy footfalls head my way. Several people approach but they don't seem the least bit concerned about being heard.

"Where's the new one?" A man asks.

"At the end. She's been...resisting."

A disgruntled harrumph greets me less than a minute before I sense movement in front of me. I wish that I could open my eyes, sneak a glimpse of my captors. Instead I rely heavily on my other senses.

I note the ticking of a watch. Smell the scent of cologne attempting to mask alcohol. I feel a cold breeze on my arm and wonder if the door they entered through was left open.

"Is she awake?"

I keep my breathing slow and steady. A hand presses to my neck and I force myself not to react. The man steps back. "Her vitals are steady. It is possible that the sedation has begun to wear off again."

Again? I don't remember waking up here before.

"How much have you managed to collect?" The gravelly voice belongs to a seasoned man, perhaps in his fifties or later. His words are clipped, no nonsense. This is a man who is obviously used to giving orders and having them instantly obeyed.

"We have removed two pints so far, but I'm still waiting for the test results to come back." A meek voice speaks up. I hear the rustling of papers and imagine him to have a clipboard in hand, sifting through my charts.

"Not good enough, Doctor. I want triple that."

"But sir–" his protest is cut off.

"No excuses. We are running low. Our soldiers' lives depend on it."

I have to fight not to react to that. I remember giving blood when I was a bit younger at a mobile red cross unit that stopped at a church just down the street from me. To be honest, I went for the food afterward, not for some noble notion that I was helping people. I was hungry. My mother had been on one of her drinking binges again and the only things in the fridge were baking soda and butter.

That day they took one pint of my blood and it was enough to leave me woozy for a while. I didn't like that feeling. In the end, I decided the food wasn't worth it.

Now this guy wants to take half of my blood and call it a day? Oh, hell no!

"I have rights," I croak, lifting my head.

"Rights?" Thick fingers paw at the blindfold over my face, tearing stands of hair from my scalp. The blindfold slides down around my neck and I'm forced to blink several times before my eyes adjust to the brilliant light overhead.

It is a medical light, round and domed, like what you see on TV. My mom used to have a thing for watching reruns of ER. As I look around I see several machines that look vaguely familiar.

"And what rights do you think you still have?"

I turn my head to the right and glare at a stern looking man. His temples are flecked with white against his cropped graying head of hair. Lines mar his face, streaking his forehead. His eyes are dark and cold, demanding.

A green uniform encases the man, tailored to perfection right down to his shiny black shoes. A colorful array of medals dangle from his chest. He must be high ranking to be decorated like this. Perhaps a general or commander of some sort.

"I'm an American citizen. You have no right to detain me."

His throaty laugh grates against my frayed nerves. Beside him, three soldiers snicker behind their hands. A doctor, with a three-quarter length white lab coat shifts uncomfortably. He wears a matching uniform beneath his coat.

As I look beyond him I see that I am in a darkened room that stretches out before me. The ceiling is metal and domed. It looks like an aircraft hangar that's been converted into some mad scientist's lab.

I am in a long row of chairs, each with its own light, heart monitors and web of tubing. Men and women sit in the chairs, emotionless, unconscious.

I turn to glare at the man, knowing he is in charge. "This is wrong."

"No." The humor in his eyes vanishes instantly as he steps forward. His arms cross behind his back and he leans over me. "What is wrong is that my men are dying out there trying to save your sorry ass. Trained soldiers, good men fighting for freedom are being cut down by the scum that think they own this city now."

"I'm not one of them!"

He rises back up and appraises me coolly. "You're right. You're part of the cure now."

He turns on his heel and starts away. "Wait!"

The man pauses but does not turn. I grit my teeth, blowing out a breath before I speak. "I had a friend in the city. She was in danger, needed my help. I have to get back to her."

The general doesn't respond, doesn't make a sound as he resumes his march away from me, leaving me helpless and hopeless. I lower my head as tears sting my eyes.

"I'm sorry," a voice whispers beside me after the resounding echo of the door slamming fades away. I lift my head to see the doctor is the only one who remains. "About your friend, I mean."

"Then help me escape."

He shakes his head. I notice his hands are small for a man. His stature not nearly as imposing as the others. This man has most likely never seen a day of real battle, certainly not hand to hand combat. He is a doctor. A man who might still have a conscience.

"She was only a girl, a teen who went into labor," I press, praying that I can reach his humanity. "She started bleeding. We tried to stop it but she just got weaker...."

He closes his eyes. His head lowers as he shakes his head. "Please," I beg without apology. "I have to help her."

When he raises his head, I see evidence of his compassion in the curve of his lips but then he turns aside. His fingers work the buttons of the machine beside me and I watch the IV drip increase. Another increases the flow of blood trailing from my arm. As the doctor silently works, checking my feeding tube and monitoring the output of the catheter snaking out from beneath my hospital gown, I begin to feel weakness anew.

Finally he stops and turns to look at me. My head presses heavily against the headrest. His lips purse and he shakes his head. "I'm truly sorry. I'm sure you cared for your friend, but she was probably dead long before you were even captured."

He turns and starts away, my file tucked under the crook of his arm. "He's going to kill me."

The doctor pauses. "No. I won't let that happen."

My eyes slip closed as the sound of his footsteps retreats. Tears stream down my cheeks as I mourn the loss of the only friend I've truly had in a long time. Eva wanted nothing from me. She extended friendship for the sole purpose of being nice. That is rare in my life.

I have no way to monitor time as the hours pass. Lethargy comes and goes. The doctor returns twice to readjust the machines. Neither time does he truly look at me. Not like before.

The silence seeks to drive me crazy. I call out from time to time, knowing that no one can hear my hoarse cries over the steady droning of mechanical beeps filling the air. None of the other captives move or wake. Why have I not been sedated again like them?

My vision grows fuzzy, my eyes ache from peering into the dark in search of an escape route. For all intents and purposes there are no walls to this room. None that I can see or hope to reach.

Just as I'm about to drift off again I hear a sliding footstep against the floor. A burst of adrenaline shoots through me, waking my senses as I wait for another shuffle or the moan that I fear might come. Surely they have Moaners here as well. The commander said he is losing men. That can't only mean by bullets.

"Hello?" I call out and wait, straining to hear. Another sound. Followed by cautious footsteps. I can just see movement in the shadows beyond the borders of my light. They move with stealth, far too fluid for a Moaner. "Who's there?"

"Shit," a husky voice breathes out. A pair of boots enter the ring of light first, followed by a lean waist, broad torso and strong jaw. I lift my gaze and blink rapidly, sure that I'm dreaming.

"Cable?"

He pauses at the foot of my chair, his gaze flitting over me. He looks intense, perplexed and rigid. "I thought you got out."

I bark out a laugh and my head falls to my right shoulder. He rushes forward and helps me lift it again. My chest rises and falls with exertion. "Not all that different than last time, huh?"

His expression tightens in light of my attempt at humor. He glances back over his shoulder. "I have to get you out of here."

He starts to reach for the straps holding my arms down and then hesitates. He glances all around. "Why are you here?"

"I got lost looking for the bathroom," I croak, rolling my eyes. "Why do you think?"

"No." He says in a hushed voice as he peers back over his shoulder again. "I mean here, in *this* room."

My attempt at a shrug comes off as more of a slump. "They didn't exactly give me the grand tour when I arrived."

Cable's gaze narrows in on a chart hanging next to my IV pole. He steps carefully around my feet and grabs the papers, flipping through. I roll my head to the side to watch him. The effort is exhausting.

I wouldn't have thought it possible but his expression darkens further. "You're a candidate."

"For what?"

When he looks up, I can tell that whatever it is, I really don't want to volunteer. He places the chart back down and steps to my side. "Getting you out of here won't be easy. We'll need help. My men won't be back from their patrol until tomorrow. We will have to wait until then."

"I can't wait that long." Panic pinches my voice, making me sound like a terrified mouse. "That creepy general guy wants to take all of my blood."

Cable's head snaps up. "What?"

"I heard them saying they wanted to take more. A lot more."

He wipes his hand over his mouth as he blinks rapidly. "But that doesn't make any sense. You're a universal donor. They should let you rest so you can generate more blood, not steal it all and risk killing you!"

I close my eyes, feeling a heavy pounding in my head. "Maybe you need to admit the fact that your boss isn't such a good guy."

I sound sleepy. I feel sleepy. I surface only when Cable presses his palm against my cheek. He leans in close. "I won't let them hurt you. I promise."

EIGHT

They came for me in the middle of the night. I heard their heavy march first, followed by the shouted commands to prep me. I remember my arms feeling like lead when they finally removed my restraints. My arms fell over the sides of the chair, like useless limbs, but still I couldn't resist. My legs were no better. I had no energy, no will to fight back, even as I was placed on a stretcher and taken from the room.

I have only a blurry memory of a biting cold hitting my exposed skin as I was carried from the hangar. The whirling sound of helicopter rotors filled my mind as we passed by and entered another building, this one white and exceedingly sterile looking.

Hands jostled me as I was placed on a soft surface. A mask was placed over my face, though there was no need for medication to knock me out. I was barely lucid as it was.

Now I am awake. I feel stronger, though only slightly. My surroundings have changed. I sit propped up against a white wall on a small cot in the corner of an empty room. There is no other furniture save for a porcelain toilet in the corner. A large pane of glass lies on the wall before me. I'm being watched. I can feel it.

A new team of doctors monitors me now. None of them speak to me. None of them look at me, beyond a general perusal of my physical condition. They are cold, callous.

With my knees tucked into my chest, I stare at the tube feeding into my wrist. They no longer take blood from me. Now they seem to be giving it.

My hospital gown is gone, replaced by long white pants and white cotton top, the sleeves drawn up to allow access for the IV. My hair has been washed and falls in waves about my shoulders, frizzy from air drying. My skin smells of lightly scented soap, clean and blood free. The remnants of my wounds have been cleaned and bandaged. I've been sterilized too.

My questions fall on deaf ears. The two-way glass is my only connection to the outside world and a reflection of the only thing I have left to depend on: myself.

I have not seen Cable in what feels like days and know nothing of his whereabouts. A part of me hopes that he is trying to find a way to fulfill his vow. To save me from this cage. Another part of me believes that I will never see real daylight again.

During the endless hours I've spent beneath these brilliant fluorescent lights, I've begun to question Cable's intentions. I knew he worked for the government, even suspected them of being corrupt after speaking with Eva about the missing children, but is it really a coincidence that he stumbled across me in the blood bank? How did he gain clearance for what was obviously a secured room? He is a familiar face, someone that I might be inclined to trust. Has he been swayed to betray me?

"How are you feeling this evening?" a voice calls through a speaker near the door.

I turn and look at the silver box, then lower my head again. I do not recognize the voice. It is feminine. The first I have heard since arriving in this god forsaken place.

"I expect you have questions." The clank of a lock captures my attention, as does her thick, foreign accent. I place my feet on the floor and curl my fingers around the cot's frame as the door slides open. Just beyond her in the hall I see two soldiers with guns at the ready.

A tall brunette enters, her heels clacking against the tile floor. Her hair is piled in delicate curls around her face. Her eyes bear a hint of eye shadow. The overwhelming scent of her floral perfume makes me wipe my nose as the door closes behind her.

I scan her button down dress shirt, the white a near perfect match to the walls behind her. A tight, navy blue, knee length skirt hugs the curve of her hips. Four inch heels carry her toward me. As I stare at her, I can't shake the feeling that I've seen her before.

She pauses a few feet away and clasps her hands before her. Up close I notice a thick sheen of foundation pasted onto her skin. "You have nothing to fear from me."

"Why do I think *that's* a lie?"

She ignores my sarcastic remark and motions to the end of the bed. "May I?"

"It's your bed. I'm just visiting."

The bed creaks under her weight. She curls her legs back under, crossed at the ankle as she shifts to look at me. "We are not your enemy, Avery. I realize that all of this might seem a bit extreme, but it's for your own good."

"Really?" I turn my torso to look at her. "Cause I'm pretty sure kidnapping an innocent person, stealing her blood and then performing experiments on her is still all sorts of fucked up, even in this new world."

The corners of her lips twitch, almost hinting at a genuine smile. Her hands lay one over the other in her lap. I notice that her nail polish is cracked, the glossy tips recently colored over. Upon closer inspection I realize that my first impression of her Barbie doll exterior was wrong, though I'd give her points for trying to pull off the look.

"Rough day?"

She blinks. "Excuse me?"

"You have bruises on your arm. Kinda look like mine." I raise my forearm to show her a nearly identical set of marks, bearing evidence to the manhandling I received when I was brought here. "My mom used to date some pretty nasty guys. Always had a knack for finding the beaters. I know a thing or two about cover ups and yours is pretty decent."

The woman's gaze darts toward the glass then falls to the floor. She clears her throat and straightens her spine. "You are a very special girl, Avery. We have no intention of harming you."

"Not exactly feeling the warm fuzzies right now." I draw my legs up into my chest and cradle myself. The surface of the cot is hardly what I would call comfortable, but after weeks spent camping out on the hard floor beside my mother's bed or sleeping next to Eva in that warehouse, it feels like a five star hotel.

She nods. "I imagine all of this must be hard to understand. My name is Natalia and I've been commissioned as your liaison, your go between."

"Between who, exactly? Me and the US government? Russia?" Her gaze narrows. "You're not American. The crappy accent was a dead giveaway."

She glances toward the window again and stares for a moment. I follow her gaze, knowing there is no way she can see through that glass. After a minute of silence passes, she lowers her head.

"Twenty minutes," she murmurs under her breath and rises.

I stare after her as she moves swiftly toward the door. She slams her palm against the metal twice. The door opens an inch. "I'm finished with her."

A tall, heavily armed soldier sweeps his gaze past her to me as he opens the door. I smile and wiggle my fingers at him in mock greeting. His scowl deepens as he allows her to pass then slams the door.

What just happened? I lie down on the cot, rolling to my side so that I'm facing the wall only a few inches from my face. It would not surprise me if there weren't cameras that can see me from every angle in this room, but I feel better knowing that the faceless men behind the glass window can't see.

Twenty minutes. What is that supposed to mean? She'll be back in twenty minutes? Something terrible is going to happen? Maybe it's another experiment.

I clasp my hands and tuck them under my head, wincing at the tug of the IV in my arm, and I force myself to rest. A mock rest, one with the sole intent of appearing to sleep, but my mind dashes through countless scenarios. The more I try to puzzle through Natalia's conversation and the change in her demeanor, the more frustrated I become.

Minutes tick past slowly. I count the seconds in my mind, wondering just how many were lost or miscounted during my mental rants. Surely it is nearly time, yet no one has come for me. I hear nothing beyond the walls of my cage. The painted concrete block is soundproofed, probably so no one has to listen to my screams.

I roll onto my back and stare unblinking up at the ceiling, unwilling to feign sleep any longer. *Idiot. She was just trying to get a reaction from me. Another stupid mind game.*

Rubbing my hands over my face, I rise to the edge of the bed and cradle my head in my hands. My elbows dig into my thighs as I release a deep breath. *When am I going to stop falling for this shit?*

I hear something. Raising my head, I glance around. A tremor works up through the floor into the soles of my bare feet. I start to rise but pause as I see a vibration in the glass window. Cocking my head to the side, I watch the mirrored surface appear to ripple.

The blast catches me off guard. I throw up my hands to shield my face as thousands of shards explode. Small nicks appear on my arms, slicing through the thin fabric of my clothes. Lines of crimson begin to appear along my body as I slowly uncurl to see a darkened hole where the glass once was.

A man stands there, waiting. "Cable?"

Placing his hands against the window frame, he launches himself through. Glass shatters beneath his boots as he rushes to my side. He offers me an apologetic grimace before ripping the IV from my arm, disconnecting me from the monitors. They beep loudly just before he kicks the cart over. As he reaches out to cup my face, I realize his palms are wrapped in fabric. "Can you walk?"

"Not exactly." I glance at the sea of glass all around. Cable follows my gaze to my bare feet and instantly sweeps me into his arms.

"Be ready to run. Keep your head down. Stay close behind me."

He hoists me through the window and into what looks like some sort of operating room. An array of scalpels, needles and monitors stand before me. A bin of tubing wrapped in protective sealed bags hangs along the wall. A heart monitor's green flat line trails silently across the screen at the head of the bed. Three clipboards with charts, printed cardiograms and who knows what else lies on the table to my right. I fall still at the sight of the name on the top of the page: Avery Whitlock.

"Oh god!" Flashes of memory seizes me as I stare up at the darkened dome light. "I remember."

I step back into Cable, stopped by the breadth of his chest. "Don't think about it. Just move."

"They know my name," I call after him as he rushes to the door. As he tugs it open to look out, I hear the blaring of sirens for the first time. "How do they know my name?"

"I told them." His response is flat, unemotional.

I close the gap between us and seize his arm. He glances back at me with mounting agitation. "I only ever told you my *first* name."

His gaze softens as he places his hand over mine. "Do you really think they wouldn't know everything about you by now?"

His words leave me cold as he ducks his head back into the hall. I curl my toes against the frigid tiles, wishing for a pair of warm fuzzy socks. Heck, I'd take a pair of flip-flops at this point! "Follow me."

I do, as if on autopilot. We clamber over two fallen soldiers that once guarded my door, pausing for Cable to check their weapons. "Why aren't you taking the big ones?" I ask as he tucks a small pistol in his back waistband.

"Too bulky."

Motioning for me to follow, one gun held at the ready, I weave around corners, down halls and past countless doors that all look the same to me. I don't know how he doesn't get lost. Cable marches forward, his posture tense yet confident.

Explosions rock the building. The lights flicker overhead. "What's happening?"

I duck low as another explosion hits further down the hall. A wall collapses in and we are forced to backtrack.

"Cable?" I struggle to breathe as I jog. What little energy I gained from my time spent prisoner in my white room is rapidly fading.

"You want the long version or the synopsis?

He grabs me by the arm and I slam into his chest. His arms curl around me, his body a shield against a collapsing ceiling less than ten feet in front of us. When the dust settles he draws back up. "I think short!"

Brick and drywall dusts his hair gray but it doesn't dampen his smile. "It's an old fashioned mutiny!"

"Mutiny?" The word is torn from my lips as he tugs me toward a door. He slams through it and pulls me into a hall almost identical to the last, but this one is decorated in beige tones. Bodies dot this hall but none appear to be moving. The hallway lights flicker overhead, some damaged by the shootout. A spray of bullet holes lead past us and around the corner but I hear nothing in that direction.

Cable releases my hand and sprints ahead, pausing at an intersection and for the first time he looks lost. I spy a red glowing exit sign to my right. "Over there!"

He turns back and shakes his head. "We aren't going out there."

The desire to turn tail and race for that door is nearly unbearable. Exit means freedom. I watch as Cable turns a corner up ahead and bite down on my lower lip.

Can I really trust him? Should I?

"Avery," he hisses down the hall toward me. I look up to see his head poking around the corner. "This way."

I hesitate a second longer before making my decision. "Shit."

My bare feet slap against the cold floor as I rush to catch up. I'm only distantly aware of the fact that my side no longer aches. My ribs are bound tightly but the bruising must have begun to heal. *How long have I been here?*

Cable waits for me at the end of a dark hall. "Watch your step," he calls out just before I spy a pile of glass from the light overhead.

"Where is everyone?"

"This building was on strict lock down from all non-essential personnel. Only the doctors and scientists come here at night to check on patients. Once the battle began they took off. They're not here to fight but to research. Most of them have never seen a day of combat."

"Lucky them," I mutter. Another explosion rocks the building. A crack forms in the wall beside me and I rush ahead, not wanting to stick around for the next blast. "Friends of yours?"

"Something like that." He takes my hand and raises his foot, booting the door before him open. Darkness and a frigid cold reside on the other side.

"Where are we?"

"Shh." His fingers tighten around mine as he leads me into the room. He pauses a few feet in. There is a clattering of metal then silence as he pulls me forward. The echo of the door closing behind me feels out of place as he leads me through the dark. I hear shouting now. Gunfire covers the sound of sirens in the distance

The floor feels like ice beneath my feet. A chill rises up through my legs and it doesn't take long for my teeth to begin to chatter. I hear an odd click and sense movement before me.

"Here. Grab hold." Cable places my hand on something cold and metal. I stiffen as his hands slide down my waist and he hoists me up. "Buckle up."

It is only when I feel the material of the seat and jerk at the sound of the door closing behind me that I fully realize that I'm in a vehicle. I wait in the dark as Cable feels his way around the front of the car and hauls himself into the driver's seat.

"How can you see?"

When the headlights flick on I find myself staring at the contraption on Cable's head. They look like a set of binoculars, but not nearly the same. "Night vision," he grins and tosses them into the floorboard.

The throaty growl of the engine vibrates in my chest. Cable taps the steering wheel, peering out into the light. "What are we waiting for?"

He doesn't respond but instead watches the dark intently. I wrap my arms around myself, rubbing to keep warm. A couple minutes pass before a rectangle of light appears in the far corner of the room. Two dark shapes slip inside before darkness prevails once more.

"Who is that?"

A moment later the back door opens and I see a familiar face rise into the vehicle. "No way! I'm not going anywhere with her!"

Natalia's eyes widen as she looks between me and Cable. He grits his teeth before meeting my glare. "She helped save your life. She's coming too."

"She experimented on me!"

"No." I turn fully in the seat to look at her. "I had nothing to do with that. I told you the truth. I was merely a liaison."

"I remember you."

"Of course you do," Cable says, hiking his thumb over his shoulder for her to get in. "She watched over you during your recovery."

I refuse to look away as Natalia buckles her seat belt. I don't care what he says. I can smell a rat when I see one and she is all kinds of rotten.

Another man climbs in after her. He has baby smooth cheeks, clear blue eyes, and a grin as broad as his shoulders. He holds out his hand to me. "Eric Phelan. Heard a lot about you."

"Sit down and shut up," Cable growls as he shoves the vehicle into gear. I'm thrown back as he slams on the accelerator. Eric cries out as he tumbles to the floor, flailing to grab hold of the seat.

"Are you insane? You couldn't give him another minute to strap in?" I press my hands to the dashboard as the tires squeal and we barrel toward a wall.

Glancing at the green glow of the clock on the dashboard, he shakes his head. "Not unless you want to stick around for the barbeque."

I brace myself as we crash headlong through the hangar doors. They crumple away, peeled back like the lid of a sardine can. My head ricochets off the headrest. The Humvee rattles and shakes as Cable fights for control of his wild skid.

A huge dark shape looms ahead of us. "Look out!"

Cable swerves to miss the dangling propellers of a copter, only to take out a collection of gasoline barrels. They spiral across the tarmac, spilling fuel.

"Haul ass, Cable!" Eric's hands grip the seat behind me. His face looks pale as he leans between us, shouting out directions. I grab onto the door and hold on. Natalia buries her head in her arms. A scream escapes her lips from time to time.

As we race between two hangars, my head whips around at the sight of a large yellow vehicle. "A school bus?" I turn on Cable. "So it's true? The military really were stealing kids?"

"Now is not the time," Cable says through gritted teeth. He spins the wheel and I'm thrown against the door.

I watch as he glances frequently from the road to the clock and pray that whatever is supposed to happen hurries up. Soldiers pour from the buildings. A heavy gunfight rages all around. I don't know how on earth they know who is good and who is bad when they are all wearing the same uniform!

Lights on the guard towers sweep the grounds, zeroing in on us. A twenty foot high concrete wall looms before us, filling the windshield. I glance at Cable, noting the lack of color in his knuckles as he grips the steering wheel and guns the accelerator. "Cable?"

"Wait for it. Wait for it!" From the corner of my eye I see something large emerging from the shadows. I spy the long barrel as it swivels and takes aim.

Boom.

The windows rattle as a fireball erupts before us. Smoke and dust roll over the window. Debris rains from above, denting the roof of the Humvee. Natalia wails as we burst through the wall and into the night. Our headlights illuminate trees and an overgrown path as we bounce and skid to a halt.

"You have a tank?" I gasp, clutching my chest.

"Sure do." Eric lets out a whoop as another blast echoes from behind us. I imagine the tank must be securing our departure.

Cable breathes hard as he reaches out for me. "You ok?"

"Pretty sure I just wet myself, but yeah. I'm good."

Eric laughs and pounds Cable on the arm. "Nice moves, dude. You were right. You are the better driver."

"I'll collect on that bet later."

I tense at the hard line in Cable's voice. As the last of the smoke clears I see a bright light lock onto to us from above. I lean forward to see a chopper in the air.

"Stand down." A voice calls over a loudspeaker. "Turn your engine off and evacuate the vehicle. We have been authorized to use force if you resist.

Natalia huddles low in her seat. Her hair is a disheveled mess. Her pristine clothes rumpled and dark with sweat. The sound of her whimpering fills the vehicle.

"What do we do?" I turn to find Cable glancing back at Eric.

The baby-faced soldier pulls up his sleeve to reveal a watch and shakes his head. "We gotta delay."

"Is this thing bulletproof?" I ask, staring at the large manned gun above.

"Not like you'd hope it would be."

"What's that supposed to mean?" I grab onto the door as he spins the wheel, gunning the gas as he steers the vehicle off the road. Bullets ping against the hull. Several deep dents appear in the side. Natalia screams but I ignore her as I try to keep my eye on the chopper.

"It means we are armored but only to a point. Keep your head down!" he shouts back as he spins the wheel again.

The spotting light is blinding from above as the chopper banks to pursue us. Cable cuts the headlights and drives under a cluster of low hanging branches of a large maple tree. The tires skids to a stop, the engine settles into a deep rumble. The patch of trees won't give us cover for long. "You seriously think they can't see us here?" I gawk.

Cable ignores my comment and keeps his eye trained to the broken light overhead. Bits of bark tumble down as another round of gunfire strikes the tree. A loud ping of gunfire behind me makes me cower against the door. I hear a cry of pain and look back. Natalia clutches her shoulder.

"Shit." Eric reaches over and presses his hand to her arm. "She's hit, Cable."

"We all will be soon if we don't get out of here." Cable puts the car in reverse and sneaks between two trees. "Eric?"

"One minute!"

I spot other vehicles barreling toward us from the outside of the wall. Their headlights bounce as they hit deep ruts. The chopper overhead circles once more. Dust bursts up from the ground as I watch the trail of bullets approaching from directly ahead of us.

"Now?"

I turn to see Eric staring intently as his watch. His lips part and mime counting. Three. Two. One.

The sky behind us erupts with fire. The ground rumbles as half of the base goes up in flames. The outer wall crumbles and collapses. I watch out my side window as the pursuing vehicles swerve to miss the falling debris. A large chunk of the wall smashes into the hood of the front car. Its back end flies up into the air. The second car brakes too late and slams headlong into the underside of the lead vehicle. Both erupt into flames. I watch in horror as flaming bodies thrust themselves out of the vehicle and writhe on the ground.

"Oh, god!" I grasp my stomach as I turn away. I wanted to escape but not like this. Those men were probably just following orders.

The chopper veers off. Cable punches the accelerator and guns for the forest in sheer darkness, lit only by the scattered light of the moon peering behind clouds overhead. My head rocks from side to side as we navigate the uneven terrain. The ride is rough, but I feel safer than I have in weeks.

"Get us out of here," Eric says, pointing away from the path before us. "No main roads. We have to find somewhere to lie low."

"What about that chopper? Won't more come back around for us?" I glance over my shoulder but the skies seem clear apart from the huge plume of smoke from the fire.

Eric grins. "Nah. We just blew up all of their big shiny toys. It'll take them a few minutes to regroup."

I turn forward as Cable reengages the headlights. "Now what?

Cable takes his eyes off the road only for a moment to look at me. "We run and don't look back."

NINE

I stare at the black radio handset in my hand, listening to the static. I have tried every channel, even ones I know the military would be scanning, but I had no choice. I gave Alex my promise that I would find a way to reach them, no matter what.

"This is Avery calling for Alex. Do you read me?"

Static fills the cab of the Humvee. I call again several times, switching through the stations. "I promised I would call you. I'm sorry I couldn't get back to you. I was...I was delayed, but I'm waiting for you now," I say, leaning my head against the window. I feel stiff and cold from sitting so long.

"If you hear this message, please leave the city. We are located thirty miles east of your last position. We have to leave soon." I release the button and press my hand to my lips to still their trembling. The cold is brutal today.

"Alex...come find me."

The door to the barn opens and I raise my hand to shield my eyes from the light. I spy Cable's elongated mask first as he slips into the dark, leaving the door open to the outside.

"You've been out here all day. Any luck?" Cable slings himself up into the driver's seat beside me and removes his gas mask only once secured inside. His face is clean, his hair freshly washed. A shadow of stubble darkens his square jaw. He looks refreshed despite spending a night tossing and turning in his sleep. I heard him cry out in the dark. Nightmares from the past plague him. I wonder what it is that he dreams of.

"It's been three days and I'm no closer to finding them than I was."

Cable nods, lowering his head. I sigh, resigned to trying again later. I turn off the ignition and hand him the keys.

"You know we can't stay much longer." He fiddles the keys between his fingers. "Sooner or later someone is going to hear that message and figure out where we are."

"I know." I flex my fingers then clasp them before me, wishing for the hundredth time that I had a pair of gloves. The abandoned farm house we crashed in the night we escaped from the military base smelled of old people and moth balls, but it had basic supplies. Sweaters that were a bit too snug on the men. Floral blouses that I would rather die than wear, but Natalia didn't seem to care. Come to think of it, she hasn't cared about much since we arrived.

At first I thought it was some sort of post-traumatic stress. Cable said that it's possible. People handle death and climatic situations differently. Eric has stayed by her side since we arrived. He leaves her unattended only long enough to pop open a can of soup and returns to spoon-feed her.

Cable and I searched the attic and found trunks of old clothes, photo albums and keepsakes but no trace of winter outer wear. I tucked all of the floral shirts aside for Natalia and grabbed a fluffy sweater. It's way too big on me and has a tendency to billow in the wind, but as long as I keep my white shirt tucked into my pants, it works fairly well.

Shoes are one area that I lucked out in. I guess me and the grandma who lived here share a size 8. I found a pair of brand new tennis shoes hidden in the back of a downstairs closet and enough hand knitted wool socks to keep my feet toasty for a long time.

Cable thinks the old folks probably left when the world went down the crapper. There are tire tracks in the yard. The barn doors were left wide open. Even some of the cabinets were emptied. I hope he's right.

"Do you think maybe you should let it go?" Cable asks after several moments of silence.

"I can't." I stare out the grimy windshield. The sun is bright today, breaking through the cloud cover for the first time in what feels like months. I long to feel it on my face but it's too dangerous to go out during the day. We are still too close to the military base. From time to time we hear the choppers as they work in a grid, searching. Eric seems to think they have bigger problems than hunting for us, but I have my doubts.

It's the way Natalia looks at me when she thinks I don't see. Piercing. Searching.

I've yet to find out exactly what it is that she did for the military. Whatever her relationship was with them, there is one thing that is certain...Eric is far too fond of her. I suspect that's the reason Cable let her hitch a ride out, not because of anything to do with me.

"I have to know," I whisper, turning away from the sunlight that ends just at the edge of the barn we are parked inside. "Eva needed me and I left her. I can't do that again."

Cable taps his fingers against the steering wheel, deep in thought. He does that a lot. At first it was a bit off-putting, making me wonder what secrets he might be trying to worm his way around revealing. The more time I spend with him I realize it's just his way. He's a thinker.

"You know their chances of survival were slim. That entire section of the city was overrun two days after I found you. If they didn't get out before that then they are lost."

I close my eyes and press my forehead against the window. The cold glass bites my skin but I ignore it. I told Cable all about Eva, about the group and my promise. He has actively supported my decision to remain behind, until now. I know we can't wait any more but I can't willingly leave either. I just don't know how to make him understand.

"Eva couldn't have been moved," he whispers, running his finger along the curve of the mask.

"I know." Exhaustion and remorse fall over me. I have so many things to be thankful for. Shelter. Food. Protection. People. Why isn't that enough? Why can't I adapt to this new world of loss and pain, to let go of the things that would seek to hold me back? "I knew better than to let myself care."

I stiffen as Cable grasps my hand. Lifting my head, I turn to look at him as tears that I've been resisting escape down my cheeks. "You're human. It's in our nature."

"So is murder, theft and a million other atrocities. Is that in me too, Cable? Am I going to become someone I don't even recognize just to avoid becoming like them?"

I point out the window and he turns to look at a Moaner shuffling through the yard. Several more follow behind, some leaving a path of entrails in their wake.

"I don't know," he answers with brutal honesty. His gaze is conflicted as he turns to look at me. He tries to offer me a reassuring smile but it falls flat. "I hope not."

I pull my hand away from him, tucking it into my side. "I thought you were like those other soldiers."

Closing my eyes, I refuse to see the look of pain that mars his face. Cable is a good guy, I understand that now, but being a good guy doesn't mean I can trust him.

He shifts in his seat. I hear him hit the pedals as he turns to face me. "I guess I deserve that. If roles were reversed I'd have a ton of questions too."

I open my eyes to see that he is leaning toward me. The planes of his face are hard but in a good way. The new stubble enhances his good looks. In this confined space I realize just how aware I have become of him over the past few days.

"I saw the bus…"

He swallows hard. Turning away he places his hands on the steering wheel and sighs. "I don't have all of the answers. I'm sure that surprises you." He smirks but I'm in no mood. "Look, I heard rumors but never saw any kids myself. They weren't where I slept, ate or worked so if there were there, they were buried deep."

My breath hitches as the memory of the base exploding floods back in. My hands begin to tremble as I press them to my stomach. "Did we kill them?"

"What?" He twists toward me. "No. Of course not!"

"How do you know? They could have been forgotten in the fire fight. The tank could have misfired and crushed them. They could have--"

"Stop." He grasps my hands and squeezes. "Worrying about this will only make you sick. It's best to think positive and trust that they got out."

I stare down at his hands, clasped around mine and I'm desperate to believe him. To soak up an ounce of his optimism, but I can't do it. "Eva told me that her little sister was taken by the military."

Cable nods. "Natalia worked with a few kids at a different base somewhere up north. Said it was all routine tests. Nothing weird that she could tell."

"Do you trust her?"

"Natalia?" He shrugs and releases my hands, sinking back into the seat. He draws his leg up and rests it against the wheel. "I don't really know her. Eric vouched for her so that's good enough for me."

"Really? It's that easy for you?" I cross my arms over my chest to ward off the cold. "I think we both know that I've got every reason to have trust issues right now. You seem to care about keeping me safe. Eric seems decent too. If you want me to play nice with Natalia I'm going to need more than just a friendly handshake that she's good."

"Like what?" I can tell he is hedging and that makes me all the more suspicious.

"How did she have clearance to come speak to me? What does she know about what they did to me? Why did she aid us in escaping? Who beat her?"

Cable leans back away from me and turns his gaze outward. When he reaches up to stroke his throat, grimacing at the windshield, I turn to see a woman stumble less than ten feet from the hood of the Humvee. Half of her arm has been torn off. The bone protrudes from the rotting flesh. White maggots crawl over the open wound. My stomach churns but I force myself not to look away. To truly see the horrors that have consumed this world.

"Eric says that Natalia is complicated."

I return my attention to Cable as the woman disappears around the edge of the barn. "That's not good enough."

"Well for now it's going to have to be–" he turns his head at a raised cry and leaps from the vehicle, pulling his mask into place as he goes. I'm right on his heels as we sprint toward the house. "This isn't over," I call to him as we hit the porch.

"Kinda figured you'd say that." He takes the stairs two steps at a time. I'm winded by the time I reach the second floor but he's hardly broken a sweat. "What is it? What's wrong?"

Eric appears in the doorway, his face a mask of sorrow. His chin trembles as he steps aside. I can tell by the swelling around his eyes that he's been crying. "Her fever is gone."

I pause in the doorway as the two men go to her bedside, not wanting to intrude. Cable sinks down beside Natalia and takes her hand in his. He presses his free hand to her brow. "She's freezing."

"I know." Eric tosses his towel aside and brushes past me. I watch him leave, his shoulders sagging and his steps heavy as he descends to the lower floor.

When I turn back I see Cable's head bowed low. Four blankets lay draped over Natalia. Dark shadows line her eyes. Her cheeks are sunken, as if she's been without food for weeks instead of only a day.

After a moment of silence Cable lifts his gaze to look at me. "I didn't take you for a praying man."

"Never used to be." He places her hand beside her and then lifts her bandage. The bullet that entered through her shoulder in our mad dash to evade the chopper was a clean hit. Eric and Cable have been diligent to keep it clean, but the fever began within a day of our arrival here.

Her skin is unnaturally pale. Her veins prominent against her frail arms. When he opens her mouth I see that her tongue is coated with a thick substance. He opens her eyes and they stare back at him with no reaction. She looks as if she's begun to wither right before our eyes.

My breath catches as I close my eyes. "Of course," I murmur and lean against the doorframe. "She's turning, isn't she?"

Cable clears his throat but doesn't answer. He doesn't need to. I sigh, rub my forehead and look at him. "I'm sorry. I've never seen it happen before. Not this close at least. Last time it was in the hospital and they kept the woman secluded for the most part."

"Well," he turns his face up to look at me. Cable looks exhausted. Lines carve deeply into his face. His hair hangs limp against his forehead. He shakes his head slowly and I'm touched by the sorrow that he feels for a woman he barely knew. "You're about to get a front row seat."

He continues to look at Natalia, seeming to be willing her lungs to continue to expand, her brain to continue to function. He reaches to his side and retrieves a knife. It isn't long or particularly nasty looking, but it looks sharp as he withdraws it from a black leather sheath.

"What are you doing?" I call out as he grips Natalia's arm and presses the blade to her flesh.

"Testing."

With a flick of his wrist, a thin but deep wound appears on the back of her forearm. No scream. No flinch. No sign of pain. He hangs his head and the knife goes limp in his hand. I enter the room and kneel down beside him, tucking the blade away.

"It's not your fault."

He wipes at his nose and shoves the blade into his pocket. "I'm just sick of losing good people."

I know the feeling. Even though I may not have anyone else in my life, I've grown to care about a couple of people and I don't want to see them get hurt. "You hungry? I was thinking of making soup for dinner."

"Nah." He shifts on the edge of the bed. "I'll stay for a little longer."

Feeling like a bit of an outsider, I rise and close the door behind me, heading downstairs. I find Eric sitting on the hideous pink couch, staring out the window. He doesn't notice me until I sink down beside him.

"Hey, Avery." He offers me a forced smile and brushes his hands through his hair. He looks terrible. A splotchy beard has consumed the thin growth of stubble he arrived with. Eric hasn't slept, hasn't taken the time to eat. His vigil at Natalia's bedside was constant. "How are you doing?"

I release a breathy laugh and shake my head, resting it in the palm of my hand as I lean on my knee and stare at him. "Shouldn't I be the one asking you that?"

He slumps back into the couch and grabs a pillow, hugging it to his chest. His black hair falls in waves over his forehead and not for the first time I wonder why he was never told he had to shave his head like the rest of the soldiers. His style just seems too...messy.

"She knew it was coming. Started developing the symptoms a few days back but didn't want to say anything. She knew the consequences if she did."

I purse my lips. "So that's why she was caked in makeup."

He nods and fiddles with a stray thread that has come loose from his jacket. "I told her to do it. Thought it could give her a few more days before someone found out. The doctors should have noticed right away but they were preoccupied."

"With what?" He glances over at me and I grimace. "With me?"

"You caused quite a stir back there."

"But why?" I lower my leg and turn to face him. "What made me so different than all those other people? Is it my blood?"

Eric tilts his head side to side. "Not so much your blood, but your plasma."

"And to those of us who aren't doctors in the room that means what exactly?"

"Alright," he twists his torso to face me. From this angle he looks even worse. Deep bags hang under dull eyes. He is pasty and thin. Thinking back, I'm not sure I've seen him eat more than a spoonful of soup since we arrived. "You've heard about universal donors, right?"

"Sure. Some people have a blood type that can be transfused into anyone."

"Exactly." He holds up his fingers, gesturing with surprising animation. "The number of people who have this sort of blood is right around 40%, give or take a few thousand."

"So I'm one of those?"

"Nope." He ducks his head in low and speaks in a hushed tone, as if someone might overhear. "You're even better."

He reaches out and grasps my wrist, turning it over. I watch as he brushes his thumb over the bluish veins in my wrist. "You, Avery, have something very rare. A blood type that allows you to be a universal plasma donor. Only about 1% of people have that, and since we've lost a considerable number of those people recently, you've become even more valuable."

"But why?" I draw my hand back from him. I trace my finger down the curve of a vein, lost in thought.

"Because the government thinks your plasma could be used for a cure." I turn to see Cable hit the bottom step. He wipes his knife across his pant leg before meeting our gaze. A wide patch of blood stains his right side. Small splatters dot his face. Eric tenses beside me. He wavers in place but remains upright. I reach out and grasp his hand as he closes his eyes. A guttural groan rises from his throat but he doesn't say anything.

Cable sinks down before us and clasps his friend on the shoulder, squeezing tight. I watch Eric fight back the tears, battle his grief. I don't know what to say, what to do so I just sit and wait. Slowly, Eric regains his composure. He takes deep breaths, his fingers clenching tightly against his knees. Finally he nods and Cable releases him.

"Plasma is a pretty amazing thing," Eric says with a pinched voice.

"Eric," I whisper, shaking my head. "You don't have to…"

"Yeah, I do." He wipes his nose with his sleeve then the tears from his face and raises his chin as he continues. "Easily put, it's a life-saving resource that we are sorely in need of now."

Cable sinks back onto the floor before us. Over his shoulder I see that the sun has begun its descent. Night will soon fall and we will be forced to barricade ourselves in again. Last night a chopper came too close for comfort to our camp. I overheard Cable and Eric talking this morning about the likelihood that tonight's search would expand to include our farm. Chances are we may have lingered one day too long.

Eric stares out the window, emotion seeping from his face as he comes to the same conclusion I just did. It's too late to bury Natalia. We will have to wait until morning.

"How do you two know so much?" I ask, trying to pull him back

Both look toward the ceiling and I mentally kick myself for not thinking. Eric returns his gaze to me. "She was trying to help, Avery. She wasn't like the General, driven by a need for results. She saw the person as well as the problem. I wish you'd had the chance to get to know her. I think you would have liked her."

I'm not sure what to say, how to respond. It is true that I didn't know Natalia. It's also true that I didn't want to, not after she became connected to those experiments. In my mind she was guilty by association.

A muscle running the length of Eric's neck tightens as he clenches his jaw. "I'm very sorry for your loss."

He nods but doesn't speak. His fists clench in his lap. Cable leans forward and plunges his hands into his hair and an uncomfortable silence hangs between us as twilight falls over the farmhouse. The door to the barn was left wide open. One of us will have to go and secure it before the choppers come. Looking at Cable and Eric, I decide it will be me.

"We can't stay here any longer." Cable says, staring first at Eric, then at me. He winces before he speaks, knowing that his words will be salt in our open wounds. "The past will only slow us down."

A gargled sound erupts from Eric. He surges to his feet. "Sorry," he mutters as he staggers toward the bathroom. I collapse back into the sofa as I hear him retching.

"Was that really the best time to bring that up? And what's with you not cleaning your knife before you came downstairs? Are you trying to give him a mental breakdown?"

Cable's jaw clenches with each accusation. This is a hard death to accept for both of them, but this...it just seems callous. So unlike him.

"Natalia is gone. Your friends aren't answering. I can't risk all of our lives for what if's, Avery. It's my job to protect you."

"No." I push to the edge of the couch. "It's my job to protect me."

"And where will we go?" I ask before he can contradict me. "Which road will lead us somewhere safe? You still wear your mask, for goodness sake! What if we head north and the air is contaminated there? Or West and the food has gone bad? What if we hug the coast and realize the seas are poisoned too?"

"I don't know," he shouts, rising abruptly to his feet and begins to pace. His voice is thick with emotion when he speaks.

"I don't have the answers. I just know that we can't stay here. It's too dangerous."

"We can't leave her," Eric whispers from where he leans heavily in the doorway. He wipes his mouth and spits to the side.

My heart goes out to him. The strong man that sat beside me looks lost and broken. Cable sighs are he turns toward his friend. "Natalia would have ordered you to go."

At his words, a pained smile stretches along Eric's face. "And I would have ignored her, like I always did."

I rub my hand over my face, weary and tired of saying goodbye to people, even the ones I may not have liked. "One more day," I whisper. "Give us one more day to give Natalia a proper burial. If I can't reach Alex by tomorrow night then I'll leave with you."

Cable leans forward, his hand covering his mouth as he surveys me. His gaze is intense but I meet it all the same. Finally he nods. "Ok. One more day."

TEN

Sweat beads along my brow. I duck and swing. Pain bites into my knuckles, splitting the skin but I swing again, and again. I spin and weave, thrusting my fist up. It connects with the grain bag with a deep, gratifying thud

"I think you got it." I spin around to find Cable standing behind me, leaning lazily against the barn door. "What'd it do to tick you off?"

"Nothing." It feels good to sweat, to move without having to cushion my ribs. For the first time in weeks I almost feel whole again. "I just needed to let off a little steam."

Cable tucks his hands deep into his pockets. "The funeral was pretty rough, huh?"

I nod. "It was my first."

"Really?" He straightens slightly at that. "You never lost a grandparent or neighbor?"

"Nope."

"What about a goldfish? Tell me you at least flushed one of those."

I laugh and look over at him through strings of hair. I found a bit of yarn to tie back my mass of curls but several chunks have fallen free. "I'm pretty sure Goldie doesn't count."

"Goldie, huh? And I pegged you for an unconventional sort of girl."

"Sorry to disappoint." I place my hands back on the grain sack and prepare to begin again. After a moment, I turn and find him still staring at me. "I usually vent in private, if you don't mind."

His expression is obscured behind his mask but I'd wager he's grinning.

"Why do you still wear that thing, anyways?" I wipe my brow clean with the bottom of my shirt. The chill morning air nips at my stomach as I let the material falls back into place. I switched out my sweater for a frilly floral shirt when I woke in respect of Natalia's final moments. The instant it was over, I chucked that shirt in the trash and traded it for a men's long sleeve cotton V-neck shirt that is two sizes too large. I knotted the material at the base of my back and rolled the sleeves.

Cable watches me for a moment as I turn my back on the bag and plant my hands on my hips. My knuckles sting where the skin has split. I can't help but feel smug as Cable slowly removes the gas mask. "Habit, I guess."

"Still think this crap is in the air?"

His broad shoulders rise and fall in a shrug. He uncrosses his legs and walks toward me, leaving the sun at his back. I spy large patches of shadow moving across the field beyond. The clouds have begun to move back in. I can feel a change on the air but keep my fears to myself. The last thing I want is to be caught in a winter storm while on the run, but I gave my word. One day and I would leave and never look back.

"I reckon it won't make much difference now." He tosses the mask aside.

"Why's that?"

Cable hikes his leg and sinks down onto a square bale of hay. The whole barn smells of it. That and spilled oil from the relic of a tractor in the far corner. He kicks out his leg, his boot slamming back into the hay. He rubs his hands together, losing himself to that inner world that nothing can penetrate, then grabs my pistol and begins methodically cleaning it.

I sigh and turn back to the feed bag. My grunts are the only sound in the barn for several minutes. I duck and weave, as if matching wits with an opponent. I'm sure Cable knows that I'm faking most of the moves. A soldier with any decent training would see right through my bravado but I can't just sit around and wait. I need to prepare. If what Cable and Eric said yesterday is true, my life is in danger from far more than this contamination. What started out as a need to vent has become something like borderline desperation.

Glancing over at Cable, I consider asking him to teach me how to use that pistol, but we have very few weapons as it is and far fewer bullets. I notice that he's laid the gun in his lap and is busy scratching at his palm. I squint to look closer, wondering if he's picked up a splinter while hunting for supplies, but when he sees me staring he shoves his hands in his pockets. "I'm sorry about Natalia."

"Me too."

"I uh…" I rub my hand along the back of my neck. "I just want you to know that I support your decision to move on. It will be good for Eric to say goodbye but not linger."

Cable looks around the barn, leaning back to look up into the rafters overhead. Tools hang from rusting chain: hoes, shovels, pitch forks and something that looks like a handheld tiller for a garden. "She genuinely cared about people," he finally says when he returns his gaze to me. "Eric most of all. I think they could have made it, you know? A decent couple."

I sink down into a crouch and wait for him to continue. For once he might actually be in a talking mood. "Eric knew her from before all of this. I guess he was kind of sweet on her back then but she never really had time for stuff like that. Her work was her life. By the time Eric figured that out, it didn't matter anymore."

Grabbing a handful of hay, he shoves a long strand between his teeth, as if he's always done it. There is a weird familiarity about the action, making me wonder what Cable was like in a previous life, before the mutations, before the Marines. I can't recall if he ever told me where he was from. Only that he was from the South.

"Why did she help me?"

Cable leans back, crossing his arms over his chest as he rests his weight against the wall. The weathered wood holds firm, despite the knots and evidence of termite damage near the floor. "She was a scientist. One of the best, according to Eric. She spent her life devoted to helping people, to discovering cures to unspeakable horrors. You were a piece to a larger puzzle but she knew if you remained there you wouldn't be able to help the world."

"Help the world?" I scoff, rolling my eyes. I sink down onto the ground, tucking my legs before me. I dust my hands off on my pant legs, leaving dirty hand prints behind. "I'm just one person."

Cable's expression tightens as he leans forward. "For all we know this whole thing started with a single person, a single virus, a single mutated gene. Why would you think one person couldn't fix it all?"

Blowing my hair out of my eyes, I shrug. "Because I'm no hero."

"How do you know?"

I avert my gaze, focusing intently on the bald tractor tire sitting beside him instead of his piercing gaze. "I just do."

"Hmm."

I listen to his steady inhale and exhale, wishing that he would leave. He makes me uncomfortable at times. Usually when he's trying to get some deep message across to me. It's not that he lectures me, but it's pretty darn close to it.

"You don't know me," I whisper, turning my cheek to press it against my knee. My muscles ache from training. My head feels light and airy. I've pushed myself farther than I should have. I'm still recovering, but I will go crazy if I do nothing but wait and pray for a miracle.

My pleas on the radio have gone unanswered all day. Last night, not long after the moon hit its highest peak in the sky, we heard the choppers fly over. Their light shining in through the windows would have woken me if the noise hadn't. We'd planned for that, made sure we hide in interior rooms just in case. They couldn't have seen us from the air, but that won't stop them from checking all the same. The question is: how many other homes do they have to search before ours?

"You're a good person, Avery."

"What is good? Helping an old lady across the street? Giving a kid a balloon just to see them smile? Handing out money to a homeless person who is hungry?"

I raise my head. "None of those things matter anymore, Cable. There is no good left in this world. Only greed. Only murder and evil and nothingness."

"You're wrong." He slides off the hay bale and scoots toward me. He never breaks eye contact with me as he draws near. I can smell the scent of sweat on him, see the sheen on his skin. He spent most of the morning helping Eric try to hotwire the old Ford truck in the yard. A hose sits near the front of the

Humvee that was used to siphon gas in the hopes that it will work in that old clunker. He also worked to stash our supplies in bags for us to carry out of here if we had to leave on foot. Planned tirelessly on securing the house, wiping all evidence of our presence except the Humvee. Not much we can do about that.

He has hardly stopped long enough to close his eyes for a few minutes since we arrived here. He's done the work of five people. I could never fault him for not caring about our protection. No. I'd almost fault him for caring too much. I know where that path leads and I wouldn't want that for him.

Cable motions with his hand between us. "You and me, we're still good. We give a shit." He points toward my chest. "I've watched you these past few days and have witnessed your desperation each time you switch on that radio. You risk your own life each day we remain here and for what?" He ducks his head to meet me in the eye. "For a friend."

I wrap my arms around myself and rock slowly. "She's probably gone."

"Yeah," he nods in agreement. "She just might be, but you never gave up hope."

"I should never have let myself care. I've spent my whole life keeping people at arm's length. It was safer that way."

"That's a hard way to live."

I shrug. "It's how I survived."

"And that?" He turns to look at the grain bag. "You learn that along the way too?"

"Maybe."

He stares down at my hands, no doubt noting the bruising and cut skin. "I could teach you to shoot."

"No." I shake my head, knowing that I'd only waste precious ammunition. Maybe if we come across a pawn shop or gun cache somewhere then I'd be willing to learn. "That's your thing."

"So, what? You think you're going to pummel them to death?"

I smirk, laughing at his grim expression. "I've learned a thing or two living on the streets."

His mood shifts as he rubs his jaw, his nails grazing another day's addition of growth. "Killing someone, even in self-defense, isn't easy, Avery. Don't fool yourself into thinking that it is."

Cable's words fall heavily over me, stealing away the smile that teetered on my lips. "Have you done it?"

His nod is slow and forced. He refuses to meet my gaze. "Seventeen. That's my count so far."

"Before or after the world fell apart?"

His adam's apple bobs. "Fourteen after."

I blow out a breath and lean back. "And the other three?"

He shakes his head. "They were a mission. Nothing more."

"As easy as that, huh?"

Cable falls still. "I didn't say that."

"No, you didn't, but you're sure as heck trying to make it sound like that."

"What do you want me to say? That ending a life gets easier each time you do it? Well, I hate to tell you, but it doesn't. Each time is just as fucked up as the last."

I lean forward and wait for him to re-engage with me. "You killed twice for me. I know that cost you something."

A vein pulses down the center of his forehead as he struggles to control his emotions. Guilt? Shame? Fear? I can't tell. Probably a mixture of all of those. "You did what you had to do. There's no fault in that."

He drills his gaze right into me and for a split second I recoil. "There is always fault in death. Especially when it's face to face. Those final moments haunt you forever."

I reach out and place my hand on his forearm. He looks down at it. "That's what makes us different than those people out there."

He follows the direction of my arm as I point to a small cluster of Withered Ones emerging from the dense tree line. The wooden fence proves too tricky to maneuver for the two on the far left side of the group. The others walk on, leaving their companions behind to repeatedly march into the fence.

"They aren't people," he says.

I purse my lips, hesitating before I speak. "Maybe they still are."

"What do you mean?"

I jerk my head toward them. "What do you see?"

He clears his throat and pulls his hand out from under mine. The warmth of his skin lingers only a moment. I rub my palm against my leg to remove the feeling of his touch. "Six Moaners out for a stroll."

"They aren't strolling, Cable." I wait for him to tear his gaze away from the Moaners to face me again. "They are walking, in the same direction, at the same speed."

He slowly turns back toward the doorway. I lean forward, near enough to see the pulse thrumming against his neck. "They are in step with each other."

His breath hitches as he finally sees exactly what I have seen for the past several days. "That's not possible," he mutters under his breath.

"And yet it is."

His brow furrows as he turns to look at me. His eyes widen as his nose brushes against my cheek. I quickly sit back. His gaze searches mine but I turn away, tucking my hair behind my ear. Clearing his throat, he repositions himself, placing space between us. "I never noticed before."

"I did." I trail my fingers through the dirt. The barn floor is a mixture of dust, old fallen leaves and stray bits of hay. Beneath is a layer of hard dirt. "I think one of them grabbed me."

Cable's head whips up. "What?"

I chew on my lower lip, digging my nails deeper into the ground. "Before I was taken by those soldiers, I was in this pharmacy looking for supplies. I heard it when I entered. It was dark, pretty much impossible to see. To be honest, after the herd I passed through in the street I'm amazed I went in there at all."

A smirk tugs at his handsome features and I know he's about to toss out some crap about me being stronger than I think I am, so I rush ahead. "It grabbed me by the wrist. I could feel how cold its skin was, like a tepid bath on a hot summer day. It felt...wrong. The skin was loose, kinda floppy I guess."

"What happened?"

"A bag came down over my head and the next thing I knew I was being tossed in the back of a truck. Woke up in that blood bank a while later."

I stare at dust motes floating through the air instead of him. I feel him watching me, weighing my words. "I know it sounds crazy. Trust me, I've wondered if I'm losing it so many times, but I know what happened."

"I believe you."

"Do you?" I lower my gaze toward him. He stares back with an unwavering gaze.

"Yes. I do."

"Why?"

"Because you said it."

I laugh, shaking my head and the moment of tension passes. "Are you always so trusting?"

"Pretty much."

"Must be a southern thing."

"No. I just prefer to think good of people."

"That could get you killed one of these days."

Cable smirks and pushes himself up from the ground. "Well, then let's hope today is not that day."

He offers me a hand. I brush my hand over the ground to cover my doodling and pause. "Wait a second."

Rising to my knees, I place my palm against the dirt and sweep my hand wide across the ground. Cable crouches down beside me. I trace my hand along a deep groove in the dirt, hardly unusual to find in a working barn but something about it feels to straight, too perfect.

"Look!"

Leaning low I blow against the dirt and reveal a distinctive wood grain beneath the layer of dirt. Cable begins to follow my lead and a couple minutes later we uncover a trap door. "Well, how about that."

I loop my finger through a small hole cut into the wood, but Cable places a hand on my arm to stop me. "Maybe we shouldn't."

"Shouldn't what? It's not like we would be trespassing any more than we already have."

"I know, I just think–" he cuts off as the sputtering of static bursts from the open door of the Humvee. I scramble to my feet and race for the radio.

"Hello? Is anyone there?" I lean in close, fighting to hear the garbled voice, distorted and faint. "Please repeat. I can't understand you."

"This...Alex...coming...you…"

"It's them," I call back over my shoulder to Cable, only to find him right behind me.

"I heard. Let's see if we can clean it up a bit. Go grab Eric. He's better at this than I am."

I toss Cable the handset and tear out of the barn. My shirt billows around me as I race across the lawn, grabbing hold of the porch post to swing myself up the steps. "Eric!"

The screen door screeches and slams behind me as I search the bottom floor. I move swiftly up the stairs and check the bedroom we shared the night before. The bathroom is empty, as are the spare rooms. I fight to still my breathing as I turn toward the only door left closed.

"Oh, Eric." I reach out to push open the master bedroom door. The morning light filters in through the white eyelet curtains, graying with dust. The pale rose colored rocker that sits beneath the window is empty. The pictures of a smiling man and woman standing proudly on their front porch stare back at me. White hair and big smiles contained within a frame boasting the 'best grandparents in the world.'

The bloody bed covers dangle on the floor. The pillows bear evidence of two heads, a dent on either side of the bed. I step toward the partially closed bathroom door and hold my breath as I listen to the steady drip of water. The door squeaks on its hinges as it slowly opens. Grimy white tiles offset the pink soaker tub and vanity. Wilted flowers droop from a glass vase residing on the double window beside the bathtub. Droplets fall from the tap into the bath, collecting into a tiny stream as they trail down into the drain.

Spinning around, I look into the linen closet and behind two sliding doors to reveal an old side by side washer and dryer that has a manual dial.

Eric isn't here.

"Avery?"

I turn at the sound of my name and head for the door. I pause in the doorway, casting one last glance at the room.

"Cable?"

"Downstairs."

My feet feel like lead as I descend. I should have paid attention to Eric's mood shift. I should have spoken to him, expressed my sympathy. I knew he was hurting, mourning in his own silent way. I assumed with the way he poured himself into fixing up that truck that he needed to get away...

I hang my head. "He's gone," I whisper, realizing that he probably slipped away while I was beating up the grain bag, when my grunts masked the hum of the engine starting. We should have seen this coming. Cable helped him get it ready. We gave him the perfect opportunity and he took it, leaving us behind.

"He took the truck," I say as I slowly descend the stairs. Cable nods, placing his hands on my arms as I stop on the final step.

"I know. It's what he would have wanted."

I sink down onto the step, feeling numb, cold. "Why would he just leave us like this? He took our supplies and our only transportation."

Sinking down into a crouch before me, he shakes his head. "He couldn't let go."

I wipe at my eyes, realizing that my emotions have betrayed me. It angers me that I'm crying, that I'm feeling weak when I should be strong. I swallow hard. "He was a fool."

"Why? Because he loved her?"

"Because he let her drag him down."

I rise and try to push past him, but Cable stops me, grasping my arm. "Don't shut down. Not now."

"Why not? What good has caring ever done for me?"

His grip loosens, his hand slides down my arm to take my hand in his. I stare at it, knowing that I should pull away, but I don't. "Because your friends are coming."

ELEVEN

I watch Cable shove cans of food and packages of homemade dried jerky into a spare pack, digging deep into the back of the cabinets for food we never thought we would need. He rushes through the kitchen, opening and slamming cabinet doors in search of more supplies. Spare canning jars, filled with water from the well out back, line the counter. He moves with purpose and speed. This worries me.

"Do you need any help?" He hasn't spoken in nearly three hours. Not since he told me my friends were coming. He doesn't seem all that happy about the idea. "I could help, you know?"

Cable looks back over his shoulder at me, as if realizing for the first time that I'm still here. "I need you outside. Keep watch on the west. That's where they should be coming from."

Something about the way he says *they* makes me wonder if he actually means Alex's group. I close the gap between us and grab onto his arm, noticing how the early evening light filtering in through the kitchen window has begun to wane. Twilight will be upon us within the hour. We need to be gone by then.

"Stop." He resists and I tighten my grip. "Stop, Cable."

"There's no time for that," he grumbles, pulling away. He ducks low and searches under the sink. He grabs a box of matches, shaking it to see if it is full then stretches to reach a half empty pack of batteries that look as if they may have begun to corrode. "We have to be ready to leave the moment they arrive."

"Why? What aren't you telling me?" He goes still, the backpack falling slack at his side.

"Look, I know you're upset about Eric. I want to go look for him too, but you're wasting energy. He's probably halfway to the Illinois and Kentucky border by now. When Alex gets here we can all help fill the extra packs. Who knows, maybe they have their own supply stash."

He rubs his hand across the top of his head, mussing his hair as he grimaces down at the floor. "It's not Eric that I'm worried about. He can take care of himself better than most people."

I duck down beside him, our knees nearly touching. "Then what is it?"

He swallows hard and focuses on his hands after briefly meeting my gaze. "I think your friends are being followed."

"By who?" My grip tightens on my knees as I balance beside him.

"I'm not sure. I've been worried for days that someone will have heard your messages. Worried that if the military did trace the call that they would bide their time. They could have busted in here at any time if they wanted to."

"But why would they wait?" Cable stares hard at me and slowly his meaning sinks in. I blow out a breath and sink back onto the floor. "More people. More blood."

He nods, looking as sickened as I feel. "So what do we do? We can't just leave them for bait."

"I know." He grabs a rag from under the sink and wipes his brow. Despite the chilled air in the house, sweat beads along his forehead. His cheeks hold a faint flush. "I've been trying to figure it out. To find a way to minimize the damage if there is a show down."

"You don't have to do this on your own, Cable. I know I'm not a soldier, but I've been through a lot in my life. I've learned a thing or two about taking care of myself when I need to."

"I can't risk that. If it comes down to it, we're going to have to fight."

I glance toward the barn through the kitchen window. The doors are closed, concealing the Humvee within. It won't do us any good now that we siphoned the gas and switched it over to the truck that Eric stole. That was our solution, our way to hide out in plain sight. Now we are stuck.

I don't blame Eric for his decision. Not really. I guess, if I stopped to think about it, I might have done the same thing in his position if I were consumed with grief.

Shaking my head, I know that's not true either. I couldn't just leave someone behind like that, no matter how much someone's death affected me. "Fine. So we fight."

"It's not that easy, Avery. If the military are on their tail then they will come heavily armed and with far more men than we could take out."

"So what do you want to do? Leave?"

This question places a heavy burden on him. Cable is a good guy— almost too good. He places the weight of the world on his shoulders and no one is strong enough to carry that.

"No. We don't know for sure that anyone is following them, but I'd rather be cautious."

"Agreed." I nod in agreement. "What do you need me to do?"

"Hide." He slowly rises to his feet and turns his back on me. I hear him resume shifting through things on the counter.

"No way!" I push up from my knees. "I'm not going to just go bury myself in some dark hole while you take all of the risk."

He sighs as he turns to face me. "I was afraid you were going to say that."

My eyes widen in shock at the flash of silver he swings down in an arch toward my head. Pain splinters at my temple and I crash to the ground.

When I wake, my head feels as if it's been smashed in a trash compactor. My nose feels slightly ajar. Dried flakes of blood mat my hair to my temple. My eye is tender and slightly swollen.

"Why is it always my head?" I groan as I roll to my side.

A moist cloth falls away from my face. Small chunks of ice patter against the ground beside me. Pressing my palm to the side of my face I feel a chill. "A jerk and a gentleman at the same time," I grumble as I slowly rise.

The throbbing in my head increases as I sit up. The air feels cold and thick, making it feel as if I can't catch my breath.

I push back slowly and cry out as I hit a wall. My fingers search about me in the dark. Splinters of wood burrow into my fingertips as I trace along the wall. I ignore the pain and slowly work my way around the small space.

From above, a rectangle of light can just be seen. The light darkens. I raise my face toward the ceiling and cough as dirt rains down. My fingers guide me along a set of wooden steps that lead up. I can feel cold seeping through the space beyond the steps and hurry to sink into the dark hole behind. Earth presses against my shoulder. I lean my head against it to ease the pounding as shouts reach me for the first time.

Overhead, I hear the grinding wheels of the barn doors sliding open. My pulse thumps in my chest as I listen.

The voices above are muffled. I strain to hear what they are saying, to determine if they are familiar to me. *What if it's Alex and he doesn't know we are here? What if they haven't been followed and they think we've left them? What if Cable is hurt and can't tell them where I am?*

Indecision keeps me stalled in place. I want to see, to find my former group to make sure Eva is safe, but something holds me back. In the distance I hear the ping of gunfire and shiver.

"Shit." The person standing overhead shifts away and the light reappears. I crane my neck to see, listening to the return fire.

Cable was right! They were being followed!

Chaos erupts around the farm. Gun fire fills the air. I hear screams of pain drowned out by the roar of engines. The scent of smoke slowly begins to filter into my hole. I press my sleeve to my face, taking only shallow breaths.

I can't see repeats through my mind as panic begins to overwhelm me. The dark is thick and suffocating. *It's a big room with windows. Lots of doors. A high ceiling.*

I used to do this when I was a child, when fear of small spaces would seize me. My mother never locked me up. She may have been a crap mother but she wasn't cruel in that way. No, my captivity was self-inflicted. I would hide to be alone, to escape the crushing fist of one of the jerks she brought home with her after work. Some of them weren't too bad. Others...it was better to be afraid of the dark than be within their reach.

I duck at the sound of a loud thud overhead. I hear footsteps, slow and controlled. Something heavy is rolled over, dragged a few feet.

"No. Please!"

A close range gunshot covers my scream as I cower back. Something wet slaps my forehead. I reach up and touch the warm liquid. It is thicker than water. Blood.

Holding my stomach, I double over and try to block out the sounds of a struggle overhead. Grunting. Swearing. The repetitive thuds of blows landed.

Please don't be Cable!

More shouts rise in the distance. I raise my head and listen, realizing that the rapid gunfire has lessened. Have we been overrun? Have they called a ceasefire to hunt for me? It was all over far too soon to have been the military, but who else could have attacked? Maybe survivors from a nearby town looking for supplies?

I hear the snapping of bone above and hold my breath. There is a long, pained groan and then silence. The victor stumbles back and the wooden trap door creaks underfoot. The person halts. The thrumming of my pulse against my neck intensifies as seconds pass. Then I hear it. The sweeping of a shoe against the ground. Someone above me searches for the edge of the door.

As the creaking of the wood comes again I dart from my hiding place, rising to my full height, arms stretched out before me as I head toward where I think the far wall is. My fingers clash with rubber tipped handles, the metallic clanking of tools sounds loud and echoey in the small space. I know the person above heard.

I grab wildly at a handle and yank but it doesn't budge. Raising my foot, I press back against the wall, tugging with all my might. *Release, dammit!*

The wall emits a loud wooden groan a second before the tool releases and I'm thrown to the ground.

"Hey!" I freeze at the shout overhead. "There's someone down here!"

I press back into my hole just as the trap door is yanked open. Unnatural light spills into the hole. I cover my eyes until I adjust to the sudden brilliance. Heavy steps descend into the dark. The earth crumbles against my shoulder as I flatten against the wall.

"Hello?"

I hold my breath, clinging to the tool with sweat slick hands. The dual handles feel heavy in my grip. I run my finger along the wooden handle and down the long length of the metal head and realize I grabbed a pair of pruning shears. The metal feels gritty, worn. Most likely so rusty I won't even be able to open them. *I have the shittiest luck ever,* I silently bemoan.

The man reaches the final step and pauses. I watch from beneath the stairs as he ducks down and surveys the room. He raises his hand to try to peer around the light spilling over his back. "I know you're down here. I'm not going to hurt you."

I reaffirm my grip. Beads of sweat drip from my brow and land on my nose. Despite the cold, heat flashes through my body, setting me on edge.

"It's safe to come out," the man calls again.

I raise my sheers and poise the curved metal end through the stairs, aiming for his upper thigh. Soon he will move and I'll lose my chance.

I allow myself a brief inhale and hold it, wishing that time could slow so I would have more time to think, to plan, but it doesn't. It speeds up. The muscles in my arm constrict and I draw back my arm to strike.

A shout from overhead startles me. The shears slam against the wooden step as I recoil. A shadow hurtles down from above. "Get away from her!"

I crawl out of my hiding place at the sound of his voice. When I rise, I find Cable on top of the man, pummeling him with his fists. I feel paralyzed as I watch the muscles in his back constrict with each swing. The scream of pain snaps me out of it. "Cable!"

His arm pauses, cocked back as he turns to look at me. His face is flushed and glistens with sweat. His hand is bloodied, his face covered in scratches and dirt. His hair is matted with blood but I can't tell if it's his own. "You...ok?" he grunts.

The man beneath him groans. His leg shifts, bending at the knee before it falls still against the ground.

"I'm fine." I look down at the man's torso. Though it rises and falls with breath, I can tell he's badly wounded. "I could have taken him."

Cable wipes at his face, managing to smear the blood rather than clean it away. "I know. The thing is, I didn't want you to need to."

"Still trying to save the world, huh?" The erratic beating in my chest slowly abates as he stares at me. I feel an odd flush rises along my neck under his intense gaze. It feels intimate.

He nods and a small twitch tugs at the corner of his lips. "Yes, Ma'am. One pretty gal at a time."

A tell-tale blush betrays the impact his statement has on me before I turn away, dipping low to retrieve my shears. Cable looks down at my weapon. "Haven't seen that one used before."

I shrug. "I improvised."

"That's good." Cable grunts as the man beneath him begins to stir. "Why don't you go on up? There's someone waiting to speak to you."

I look toward the light as hope flares in my chest. *Eva!*

I set my shears down, propping them against the wall and rush for the stairs. I'm nearly topside when I hear a grunt of pain and turn to see Cable crashing to the ground. The man kicks out at him as soon as he falls.

"No!"

"Stay there," Cable grunts as the man throws himself on top.

The two men roll side over side, their legs entangled as they disappear into shadow. I peer into the dark, ducked low, desperate to see. "I can help."

"No." Cable's voice sounds strangled. My legs go weak at his howl of pain. Standing there, knowing that he is in trouble, that I could help, is maddening, but there is little room down there. If I were to go back down I might take away any advantage Cable may have of getting the upper hand, so I obey.

Another cry of pain brings them back into view. Two pair of feet kick out. A low punch strikes at someone's kidneys.

"No!" My heart stops in my chest at the plea. A piercing cry cuts off and silence falls over the space. One set of legs collapse to the side. Only the sound of heavy panting can be heard.

"Cable?" My call is too soft to be heard so I try again. I watch the survivor roll away, knees bent, chest heaving with exertion. I close my eyes at the sound of vomiting. The scent wafts toward me, turning my stomach.

"Cable? Dammit, speak to me!" I grip the edge of the trapdoor as my mind flies through escape scenarios. If the other guy won I'm in a world of hurt!

"I'm here," comes a hoarse response.

My shoes clatter against the wooden steps as I rush down and find him curled onto his side and pull him toward me. My grip falters on his arm as my hands become slick with blood. "You're hurt."

"Not...mine," he rasps, clutching his ribs. I spy his glock lying on the ground beside him.

"I don't remember hearing a gunshot."

He coughs and rolls, grimacing. "Out of ammo. Took out a few of the raiders outside."

"And my pistol?"

"Gone. I used everything."

Cold dread washes over me as I look to the light above. I don't blame Cable for using what little ammo we still had to protect us. It was the right call. I'm just worried about what happens once we hit the road without any bullets.

As I lower my gaze, I notice the dark pool growing beside him. I tug Cable away, disturbed by the idea of it touching him. He grunts in pain as I fight to prop him against the wall.

I turn to look at the other guy. Now that my shadow no longer conceals him, I spy the set of shears plunged deep into the man's chest. "Oh, God!"

Cable grips my arm, keeping me from moving forward. "Don't."

"He could still be alive."

"Avery..."

The waiver in his voice breaks through my growing need to see, to check that we are safe. I hear his grief and stop resisting. Cable killed a man in cold blood. I can't begin to imagine what must be going on inside his head.

"He's not wearing a uniform," I whisper, staring at the pair of white tennis shoes lying in the light. I turn to look at Cable. "He's not military."

Cable shakes his head. "It wasn't them."

My voice catches in my throat. I yank out of his grasp and dive toward Cable's attacker. His face is buried in shadow but when I reach his side I see his dark skin and the gold nugget ring on his finger.

I close my eyes and collapse back onto the floor. My breathing catches as I recognize the ring. "You killed Devon."

Cable coughs, his feet digging into the ground as he fights to stand. I turn away from Devon and throw my arm around Cable's waist to help him rise. "Couldn't see," he rasps.

"Shh," I whisper, easing him toward the steps. His limp is pronounced, making it hard for me to help from my shorter height. He is much heavier than he looks. "It was an accident."

His grip on my shoulder tenses and I pause. "I thought he was trying to attack you."

I don't tell him that Devon tried to coax me out, claiming that I would be safe if I did so. I also don't tell him how close I came to taking Devon out myself. "It was dark. There was no way you could have known."

Cable hisses as I squeeze his side to help him up the steps. "I should have known. Should have stopped. I just sort of lost it…"

"No." I grunt as we take each step at a time. He is hurting. His steps move with exaggerated caution. "It was my fault. I should have recognized his voice. Should have come out sooner."

He pauses, forcing me to halt. I look up to find him glaring down at me. "You are not to blame. It was my job to protect you, not the other way around."

I ease Cable down onto a stack of wooden crates. They were filled with sand and carrots when we first arrived, making me think that the old folks who used to live here probably had intentions of turning that trap door space into a food cellar.

Maybe that's why there were so many empty wooden shelves down there.

"I told you earlier that I'm not your job." I step back and cross my arms over my chest, watching as he clutches his stomach. Blood seeps from his nose. His eye has already begun to swell. His lip is split. Who knows what other injuries lie beneath his shirt. "You don't have to always come to my rescue."

A slow breath whistles between his teeth before he responds. "Maybe I want to."

I start to speak, to tell him that I'm just fine on my own, but I hesitate. If Cable hadn't come to my rescue it would have been me with blood on my hands, with remorse that could never be removed. I would be tainted. A killer. Devon was innocent. I may not have liked the guy but down in that dark room, I would have done whatever it took to survive. If Cable hadn't come for me, I would be the murderer.

I look toward the barn door and realize the light flooding in comes from the remains of four large vehicles. I raise my hand to shield myself from the firelight and spy bodies prostrate on the ground. Smoke filters past the door. An orange glow flickers off to the left as well.

"You set the house on fire?"

Cable slowly nods. "It was a distraction."

"That's why you were so anxious to gather the supplies."

He nods again, wincing as he coughs. I sigh and sink down beside him. "I forgive you for knocking me out."

"Really?" His eyebrows arch in surprise. "Figured you'd hold onto that grudge for quite some time."

"Don't you think for a second that I didn't consider doing just that." I grin and place my hand on his knee. "I know you did all of this for me."

His gaze falters and he looks away. "You're the only person I've got left."

"Well," I smile and pat his leg. "I guess that makes us family."

Even as I say *family* I recognize that the word doesn't fit. Not for us. Not now. I have begun to care for Cable and that scares me. In more ways than I care to think about.

TWELVE

I walk in silence, listening to the fire spit and crackle behind us. The woods are illuminated by the flames, both directly behind us and further into the distance. I remain by Cable's side, his arm around my shoulder, allowing me to assist him.

The pack on my back is heavy, filled with hammers, chisels, a small ax and a pretty wicked looking mallet, but it is not nearly as heavy as my heart. Eva was not with Alex's group when I emerged with Cable from the barn.

I spotted Alex first. He worked with Sal to toss unfamiliar bodies into the flames. The two story farm house was ablaze, sending a plume of smoke into the night air that would easily be seen for miles around. Victoria puttered about, randomly kicking at the deceased. I'm not exactly sure what her point in doing that was, but the old bat wasn't exactly all there the last time I saw her. She seems worse off now.

When Alex looked up and saw me under Cable's arm, a sad smile lit his face, but it quickly vanished when I told him Devon had fallen. I didn't say how or why. Cable noticed but didn't say anything.

It didn't take long for the barn to catch fire. In the flickering flames I could see some of the Withered Ones in their moaning march across the fields. I knew they wouldn't make it with the flames setting bits of hay in the yard alight, but there was no point in trying to stop them. They would probably continue marching until the flames finally consumed them. A part of me felt that was a better fate than their endless, mindless walk.

Now, Alex leads the way through the dark woods. He has two packs on his back. As does Sal. Victoria refused to take more than one, garnering her another livid glare from me. When

I first met her this might have bothered her, but now...she seems different. Like the last cog on her gears finally popped off.

None of us speak as we head into the woods. The forest feels safe and I for one want to stay clear of people for a good long while. We have supplies enough to last us a few days and some crude tools that can be used as weapons if it comes to it. We will make it. The question is...for how long.

It's not just the military we have to watch out for, or the gangs tearing apart St. Louis brick by brick. Now it's the survivors in small towns that we will meet. Those people desperate enough to put a gun to our head when they want something.

And what about the virus? We are no closer to discovering how it ticks. Hiking through the forest isn't about to help that situation either, but none of us are ready to face another slaughter. Ours or anyone else's.

From time to time I look toward the other fire well off in the distance, wondering who started it and if there were any survivors. Is it a coincidence that both fires started around the same time? Did the same men who follow Alex's group follow another?

The moon rises high overhead. A bitter cold descends but we don't stop. Moving keeps us warm. Cable shelters me from much of the brutal wind. He must be suffering. His coat was lost to the battle. He has only a thin long-sleeve shirt to protect him from the winds now.

"Wait up!"

Alex pauses and circles around to me. Cable's teeth chatter. "We can't stop."

"Cable is freezing. Do you have anything to spare?" Eric took all of our supplies, including the last of the clothes we'd scavenged.

I look to Alex and follow his gaze as he turns to look at Sal. The sleazy creep crosses his arms over his shoulder and shakes his head. Anger simmers low in my belly but Cable's weight holds me back. "Alex?"

"Let me see." He swings his pack off his shoulder and kneels. The sound of the zipper is loud in my ears. The woods are quiet tonight. Far too quiet for normal. It is unnerving.

I watch as he shifts cans and used bottles half empty with water. He removes a worn cloth that is stained pink. When he looks up at me there is pain in his eyes. I look away, biting my lip to keep back the tears. I want to ask about Eva, to hear what happened at the end, but I'm afraid of hearing it. I want to believe that she survived, that she lived to hold her baby, but I don't believe it anymore. Not really.

"It's all I've got." Alex holds out a small blanket. It is threadbare and tattered on the edges but large enough that it could shield Cable's back and arm.

"Thank you." As I take the blanket from Alex I realize that his hands are shaking. He meets my gaze briefly before quickly turning back to his pack. The weight of Eva's loss sits heavily on his shoulders. There is anger too. At himself? At me for leaving them behind? I honestly don't know, and I don't have the stomach to ask. Not yet.

Alex zips his backpack and slings it over his right shoulder. The second pack is larger and heavier, weighing down his left side, forcing him to walk unevenly. He returns to Sal and Victoria's side while I see to Cable.

"Your friends seem intense." His teeth chatter so hard I fear he will bite his tongue.

I set my pack on the ground and shake out the blanket. "They aren't my friends. They just sort of took me in."

As I wrap the blanket around him, I notice how close we are. I can feel the warmth of his chest against mine as I rise onto my tiptoes to tie a knot around his shoulder. It won't do much to warm him, but it should at least be a buffer against the winds. I sink back to my flat feet. Cable grasps my wrist as I start to turn away. "Sometimes we don't get to choose our friends. Especially not now."

I glance back toward Alex's group. It is smaller now. Devon is gone, as is Eva and the two people they had locked away. Seven becomes three. How many more will be lost in the coming days?

"I know." I look down at his grasp on my wrist, remembering when we first met, how sure I was that his intentions weren't entirely pure. He has proven to me time and time again to be honorable. I don't think I could have found a better friend. I've surely never had one so good before, except Eva.

"You miss the girl, don't you?" He whispers as I ease into my pack and place his arm over my shoulder. Alex helps Victoria back to her feet and moves out. Cable and I remain a couple dozen paces back and a visible divide develops within our group.

"I just wish I knew what happened to Eva." Although Cable gently tried to pry information from me over the past few days about what happened to me between the time I left the apartment and arrived at the military hangar, I wasn't overly forthcoming with details. All except for my need to see Eva again. The rest was better left unsaid.

"Why don't you ask them?"

I shrug and feel the burn in my shoulder muscles. Helping Cable was never a question, but it is taxing. I don't know how I will be able to keep up with Alex's faster pace. He marches as if the Devil himself is on our heels. The trouble is...he just might be. "Sometimes not knowing hurts less."

"Are you so sure you want to assume the worst?"

I look up at him and notice the sheen on his forehead in the moonlight. "Are you feeling ok?"

"You mean apart from the knife in my side and the wrecking ball that slammed into my head earlier? Yeah. I'm good."

"No." I slow down, noticing how labored his breathing in. "You're sweating."

"We're walking."

"It's freezing out here."

"Is it?" He frowns and looks around us at the darkened woods. The fires have fallen behind us. The barren maple trees and towering pines spread ever before us. The terrain is uneven, dangerously inviting for a twisted ankle.

I stop completely and force him to halt. I press him back against a tree and roll my shoulder once I'm free of his weight. He doubles over, clutching his side as he breathes deep, looking as if we've just finished a long distance sprint rather than hiked for an hour.

"Something's wrong."

He shakes his head, his head bowed. "I'm fine."

"Liar."

His shoulder shakes with a deep throaty chuckle but he sucks in a breath as the pain hits. His arms quiver. "You're barely on your feet, Cable."

"I'm fine."

"Are you always this stubborn?" I plant my hands on my hips and wait for him to look at me. When he does, I see a glint of humor in his eye.

"Not so fun when it's being directed back at you, huh?"

"Alex!" I cup my hands and call out to the woods. I can no longer see them or hear their heavy-footed traipsing. It's a good thing we aren't trying to be quiet; otherwise we'd be a dead giveaway. "Alex!"

A moment later I see the swinging flash of a dim light heading toward us. I wait, using one hand pressed against Cable's hunched shoulders to keep him upright. Alex comes around the side of a tree, a frown deeply etched onto his face.

He starts to speak but takes one look at Cable and closes his mouth again. "He's hurt."

"We all are." A burn rides along Alex's cheek and down his neck. The skin looks angry. It needs to be clean but he refused. Apparently Cable and I aren't the only stubborn martyrs in the group.

"He's worse. We need to stop for a bit."

"Can't do it." He shakes his head and reaffirms his grip on the two packs. His gaze travels beyond me, back in the direction we came from. Fear pinches his handsome features, making them distorted and ugly.

I help ease Cable to the ground when I feel his legs begin to buckle then rise and stare down Alex. "I'm really getting tired of being treated like a pathetic, helpless little child. I can handle it so you might as well spill whatever little secret you two have been keeping from me."

Alex and Cable exchange a glance. Alex shrugs but it is Cable who responds. "The military base was sacked."

That I didn't expect. "What do you mean sacked? How? By who?"

"The gangs spilled over the river, took out most of East St. Louis a day ago. Guess they decided they'd like to expand their horizons without any threat to oppose them so they sacked the base. Weird thing is, it looks like someone else beat them to it."

Cable gives me a warning glance so I remain quiet about our escape from the base. Alex sinks down into a crouch and I follow, if only to keep at eye level with him. If I start thinking about how sore I am then I'll be inclined to give up completely. "Things fell apart real fast after you left...after Eva..." Alex looks away. His adams apple bobs and he wipes his hands over his face.

I bite down on my lower lip and squeeze my hands into balled fists, savoring the pain my nails inflict on the tender flesh of my palms. Alex grabs a stick and hurls it toward a tree, seeming less than satisfied by the tiny smack of wood, probably hoping for it to snap it half.

"They broke down the door less than an hour after you left. Devon and Sal nearly got caught trying to get Victoria out. Stupid, really. She moved as slow as molasses and couldn't keep her trap quiet when she was told to." He heaves a weighted sigh and sinks all the way to the ground. His hands splay over the cold earth, sifting decaying leaves. "I stayed with Eva till the end. I owed it to her."

"Did she...did she feel any pain?" My voice cracks. Cable reaches out for my hand and twines his fingers through mine. I'm grateful for his presence.

"Pain?" Alex's gaze grows distant as he slowly shakes his head. "No. Those last few minutes I spent at her side she didn't feel much of anything. She lost consciousness within minutes after you left. I didn't know what to do, how to help."

"I'm sorry," I whisper, drawing my knees up into my chest. A tree root presses against my tailbone but I ignore it. "I wanted to come back..."

"No." He crosses his hands over his knees and I see dirt buried deep under his nails. "It's good you got out."

"She didn't." Alex turns to look at Cable. "She was captured."

"By who?"

I close my eyes and try not to remember the feel of the bag over my head, the fear of waking without senses, confined as a prisoner. I hear Cable giving Alex the rundown but I tune them out. As I think over all that has happened, a new thought hits me and I break into the guy's conversation.

"You never said Eva died."

Alex blinks. "Well, no. That's because she didn't."

My fingers uncurl as I scoot toward him. "Where is she? Who took her?"

Alex frowns. "The military. I thought you knew that."

A blanket of cold falls over me. "Why her?"

"They wanted her baby," Cable says in an emotionless tone that seems out of place for him. All this time he has fought for what is good and right. Why this time would he not seem to care?

"Why?"

Alex rises, dusting his hands off on his pants. "I need to catch up with the others. We haven't put nearly enough distance between us and those gangs, and I for one don't want them coming down on us in our sleep."

"Cable isn't ready to move yet." I protest, knowing exactly why Alex chose this moment to interrupt. What happened to Eva doesn't sit well with him. How can it?

Grunting with effort, Cable presses back against the tree and rises. I follow suit. His grimace releases when he is fully upright and he nods at Alex. "We'll be behind you."

"I'll try not to get too far ahead. If we get separated just head toward the sun."

"That's hours away from rising," I say, noting that the moon still hangs far too high overhead.

"Devon told me about a town not too far from here. There's a railroad that runs right into the heart of town. Keep it on your right and you will find us. We'll set up camp and wait for your arrival."

"And if we don't make it?" I ask.

Cable steps forward and settles his arm around my shoulder. "He'll move out when he has to. That's the way things are now. You take care of your own."

I watch as Alex gives my friend an appraising glance. "You found yourself a good guy, Avery. Take care of him."

"I will." Though I have zero intention of going it on our own. Despite having grown up as a loner all my life, the past few days have taught me a very important lesson: I need people, even if I don't always want them.

THIRTEEN

I don't really know how Cable and I made it through the night. His limp as we neared the deserted town was so bad I felt as if I would stumble with each step he took. My back ached and my heart thumped, pain shooting behind my eye. When we spied a candle in the window of a brick and white sided church I prayed that it was Alex and not some stranger looking to steal supplies.

It took me less than a minute to sink into oblivion after we were inside. I welcomed it. Victoria's mumbling and Sal's snoring were not enough to wake me as the sun rose and fell once more on the land. When I finally roused the following morning, I felt rested but plagued with a penetrating ache that could not be ignored.

"Filthy stinkin' weasel," Victoria says as she putters past. I sweep my gaze behind her to see the remnants of a haughty sneer on Sal's face.

"What's that all about?" I ask, rolling to my side. The wooden pew was hardly a suitable bed. The sweater I used as a pillow has left my neck in a crook. I rub at the sore muscles, hoping that Cable has improved enough to not need me as a crutch today.

Alex thrusts his knife toward Sal, the tip dripping with juices from an apple he just sliced open. My stomach growls at the sight. They must have come through one of the orchards not far from the base. "Victoria thought she could outsmart Sal. Bet him her food ration that he couldn't solve one of her riddles. Guess ole' Sal ain't as dumb as he looks after all."

"That's terrible. She must be hungry."

He shrugs and pops another piece in his mouth before passing me a slice. The flesh is softer than I would like but still tastes sweet. "A bet is a bet. She'd have made him pay up if she'd won."

I draw my legs under me and reposition my sweater to cover my lap. The scent of mothballs has begun to fade at least.

The air in the church holds a strong chill and I stifle a shiver. "What'd he stand to lose?"

"His hair."

I blink, sure that I've heard him wrong. "His...his hair?"

Alex nods and wipes his knife on his pants. "She says it's not fitting for a man his age, and with his state of hair decline, to be wearing a mullet."

I clasp my hand over my mouth to stave off my snort, but it's not enough. Giggles erupt from my lips and Alex's grin broadens. It feels weird to laugh again. Haven't had much reason to recently. "Even though I'd hate to live with her gloating, I almost wish she'd won," Alex says.

"Me too." I raise my hands overhead and stretch, feeling each muscle pull taut. It's going to be a long day.

As I lower my hands I see Alex glancing at me from the corner of my eye. I blush and wrap my arms over myself, feeling self-conscious in my skin tight white shirt. If I'd had a better option I would have left any memory of my time spent at that military base firmly seated in the hottest part of the fire but clothing is limited now. I can't waste needlessly.

Turning to don my sweater, I find Cable's spot empty. I hadn't realized he was awake. "Where's Cable?"

Alex shrugs and pops the final bit of fruit in his mouth. "Said he needed some air."

"In his condition?" I frown and hurry to lace of my sneakers. My white pants are stained and dingy, more brown than anything now. Rubbing my fingers along my pants, I feel the dirt embedded in the fibers. I feel gross but I'll have to wait for a wash.

Slipping out of the church, I sneak down the front steps and look around. Cable is nowhere to be seen. I creep out to the road and use an abandoned car to shield my body. The road splits in three directions. Cable could be down any of them.

"Cable," I call, cupping my hands over my mouth. I duck down and wait to see if there is a response. Being out in broad daylight bothers me. Despite the frigid cold that keeps us company at night, I feel safer.

A noise from the street to my right captures my attention. I call his name as I head in that direction. The noise sounds like someone kicking a can, but I follow it. Three blocks to the south I discover four Withered Ones on the road. They stumble forward together, with only a couple of feet separating them. One tumbles over a mailbox while the others continue on, oblivious to their loss.

I creep up toward a cottage style home with blue shutters and a peeling white wooden fence. Remnants of flowers lie buried and lifeless beneath the window sill as I peer into the house. No sign of movement.

A loud crash sends me ducking low. I look all around for the sound. Slowly I rise, planting my hands on my hips as I chuckle. There, scampering through the gutter, is a small raccoon with its head stuck in a can. It runs straight ahead and bashes into the curb before scurrying off in another direction.

"Scared of a household pest. Wow, this is a new low, even for you." I turn to head back toward the church and freeze. A block down on my right I see Cable, perched atop the hood of a truck. He is bent over his knees, his head buried in his crossed arm. I run full out toward him, terrified of how exposed he is.

"Cable," I hiss, waving my arms to get his attention as he looks up. His face is ashen, his chin trembling. His eyes are watery but he doesn't try to cover his tears. I stop beside him and place a hand on his leg. "What? What is it?"

"I found it."

I glance all around. He has nothing in his hands. Nothing sitting beside him on the hood, and that's when I see it. The faded red paint on the hood of an old beat up Ford truck, more rust than metal now. "Cable," I whisper as he slides off. I wrap my arms around his waist and hold him as he cries into my shoulder.

Now that I'm close I detect bullet holes in the hood. The windshield is a mass of spider webs. Blood stains the driver's side. The door hangs open but no one is inside.

"I'm so sorry."

Cable releases a shaky breath as he pulls away. "I checked inside. Eric and all of the supplies are gone."

Why did he have to go for this walk? Why couldn't he have just stayed in bed a little longer and left this town with the thought that Eric made it to wherever he was headed? That he would find peace and happiness?

I glance at the neighborhood around us. Middle class homes. Manicured lawns. Basketball hoops standing at the end of long driveways. Even a birdbath or two decorating the lawns. Not the sort of area you would have expected a drive by in days past.

"We should get back."

He nods and turns to follow though I can tell he is reluctant to leave. Losing Eric the first time was hard. This is far worse. I can only hope that his end came fast.

As we walk back toward the church, I cast furtive glances toward Cable. He is sullen. I don't want to push him so I remain quiet as we walk side by side down the street. I keep an eye on each intersection, each window curtain but nothing moves apart from the random Moaner.

"How are you feeling?" I ask as the church appears one street ahead.

"Well enough." His response is flat.

Movement on the church steps captures my attention. I wave toward Alex, signaling our return. I pick up the pace as he waves back and heads inside.

"I don't like the way he looks at you."

I glance back at where Alex stood a moment before. The porch is empty now. "He's harmless."

"You so sure about that?"

"Yes."

Cable turns slowly to look at me. The change in subject seems to have woken up him a bit. "Not all guys have good intentions all the time, Avery."

I bristle and pull to a stop. "Are you jealous?"

"No." He shakes his head and brushes his foot along the street. He tucks his hands deep into his pockets. I can tell by the way he holds his arms close to his sides that he's still hurting. "I just see things."

"Well, so do I, and I think you're jealous."

I wait for his reaction, knowing without a doubt that there will be one, but what I see surprises me. No humor. No laughter. No crinkling of laugh lines around his eyes. Instead, he grows all the more serious.

"What's wrong?" I whisper and reach out to grab onto his arm.

Though he speaks to me, he does not look away from vacant porch. "It's been bugging me all night. Probably why I went for a walk this morning. Always did think better outside."

I wait for him to make his point. My patience is on a thin rope today. Must not have slept as well as I originally thought. Or my mad dash through town in search of him has left me frazzled. "Those men that followed Alex's group onto our farm didn't seem like they were giving chase."

I fall still. "You're saying you think they followed closely behind Alex?"

He slowly looks over at me and the anger I see darkening his gaze chills me far more than the blustery winds the night before. "I'm saying I think Alex led them to us."

I start to speak, to deny that Alex would do such a thing, but I stop myself. How well do I really know Alex? Devon? Whoever was calling the shots when they came to us.

"Just be careful," he whispers next to my ear. "Keep your eyes open. We don't really know who we can trust."

I turn to look at him and realize that our lips are scant inches apart. I breathe him in, savoring the distinctly masculine scent that surrounds him. I lick my lips and pull back slightly, unnerved. "And I can trust you?"

The hard lines of his face soften as he reaches out and cups my cheek. His palm feels rough but warm against my skin. "With your life."

I stare into his dark eyes, lost in the moment. A long time ago I trusted a guy. That had been a big mistake, one I swore I would never repeat.

A throat clears nearby and I look up to find Alex staring down at us, his hands planted on the church railing. His shoes are laced, his jacket buttoned, and both packs rest on his back. "It's time to move out."

I glance up at the sun and frown. "It's daylight."

"Yes. It will help us get our bearings. Sal and Victoria are preparing to leave. Figured I'd give you a few extra minutes to gather your things."

"Thanks." I watch as he walks away and sigh. "Here we go again."

I start to climb the steps but Cable tugs at my arm. "Remember what I said."

I do. And I will also remember everything that was left unsaid between us.

When we reach the edge of town without further incident I breathe a sigh of relief. The hours pass by just as slowly as the night before but we don't stop when dusk falls. We keep walking, trying to stay ahead of whoever it is that might decide to come looking for us. That list seems to be getting a bit too long for my liking.

Alex and his group remain well ahead of us. From time to time I spy their flickering lights. Cable and I move slowly, carefully picking our footing in the moonlight. Cable warned me against using flashlights. They are too easily seen from a distance, and who knows when we might be in desperate need of light in the days to come?

Hours turn into days. They all feel the same, look the same. The cold is a constant, so much that at times I almost forget what being warm felt like. For several days we stick to the forest, pitching rustic campsites made with blankets and spare clothing for bedding. We huddle around small campfires at sundown, squashing them out before night hits and the light could be seen from a distance. We sleep back to back, Victoria and I in the middle, Cable behind me and Alex and Sal behind Victoria.

The nights are long as we shiver together in silence. It feels wrong to rest when we should continue moving, but exhaustion weighs heavily on all of us. Victoria begins to show signs of struggle as the terrain becomes more unstable. My ankles are a constant ache as flat farm land gives way to hills and rock.

We spot stray Moaners from time to time. One of them was stuck in the mud of a river bank, sunk up to its knees. It clawed at the air in its relentless attempt to move forward. We found another caught in a hunter's trap. The metal claws buried so deeply in the bone of its leg that it could not get free.

The Withered Ones don't bother us, well...not any more than can be expected. I awoke to one trampling through camp in the early morning hours two days ago. It tripped over Victoria as she slept, sending her into a full blown panic attack as the rotting woman flailed atop her. We got a late start that morning. It took hours for Victoria to calm down.

Just outside a small town we found a landfill and spent a few hours digging through trash. Never in my life would I have imagined that I would do such a thing. At least not to this degree. As Alex and Sal sorted through a small pile of things I would consider to be questionably useful, I hunted down Cable, only to find him caking his body with mud. He said it was for the bugs. Even in the dead of winter the darn things seem to find a way of getting you.

Yesterday we found an old shack to sleep in. It stank of animal feces and urine. We kicked most of the nests out of the corners before we bedded down. I slept with my sweater tied around my nose to help with the smell, but I slept better than I had in nearly a week. I was semi-warm.

This morning I woke to find Cable feeling better than I'd seen him in days. Color has returned to his face. The flush in his cheeks has begun to fade. After a meager breakfast of cold beans out of a can, we all crowd around Alex's map. We are still heading south, but not nearly fast enough. Even if we manage to avoid military or gang detection, the elements might take us in the end.

The terrain continues to change. The gentle rises become hills with high enough cliffs that you could do some real damage if you fell. We skirt along hiking trails, realizing that we have entered a state park. We pass picnic benches and small wooden buildings hosting the first toilets we've seen in days. I won't deny that I teared up a bit when I saw real toilet paper and made sure to stuff a few extra in my pack for safe keeping.

The march through the night is hard. Although the hills block some of the winds, around a bend it funnels it straight at us. I huddle behind Cable, grateful for his height and the breadth of his chest. From time to time he reaches back to hold my hand in the dark. Though his fingers are cold, his grip is reassuring.

Just before dawn we spot an old graffitied rail car on the far outskirts of a small town. Alex and I help ease Cable inside and close the door behind us. We spend the whole day in the box, warm and snug. As night falls I can feel Alex's reluctance to leave. No one would look for us here. We are out of the way, off the main roads.

Leaving Cable to his rest, I sneak over to Alex's side. "You look lost."

He stuffs his fists into his pack, trying to shift the contents around to find a more comfortable position. "I've got a map."

"That's not what I'm talking about."

"I know." He stares up at the ceiling. Small cracks in the roof allow moonlight to filter in from above, creating trails on the floor. "Sal is acting a bit off."

"More than usual?"

He nods and rolls his head to the side to stare at the snoring man. "He's been complaining more than usual today. Small things. Like how his teeth ache or he can't stand being too close to the fire because it's too strong a smell. He's irritable."

I frown and look over at his slumped figure. "That's nothing new."

"But it is." I turn to look at Alex, peering through the dark to see him. "Normally he's just ticked about the cold, about being hungry or that his feet hurt. Now..." he sighs. "I don't know. Maybe I'm just being hyper sensitive about everything."

"No." I rub my hands together to warm them. With the sun hiding for the night the cold has returned and what warmth the day brought has been stolen away. "That's good. We need to be."

He rolls onto his side and looks past me. Victoria's muttering rises and falls, even in sleep. She is speaking to someone, her mom by the sounds of it. She keeps talking about a puzzle but it makes little sense. "How's your friend?"

"He's mending. Too stubborn to stop long enough to properly heal."

"Have you looked him over to make sure he doesn't have any internal bleeding? Looks like that other guy roughed him up pretty good."

I swallow down my guilt. Alex still doesn't know that Devon was the man who left Cable in this condition and I have no intention of ever revealing that, especially not if it could put Cable's life in danger. "I haven't had time."

Alex snorts.

"What?"

"Nothing." He crosses his legs out before him and places his hands behind his head.

"Tell me."

"What's there to tell? It's obvious you like the guy."

"I don't...no. We're friends."

He whistles low and soft. "If I had a dollar for every time I heard a girl say that."

"It's true."

"Sure it is. You tell yourself whatever it is that you need to get through the day, but I believe what I see."

I cross my arms over my chest, annoyed by his insinuation. "You're wrong."

"Could be." He rolls onto his side, placing his back facing me. "Guess you're the only one who would know."

As the silence falls around us, I return to Cable's side. His breathing is steady. His eyes shift back and forth, evidence of a deep, restful sleep. I lie down beside him and press my back against him for warmth. Cable stirs and shifts his arm. His hand falls along my upper thigh and I lie perfectly still. After that, sleep takes half the night to find me.

When I wake, I discover I'm the last to rise. Cable and Alex stand beside the open train car door, looking out in the direction of the town. My stomach clenches as I see them motion toward it. I don't trust towns. Not anymore. We've done just fine staying clear of them, but our supplies won't last long. Sal is a bigger guy and eats more than his fair share. The rest of us try to compensate, but we can only do that so long. Cable needs proper nourishment to finish healing.

I groan as I force myself to rise. My back aches and the muscles in my neck are stiff. I stretch out my arms overhead and then attempt to touch my toes.

"Sure must be nice to be so limber."

I raise back up and find Sal openly staring at me, or rather straight down the drooping neckline of my shirt. "You're an ass."

"Never claimed not to be." He chucks me a stale crust of bread and moves away. I grab it off the ground and dust it off, irritated that life has become a subsistence of such meager rations.

"He bothering you?" I look up to see Cable towering over me. His fingers loop over the bottom of his camo pants pockets, his stance portraying a casualness that I know he doesn't feel. The planes of his face are too hard. His eyes narrowed and piercing.

"I've handled worse than the likes of him."

Cable emits a throaty grunt. "I'd like to handle him a bit myself."

I laugh and stretch out my hand. "Help me up, will you?"

The muscles in his arms flex as he easily pulls me up. "You must be feeling better," I muse, standing awkwardly with my hand in his. I know I should step back, to draw my hand away and gather my pack, but I don't. I spent all night thinking about him, wondering if Alex was right. Am I starting to like Cable too much? Is it noticeable to everyone except me?

"I am, thanks to you. You'd have made quite the nurse, you know?"

I finally pull away, making sure to shove that hand deep into my pocket so he can't see how it trembles slightly. I brush my hair back from my face and tuck it behind my ear. "I never really liked blood, or math, science, or even school for that matter."

He leans in and bumps me with his shoulder. "Then it will be our little secret."

I watch as he walks away. *Should I have secrets with him?* I frown at the thought, knowing that I am heading for trouble. I need to space myself from him or risk giving him the wrong impression. Even though I like Cable, I can't afford to feel anything more than general friendship for him. Not in the world we live in now. Too many people are lost. Too many go to an early grave. It's best to not let yourself care. That's how you survive.

I turn and scowl at Sal, who appraises me openly again. "What are you looking at?"

"The only show worth watching in this shithole. I think you'll find I'm not the only one entertained."

I follow his gaze and find Alex and Victoria standing near the back end of the train car. Both watch me and then swiftly look away. I sigh and grab my pack off the ground. "I'm going for a walk."

"Need some company?" Sal calls.

"Not from a worm like you!"

As I leap down through the door, I hear his laughter. It sounds wheezy in his chest.

I tug hard on the straps of my pack and march away, head lowered against the winds. I need to be alone, to set my thoughts straight. Ever since this crap started I've been forced to be around people and I don't like it. My mother always used to harp on at me about how unhealthy it was to be a loner. She never really got that it's what I like, what I thrive off of. Not everyone can be a people person.

With no conscious decision, I head for the backside of the town, hugging the woods for cover as I scope it out. Alex and Cable were planning to do the same, but if I can save them the trip while working through my frustrations, it's a win-win in my eyes.

As I near the first building, I duck low, my back pressed against the vinyl siding. Somewhere up ahead a screen door slams shut, only to be caught up by the wind and slammed again. The foundation of this home seems a bit off kilter, as if the whole right side has begun to sink into the dirt. The neighborhood looks a bit rough around the edges. Not really the most ideal place to live, but I guess someone had to do it.

Craning my head, I peer through the window. The interior is dark. Sheets hang over the windows to block out the sunlight, or other things. Tables are overturned. A recliner sits upended. I turn to look back in toward the house and scream, rearing back from the window.

A hand claps down over my mouth and I buck against the strong grip. "Easy," a voice calls in my ear. "It's just me."

Growling in frustration, I shove Cable's hand away. "I wanted to be alone."

"And I wanted to make sure you didn't do anything stupid." He raises his eyebrows and jerks his head toward the house.

Point taken.

I rub my hands down the front of my pants, trying to ease the quaking in my fingers. "What made you scream like that?"

"Be my guest." I point to the window and step back, leaning against the wall. I watch him, waiting for the same horror that I experienced but his expression hardly changes. "Really? Nothing?"

Cable pulls away from the window. "I've seen suicides before."

"That woman's face is wallpapered to the drywall. Her brain is coating the window. How you can be so blasé about it?"

He shrugs. "Maybe because it was her choice?"

"Her...her choice?" My voice shakes as I stare at him with open incredulity. "How is that a choice? She shoved a gun in her mouth and pulled the trigger. That's not a choice. That's the epitome of cowardice."

He shakes his head. "You didn't see, did you?"

"See what?" I look toward the window.

"The baby."

My breath catches as I rush forward and peer in again. This time, cradled in the woman's lap, I spy the child. Its face is pale, its eyes open and unseeing. Its mouth opens and closes, its arms pawing at the air.

I sink back and feel Cable standing behind me, offering me help to remain upright. "She knew..."

His grip tightens on my arms. "Imagine what that must be like, to know that your child is going to become the thing that has everyone terrified and there is nothing you can do to stop it. Could you live with that? With knowing that you couldn't save your own child?"

A penetrating cold sinks into my soul at the thought. "It's always the people you love most that hurt you deepest."

Cable slowly turns me around. "It doesn't have to be that way."

"But it is. It always has been. Why should things change? Especially now?" Warm tears seep from the corners of my eyes, trailing down my cheeks. I didn't mean to cry, don't want to, but staring up into Cable's knowing gaze I feel exposed.

"You shouldn't be here, Cable."

"Why not?" He asks. His grip loosens against my arms as his hands trail down to take my hands in his. I hate that I crave his touch, that I find myself needing it.

"Because I don't need you."

His smile nearly breaks me completely as he steps closer. "I thought you would have figured it out by now."

"Figured what out?"

He leans in so close that I'm sure he means to kiss me, but he pulls up just shy of my lips. He stares intently into my eyes before his face shifts away, his breath trails along my cheek as he pauses beside my ear. "I'm more stubborn than you. I'm willing to wait as long as it takes for you to realize that you may not need me, but you *do* want me."

FOURTEEN

Sparks flicker. The hum of electricity is lost over the roar of an engine.

"Yes!" I cheer.

Cable emerges from the driver's side of a beat up quad cab pickup that may have at one time been considered a sports model, judging by the attempt at a spoiler on the rear tailgate. He leans over the wheel and taps the fuel gage. "It won't get us far, but it's something."

I rest my head back on the bench seat beside him and grin. "A day without walking is bliss. I'll take it!"

Cable grins at me and closes the door. He twists his torso gingerly and puts the seatbelt on. He starts to put the truck in gear when he senses me looking at him. "What?"

"Nothing." I smirk. "It's just that I didn't take you for the seat belt wearing kind of guy."

A broad smile crosses his lips. "Well, when you've got precious cargo on board you tend to take every precaution."

I look away, knowing that he can see the flames licking at my cheeks. My fair skin does little to hide it.

"We won't all fit in the cab," he says, as if nothing were amiss with his previous statement. "I'll take the back with Sal for a while. We can trade off later."

"Why you? You're still trying to heal. I can sit back there just as easily."

He glances at me from the corner of his eye but says nothing. He doesn't have to. I already know what he's thinking.

"We've got some supplies. A couple blankets and enough water to last us for a while. If we load the food and water near the back, I can huddle against the cab to block most of the wind."

"Are you always this logical?" He asks as the truck jerks into gear and begins rolling forward. We are on the far end of town. By now Alex, Victoria and Sal should have cleaned out the houses nearest the train car. After finding that baby, I couldn't bring myself to search the houses so I stuck to the shops.

The pharmacy offered some supplies. Antibiotics. Pain meds. Fresh bandages to wrap Cable's bruised ribs, though they seem to be improving greatly with each day that passes. My nasty bandages were used as kindling two nights ago when the cold become too much to bear. In the final store I found ointment to heal the blisters on Alex's face.

"Only when I want to get my own way."

He laughs and reaches out to turn on the radio. I don't know if he does it out of habit or if he's searching for something, but when only static bounces back at us, he turns the knob and falls silent.

I stare out the window at the faceless homes, at the drawn curtains and doors left open and forgotten. Christmas lights nailed to rooftops flap in the wind, nearly three months overdue. The cheer of the holiday season gone forever.

We weave around abandoned cars and Withered Ones wandering the streets. I watch them as I pass, realizing that in the past week I have nearly grown immune to their presence. The scent of decay isn't quite so strong anymore. The sight of torn limbs and maggots feasting on rotting flesh doesn't turn my stomach now. I never dreamed that I would become immune to it all, but I guess it becomes a matter of perspective.

Watching their endless walk brings two emotions now: sadness and wariness. Though I know no one else shares my ideas, I can't shake the feeling that something isn't right with them.

"Do you even see them anymore?" I ask, without turning away from the window.

"I'm swerving around them, if that's what you mean."

"No." I press my nose against the glass as Cable slows the truck. We inch through a herd of Moaners. Several bump repeatedly against the hood. Cable slows to a near halt in an attempt to let them veer off in a new direction. When they don't, he pushes the accelerator. The truck rises and falls over the crushed bodies and we continue on our way. "I mean, as people. Or former people, I guess. Are they just things to you now?"

Cable is silent long enough to draw my gaze back toward him. His fingers grip the steering wheel as we are forced to slow again. We went nearly all morning without seeing a Withered One and now they flock to the one street we need to be on to get us back to our group.

Putting the truck in park, Cable sighs and drops his hands from the wheel as we wait for them to pass. "I can't think of them as things."

"Why not?" I draw one leg up onto the seat and turn to face him. I note that the deep bruising along his cheek and temple have faded into an ugly yellow now. The cut on his lip has begun to heal nicely. He no longer holds his side when he breathes.

"My brother is out there." He speaks to the windshield instead of me. His gaze is fixated on the grotesque faces before us. I try to ignore the strips of flesh being torn from the passing bodies by the sharp edge of the broken side mirrors, or hear the raspy moans that make goosebumps rise on my arms.

"You never spoke of a brother before."

"Lenny and I never really got along too well. I guess that comes with the territory, though. Half-brothers tend to butt heads a lot."

"Sounds like you care about him, though."

"He's family, even if my scumbag dad decided to mess around. I don't hold that against him."

I pick at a scab on my arm where thorn bushes tore at my skin a few days ago. By the time we figured out we'd marched straight into a massive briar patch, there was no choice but to keep going.

"My dad ran out on us when I was younger. I remember hurrying home each day after school and waiting on the front step of our porch for him to come back. He never did, of course. My mother moved us to St. Louis not long after. Never really forgave her for that. I was sure one day my dad would walk up that path for me and wonder where I'd gone. When I got older I figured out the truth."

"What was that?" Cable flicks on the windshield wipers and I grimace at the smear of blood as he tries to clean away the carnage left behind.

"That sometimes no matter how hard you try, things don't work out. People leave for their own reasons. You just gotta suck it up and move on. Put them in the past so they can't hurt you anymore."

Cable looks over at me. The path before us is clear, if blurred by the red haze predominate on the windshield now. "Sounds like that didn't work out too well for you."

I blow out a weighted breath. "I'm still working on it."

The truck begins a slow roll forward. Cable ducks his chin to see through a clear patch. "You can't keep the whole world out, you know?"

"I can try."

"Sure." He yanks a bit of the fabric off the torn seat cover and leans out the window to wipe the glass before him. It helps a little but we'll have to do a better job before we hit the road. "Just make sure you don't include me in that, huh?"

I turn away so he doesn't see the tiny smile that betrays me. My eyes widen and I grip his arm. "Cable!"

The truck jerks as he slams his foot on the brake. He follows my gaze in silence. There, standing between two houses is a Moaner. Most of his face has been torn away. His shirt is ragged, his scalp bald apart from a few stray tufts of hair.

"Are you seeing this?" I ask, unable to tear myself away from the man. His eyes are a milky blue. He stands with an unblinking stare into the distance.

"He's not moving," Cable whispers. His voice sounds hoarse.

I turn to look at him. "I've never seen one do that before."

"Me either." I can tell by the color leaching from his face that he's freaked out but trying hard not to show it. "Let's get back. The others will be waiting for us."

I nod in agreement but the truck is already moving at a faster pace than before. It only takes us five minutes to maneuver around the debris in the road and arrive back at the train car. Victoria paces near the steps, her hands tucked around her waist. Her lips move rapidly and I realize that she's slipped into another muttering phase. She's been doing that a lot more lately. She's taking to speaking with her deceased mother a lot, sometimes about trivial things like the cold or how hungry she is. At other times it seems as if she's trying to puzzle through the outbreak. It's scary that some of her mutterings are beginning to make sense.

Alex looks up as we roll to a stop near the overgrown track. Sal sits with one leg dangling from the car, appearing unconcerned and indifferent to our arrival.

"You're late." Alex opens my side of the truck and helps me out. I feel a bit unsteady on my feet, still shaken by the Withered Ones.

"Got trapped by a herd in town." The driver's side door squeals as Cable shoves it closed.

Alex glances back toward town. A deep frown settles onto his handsome features. "It's been a while since we saw any of those."

"Well," I grunt as I toss a cloth grocery bag full of bottled water into the truck bed, "we found one."

"But all together?" Alex hefts two large black grocery sacks of clothes, towels and medical supplies into the back. "I know you two told me you'd seen it before but I was kinda hoping you were just yanking my chain."

"There's something else." Cable grabs a cardboard box from beside Alex. I'm relieved to see it filled with boxed foods and canned goods. The homes must not have been completely emptied.

Alex pauses. He looks between us, but I let Cable tell him about the Withered man that we saw. Alex reacts similarly to how we did. Visible disbelief that is quickly followed by a deep seated fear that begins to spread with alarming speed. He looks hollow, his face haggard.

"What do you think it means?" He asks as he shoves the tailgate closed. The supplies won't last long, but we should be good for a week, maybe more if we are lucky. That means we can head back into the woods where we can be safe.

"It means we need to stop sleeping where we are exposed," Cable responds.

"The Moaners have never been a threat before." Alex glances back at Sal and Victoria, keeping his voice low enough that it doesn't carry.

Cable looks to me. "Avery noticed they are starting to alter their behaviors. Small things, but still enough to be concerned about. I'd rather play it safe. If we can't find a house or abandoned building to crash in we need to find a way to make this truck more secure. Just in case."

Alex glances at the cab. "It's too small."

"Then we find a cover." I turn to look back into town, knowing that I really don't want to go back in. I'm spooked and not afraid to admit that. "Maybe at the next town we can find a truck cover, plywood, or something to give us some shelter."

"Agreed." Alex wipes his brow. His cheeks are flushed. I wonder how many houses they had to search through to find what few supplies they brought back. Or how much help Sal and Victoria actually were. "Do we tell them?"

"No." Cable rests his arms over the side of the truck. He looks tired. He hasn't been sleeping well. At first I thought it was nightmares but now I've begun to wonder if his time clock is all out of sorts. "There's no sense worrying them."

He looks to me and I nod in agreement, though not for the same reasons. I don't think Victoria could handle the stress and Sal...the less he knows the better.

Within ten minutes we are prepped and ready to leave. After a heated debate of who would be sitting in the truck bed with me, Alex finally wins and Cable takes the wheel with Victoria pressed in next to him and Sal on the far right. I huddle into my blankets as we turn onto a dirt road leading away from the town.

I don't know its name or anything about the people who once lived here, but I do know that I hope to never see it again.

Alex remains unusually quiet over the next few hours. We huddle close for warmth. With a blanket beneath us and one wrapped around us, we savor the trapped body heat but little can protect us from the winds that bite at our cheeks. It's slow going even on the back roads. Weaving around abandoned cars and back tracking to avoid major pileups takes up precious daylight.

The sun beats down on us from overhead, warming the top of my head. I lift my face to the light, enjoying this rare time of travel during the day.

"I'm worried about Sal." Alex breaks the silence, glancing back over his shoulder.

"More than earlier?"

He nods and tucks the blanket high under his chin. "I noticed something this morning. Something I've seen before."

I shift and knock knees with him. I start to apologize but realize he's too lost in thought to care. "There are spots on his mouth. At first I thought they were blood, maybe he bit his lip in his sleep or something, but there are more. The idiot chews with his mouth wide open so I noticed a few more on his gums."

"Maybe it was just food. I saw him tucking into a candy bar before we left." The fact that he never bothered to share with the rest of us angered me but didn't surprise me. He's not the sharing type. Sal is one of those guys who is in it for himself and holds no pretense otherwise.

"No." Alex glances over his shoulder at Sal. I follow his gaze and frown. There is a red patch of skin just below his left ear. It seems to be trailing up into his hair. As I follow the trail I see a large patch peeking out near his ample bald spot near the crown of his scalp.

"You think he's turning, don't you?"

Alex scrunches up his face then wipes his nose on the blanket. "Maybe not, but I've seen the signs before."

"In who?"

"My co-pilot, right before we were grounded in St. Louis. At first I thought it was just stress. We'd done two long hauls back to back and that was against regulation. We were bone tired. Anyone would be. I was almost relieved when they grounded us."

"But it wasn't because of your work schedule, was it?"

He shakes his head. His teeth clatter together and he shrinks further under the blanket. "Charles lost his wife and son while we were in the air. He never even knew they were sick. That was the excuse the airline gave us when we landed but I could see it was more than that. There were soldiers everywhere toting guns big enough to take down a jumbo jet. We were put in some sort of quarantine. Never saw him again."

"What happened to him?"

He shrugs. His wind burned cheeks look dry and near cracking. I duck my head under the blanket and feel around in my pack, searching for the ointment. I'd forgotten that I had it.

"Here," I hold out the bottle to him. "It might help."

Alex offers me a smile and dabs the clear medicine on his cheeks then slathers it over his burns. His sigh of relief is audible over the winds. "Thanks."

"Must hurt like a bitch."

He laughs. "I'm tougher than I look."

"A survivor."

He nods. "I've learned to do what has to be done."

As a new silence hangs in the air between us, broken only by the chattering of teeth, I can't help but wonder if that goes so far as to betraying us back at the farm. Though Alex has shown no signs of wanting to harm us, I know that the doubts Cable put in my mind about him will linger for quite some time.

FIFTEEN

We moved steadily south over the next four days, but our progress was stunted by a blown head gasket on the truck, leaving us stranded on the side of the road less than thirty miles from town on that first day. We continued by foot, moving parallel to the highway to stay on course. On the fifth day we were hit by the mother of all winter storms driving us back into the shelter of the forest. It crashed over us like a tidal wave, spilling arctic air from the North. By our best guess we have traveled nearly eighty miles from St. Louis but it is not nearly far enough to outrun winter.

By the time we stumbled across a hunting cabin deep in the forest, we were all nearly frozen through. Cable and Alex remained alert for the first two days as the storm raged, but I found myself able to relax for the first time in quite some time.

The Moaners seem to have vanished again, leaving us in peace. Maybe they don't like the cold either. If that's true, I may change directions and head to Canada!

Though I have not seen a Moaner in nearly three days, they haunt my dreams, chasing me with gnashing teeth and rabid eyes. Anger. Desperation. Condemnation. None of those emotions make any sense but waking in the early hours before dawn, each one feels real to me.

The winds that battered the cabin have fallen still, the loud howling diminished to its normal gale. The icicles dangling from the pitched roof drip onto the wooden porch, making it a dangerous skating rink at night. The ice has receded greatly beneath the heat of the sun, the first time we've spied its presence in days. It is a welcome sight, if for no other reason than to bring a bit of cheer once more.

The cabin is cozy, snug and warm. Whoever built it meant for it to be a vacation home, not some shanty used only for fishing or deer season. It is well insulated and stocked with enough wood to last us weeks. The cupboards were bare when we arrived but we have made do, spreading our remaining rations thin.

The A-frame shelter isn't large but it fits the five of us well enough. A king sized bed is housed in the loft, accessible by a leaning wooden ladder. Another bedroom sits off the small kitchen. Two twin beds fill the small space, with a single dresser between. A gas lantern sits on the empty table top.

Cable and I took the bed in the loft, seeing as how we have become used to watching over each other. Cable remains a gentleman, wrapping himself in a separate blanket before huddling up behind me for warmth. Victoria and Alex claim the twin beds while Sal sleeps on a pull out sofa, though he prefers the recliner more. I suspect he remains out there to rummage through our things in the middle of the night. I try to listen for his movements in the dark but the inviting comfort of the bed draws me into a deep, restful slumber.

Our time spent here has not been bad. In fact, it has almost felt like a little slice of home. After rising this morning, and seeing to the more basic human needs, I resumed my usual spot by the window, lounging the day away. I read a book this afternoon. It wasn't very good. Some stupid hunting how-to novel, but it passed the time well enough. I may have even learned a thing or two about setting traps.

It feels weird to not be walking, to not be fighting to survive. I could get used to that.

Now I sit in the corner of the cabin in an oversized rocking chair and watch the people in my group. Victoria buzzes like a contented little bee. The clacking of knitting needles can be heard over the crackling of fire in the stone hearth. I don't think I've ever seen her so happy. The stash of yarn and needles she discovered in the upstairs loft was all it took to bring her out of her weird depression.

"Look at her," I whisper to Cable who sits on the floor beside my knee. I rock slowly, enjoying the warmth of the nearby fire. "She looks so happy."

"She is."

"It's just yarn."

Cable turns his head to look up at me. "It's familiar, something from the past. Maybe it will do her some good"

I try not to speak to Victoria. She and I have had our differences in the past, but her most recent decline into crazy land has left her as my least favorite conversation partner.

Alex sits perched upon an old wooden barstool across the room, his gaze focused on the back of Sal's head. When he first mentioned his concerns in the back of the truck I thought he might be overacting, but even I've begun to see changes in his personality.

Increased irritability. Spreading rash along his neck. A facial tic under his right eye. He scratches in his sleep, muttering and moaning loud enough to wake all of us. In the light of day I see a change in his eyes.

Cable follows the direction of my gaze and frowns. He drops the corner of the rug that he was fiddling with and turns, speaking from the corner of his mouth. "I don't want you near him when I'm not around."

"Done."

His eyebrow rises. "Really? No argument? No 'I can take care of myself' crap?"

I laugh and resume my rocking. "The guy's a bona fide creep. I'll happily place him in your charge."

"Huh." He sinks back against the wall. "Well, I never thought that would happen."

"Disappointed?"

"I gotta admit, I am a little."

I smirk and rise from the chair. "I need some air."

Cable glances toward the window. "It's going to be dark soon. Not sure that's wise."

"This is the point where you realize I don't care." I grab a towel off the back of a chair beside the fire. Several pair of socks and shirts hang nearby. "I'm just going for a wash."

Alex looks up. "You'll freeze."

"Well," I pause with my hand on the door and glare pointedly at Sal, "maybe this time I can get a bit of privacy and I won't be gone long."

I didn't intend to slam the door behind me but the wind rips it from my hand. I shiver and rub my hands along my arms. Maybe this wasn't the best idea.

No. I need to go. To be alone for the first time in a few days.

Cable has been after me to join him for a sunrise walk since the storm broke. He claims that it's well worth losing sleep over. I still have my doubts, and zero intention of taking him up on the offer. I try to tell myself it's because I don't want to risk spending time alone with him, but this time it's a bunch of bunk. I just really love to sleep!

Alex and Cable scouted out a nearby river with a pool of water mostly enclosed by rock walls and steep cliff faces. The water is sure to be freezing but much of the winds should be blocked.

Cable was kind enough to drag pails of water up to the cabin for Victoria and me to bathe yesterday. For all of its quaint charm, this cabin was built rustic. The bathroom was just that...for bathing. No indoor plumbing. Only a large claw foot tub and a wash basin. And no lock, so Sal was happy to discover as I was in the middle of disrobing for a wash last night. I vowed that I'd rather be dirty than let him see me naked again.

After days of lying on dirty floors and tramping through mud, muck and deer shit, I'm desperate to feel clean. To wash the gnarls and dirt from my hair. What I wouldn't give for a bar of soap! The last of it was used on our clothes just this afternoon.

I know we will have to move on now that the storm has passed but I'm none too eager to go hunting around another town. The last one left a bad taste in my mouth.

Following the path in the fading light, I tread lightly, careful not to step on the few remaining patches of ice. Leaves crunch beneath my shoes. The night approaches and with it comes a flurry of activity as the forest wakes around me. It won't be long before dusk is lost to me. I need to be back before the final drops of light fade from the sky.

Picking up the pace, I clutch my towel to me and hurry down the path. It has been well used, though not recently by the looks of it. Much of the grass is matted down, but stray bits have begun to poke back through the trodden path.

Up ahead I see a glint of water. I place my hand against a tree and hoist myself over the final obstacle, a downed log whose innards have long since rotted away. Placing my towel over the tree, I quickly pull my shirt over my head. A shiver ripples along my skin.

"Why does it have to be winter?" I grumble and hop around, removing my socks and shoes. The instant I am completely bare I race for the water.

The water splashes high against my thigh as I rush into the stream to hip height. The recent storm has made it feel more like a river as it overflows its banks. My teeth begin to chatter within seconds. I scoop handfuls of water and rub it against my sensitive flesh. The frigid water is invigorating and my shivering helps to keep me warm.

A crack of a branch nearby drops me to my knees. I scan the woods before me, listening for any unusual sounds in the night. An owl hoots from the treetops. Wind rustles the leaves along the ground. Naked tree branches clack together overhead. I feel as if I'm being watched.

My lower half burns from the cold water, but I dare not rise. I can sense a presence. The question is...are they alive or withered? An enemy or a friend?

Several minutes pass without a sound. My teeth chatter as I wrap my arms about myself. I have to get out or risk hypothermia, but not before I know who or what I'm dealing with.

"Sal? If that's you out there I swear I'll tie you to a tree and leave your sorry ass behind for scaring me!"

Silence.

I begin to quake and know I don't have a choice. I'm about to turn toward my towel when I see movement about a hundred yards ahead of me. A flash of green against the dark trees and then it's gone. Its gait was halting but fast.

Shit!

Turning on my heel, I prepare to dash toward my towel and come up short. There, standing just behind the tree, is Cable. His eyes are wide as they trail over my body in the fading light. A flush rises above the stubble lining his jaw.

Standing perfectly still, I feel exposed, bare to his sight. "I uh...God, I'm sorry. I didn't mean to..." He averts his gaze when I attempt to cover myself with my hands. "I mean I intended to come find you but I didn't think you'd be like that. Shit," he wipes his hands over his face, as if trying to mentally remove the image of me from his mind.

"Did you see it?"

His hands fall away, instantly alert. His gaze floats beyond me. "See what?"

"The Moaner."

He closes the distance between himself and the edge of the water, motioning for me to hurry to his side. My feet feel like blocks of ice as I trudge through the water toward him. "It's gone now," I say through chattering teeth.

"How can you be sure?" He risks a glance down at me and then jerks back up when he looks a bit too low.

"I saw it leave."

"Leave?" His brow furrows. "You make it sound like it came, stayed for a while and left again."

"That's exactly what I'm saying." I wrap my arms over my chest and cross my legs.

"That's not possible, Avery. They don't just watch people. They don't feel anything, do anything beyond walk forward."

"I know what I saw."

He rubs his neck, slowly shaking his head. "You must have been mistaken. It's too dark to really see anyway. Maybe it was a deer or coyote?"

"I know what I saw," I repeat. It bothers me that he doesn't believe me, but I guess if our roles were reversed I'd have a hard time believing it too. "Can I have my towel now?"

He jerks around and snatches it off the log. As if realizing that he can't just toss it toward me, he hesitates. Despite the ache in my lower legs from the freezing water, and the fact that I've just been caught out in all my glory, I close the gap between us. He raises his gaze for a moment then lowers it again, the towel dangling from his outstretched hand.

"I'm cold."

"No kidding." He shakes the towel at me. I take it from his grasp and he wrenches his hand back.

Wrapping the cloth around me, I wring excess water from my hair. "You act like you've never seen a naked girl before."

He swallows hard, then raises his head to meet my gaze. "None that didn't give me previous consent."

I laugh and step toward him. "I forgot. You're not like that, are you?"

A muscle along his jaw flinches. "No."

"Well, then I guess it goes without saying that I'd appreciate you not telling the others about our...encounter."

I grab my clothes and hold them to me, wondering if I'm really going to have to ask him to turn away. His blush deepens as my intent finally sinks in. He spins on his heel. Rushing to dry myself and slip into my clothes, I hop about behind him.

He cocks his head to listen and I hear his deep throaty chuckle. "You try putting jeans on when you're wet," I snap.

He turns away but not before I notice his shoulders rising and falling with laughter. He props his arm against his side and angles toward me. "Use me."

"Well," I pause and look him over, "isn't that a fun proposal?"

He whirls around, his gaze wide and unblinking. "I'm not decent yet!"

"Sorry!" Heat stains his neck as I grab onto him and sort out my pants. With my hair still dripping, I shove my shirt over my head and nestle into the warm fibers.

I kneel down and conceal my feet in socks and shoes before standing. Though I am fully dressed I still feel exposed. Tucking my hair behind my ear, I hesitate, no longer sure of what to say.

"I guess you're wondering why I followed you..." he begins. His voice wavers and he falls silent. I almost feel sympathy for his embarrassment. Almost.

Of course that crossed my mind a time of two. Cable has proven himself to be a gentleman. I can't imagine he came for a peep show like Sal, but then why else would be have come so close? I wasn't exactly being quiet as I splashed about.

"I was worried about you." He casts a surly glance toward the woods. "I guess I had a reason to be."

A trembling begins in my fingers that I'm not entirely sure has anything to do with the cold. What I told Cable was the truth. No human walks with the same style of stunted steps as the Withered Ones. As impossible as it may be, I know one of them was watching me. I just have no way to prove it. "I'm glad you're here."

"Really?" He seems slightly taken aback by my admission.

"Ok, well maybe not in this exact situation, but you know what I mean."

A smile slowly spreads along his lips. "Do I detect a hint of need in your voice?"

"Ha. Did you hit your head on the way out here?"

Cable grins. "That would make you feel better, wouldn't it?"

"Little bit."

Water drips from my hair as we walk. I wring it again. Droplets patter on the leaves underfoot. The back of my shirt has begun to soak through. "Cable?"

"Yeah?" He turns back to look at me. I sympathize with his desire to get back to the cabin. These woods have lost their feeling of seclusion for me now.

"I think that Moaner came from around here."

He stuffs his hands in his pockets as he pauses. I can't help but wonder if he's got his knife hidden there. It wouldn't surprise me. "Ok, let's say that you are right. That somehow one of those things had the capability of thought and reason. What makes you think it's from around here?"

"Because he was wearing a camouflage jacket, just like the one I found inside the cabin for you."

"This area is bound to have a lot of hunters. There are rednecks everywhere! It might not mean anything."

"Or it could. We should warn Alex, either way."

Tugging the towel from my shoulder, I bend over and wrap it around my head. Cable's stern expression cracks when I rise back up and twirl it around my head. "Not a word," I growl and begin tromping back through the woods.

Cable follows close behind but not so close that I feel as if he's invading my personal space. *Ha. It's kinda hard not to when the guy just saw me naked!*

I glance back over my shoulder. Cable has grown quiet, introspective during the five minute hike back. I wonder what he's thinking about. Surely it can't be me. At least I hope seeing me naked wouldn't put that sort of sour expression on his face.

Why the heck do I care what he thinks about seeing me naked? It was a mistake. One I'm not about to repeat any time soon!

As the light from the cabin finally comes into view I pause and turn, placing my hand on his chest to stop him. He stares at my hand. Through the thin layers of his shirt I can feel the thumping of his heart, feel the heat trapped within. "Look, before we go back in there I just want to say thank you for coming after me. I don't blame you for seeing me naked. I mean, it happens, right?"

"Sure." He shifts his weight to his right foot and looks away. "Though that's not quite how I imagined it happening."

My lips part in surprise. Did he just say he imagined seeing me naked?

I clear my throat and try to gather my frantic thoughts. Raising my hand from his chest, I place it against his cheek until he looks back to me. "You're the only friend I've got now, Cable. I don't want things to be weird between us."

But I know they will just by the look in his eye. Cable wants me and I'm starting to think that the feeling is far more mutual than I would like to admit.

SIXTEEN

I listen to the steady rise and fall of breathing coming from the lower floor. The door to Alex and Victoria's room is partially open, per her request. Alex humors the old lady, simply so he won't have to hear her ranting about how it's not safe to sleep near strange men, apparently even at her age. Sal is sacked out in the recliner, no doubt drooling on himself again.

There's no way to tell time but I feel as if I've lain awake most of the night. The heat of Cable's back presses against mine but for once, it feels suffocating instead of inviting. Every time I inch away from him I feel emptiness and sink back.

I'm messed up. That's the only explanation. I punch at my pillow in frustration that only comes from hours of staring blankly at the ceiling. When I do, Cable stirs. I hold perfectly still as he rolls over and presses up against me. His arm winds around my waist.

My lungs go through a temporary paralysis as he pulls me closer to him. I am hyper aware of every part of his body that brushes against me as he shifts: the feel of his hand curling around my hip, the weight of his arm along my side and the gentle breath against my neck that makes me shiver.

His legs curl in around behind mine, molding perfectly to me. I suck in only tiny breaths, terrified of waking him, of shifting enough to bring him out of his dream. His fingers tense against my hip and I bite my lip, trying desperately not to think about how good it feels to be touched. It's been a long time since I let anyone get close like this.

Sure there were guys along the way, but I hardly remember their faces. They were needs that were met, nothing more. Cable is different, no matter how much I wish he weren't.

Would it really be so wrong to encourage him? Just once?

I press back into him and close my eyes, imagining what it would be like for his arms to wrap around me, to hold me. The feel of his hands on my bare skin, his lips trailing down my neck. My pulse jumps at the thought of feeling him above me, moving together in unison.

A warm tingle begins in my abdomen and grows, expanding outward as my thoughts turn to things best left to the dark. My fingers curl around the covers as I bite my lower lip. My breath catches as I imagine the feel of his hands on my breasts, kneading and teasing.

I turn my head and rock my hips back into him. I pause, waiting for a reaction. My skin is warm, sensitive to each breath that washes over my bare shoulder. My tank top suddenly feels restrictive and I long to be free. To let the cold night air soothe the fire raging within.

Cable breathes heavily behind me as I grind my hips against him. He stirs in his sleep, his fingers curling against my hip. A breathy groan escape between his lips and I nearly lose it.

There's no going back now. Not now that I'm consumed with need.

I reach back and grasp his hand, slowly drawing it over my hip and down between my legs. I press his fingers against me and turn my head to stifle a moan into my pillow.

The muscles in his forearm go rigid and I know he's awake. He angles his hips away from my ass, obviously aware of how tightly he was pressed against me. "Avery, what are you doing?"

"I can't sleep," I whisper, rolling my face so that his mouth is beside my ear.

"I can see that."

"Am I bothering you?" I bite on my lower lip and he hesitates. His fingers flinch against me and a shiver trickles down my spine.

"I wouldn't call it bothering." I clench my legs around his hand and his breath grows haggard. "Stop."

"Why?"

"Because I'm trying to be a nice guy right now and you're making me forgot my reasons for doing that!"

I smile into the dark. "Maybe I don't want you to be a nice guy right now."

He goes completely still behind me. "Avery, I don't think this is such a good—"

"No." I release his hand from between my legs and push away so that I can roll over and face him. I place a finger against his lips to silence him when he starts to speak. "Hear me out."

I wait for him to protest, to pull away and try to stop me again, but he doesn't. Maybe I've affected him more than I thought.

"I get that you care for me and you know me well enough to know that I don't let people in. Not people that I could feel for. I've lost a lot of people in my life and I've dealt with it, but sometimes I just need to be held. Not because it means something or that I'm looking for some deep bullshit connection, but because it's what I need. Just one night of not caring, of not worrying about how long I have to fight to survive in this god forsaken world. One night to feel something other than this blasted cold or endless hunger. I need this."

The darkness is so complete that I can't see his expression, read the fear or doubt in his eyes. I know it's there. He's always trying to find ways to protect me, even from himself I'd imagine, if the situation called for it. Cable wants me. I saw it plainly etched into his face earlier tonight and felt the evidence pressed against my backside only a moment ago, but there is another emotion that I saw lingering in his gaze and *that* something needs to stay buried tonight.

I push on his shoulder until he sinks onto his back. I rise beside him and extend my leg over his waist, my movements slow and cautious. His skin feels blistering hot as I settle down on him. His abdominal muscles are taut, his arms rigid on either side of my legs as I run my hands over the hard contours of his chest to hold his shoulders I wait for him to push me away, to tell me no, but he doesn't.

"Say something." I lean down and whisper into his ear. The dry strands of my hair tickle his chest.

He doesn't move. Doesn't speak. I can practically hear the battle raging in his mind and start to pull away, knowing that his honorable side will win out, but he stops me with two little words.

"One night," he vows as he reaches up and cups the back of my neck, crushing his lips against mine. My fingers curl around his shoulders as I press into him. My mess of curls spills around his face.

His hand rises from my neck and winds through my hair, holding me in place. His free hands squeezes my thigh, his fingers achingly close to where I long most to be touched. Cable's kiss is long and deep, breaking apart only when he's forced to gasp for breath. His chest heaves as I hover over him. I smile as he lifts his head to stroke my bruised lips with the tip of his tongue.

I love his scent. The taste of his lips. I don't pull away as he claims my mouth once more. I wind my hands down from his neck, tracing the muscles that flex as he pushes upright and settles me firmly around his lap.

I explore freely, savoring the rise and fall of the muscles lining his arms and across his defined chest and abdomen as his tongue explores mine. His skin pimples beneath my touch as I trail my fingers down to the path of hair leading beneath me.

I can feel him pressing urgently against me and bite my lip as he thrusts his hips. I shake my head, breaking the kiss, wanting to lengthen the moment yet desperate for release. I grind back against him and enjoy each flinch and groan that he makes.

"Shit, Avery" He rolls his head to the side as I dip my hand down between my legs and grab hold of him. "You're going to be the death of me."

I lean down and nibble on his lower lip. "At least you will enjoy it."

"More than you know." He wraps his arms around me, sealing me into his embrace. He is scorching against my chilled skin.

I've always known Cable was strong, but observing it before and feeling it now are two very different experiences. I melt against his touch as his hand rises to my waist, pushing my hips to create friction. My hips grind against him until I'm desperate for more. I break off the kiss and grasp the hem of my shirt, tugging it over my head.

"I can't see you," he growls, his fingers digging into my side.

Curling my back, I lean down and nip at his ear. My breasts graze along his chest and he arches up into me. The sensation of his bare skin against my swollen nipples wrenches a moan from my lips as I rock. "You saw me earlier."

"It's not the same." His hands move restlessly along my bare back, tugging and pushing.

Grasping his hands, I place them on my chest, filling his palms. I lean into him, resting my head atop his as he begins kneading my breasts. "Then memorize me with your hands."

My skin aches with sensitivity as his thumbs swirl around my tender flesh, pinching and tugging me into oblivion. My breath catches as he lowers his head and sucks my nipple into his mouth. My hips buck as I hold his head, begging him not to stop.

A groan rises from deep in his chest as I push back into him, grinding then pulling away. A flush grips me as I roll off him and rise from the bed, shedding the last of my clothes in a rush. I can't wait any longer.

The bedsprings squeak and I smile, knowing that he's in no mood to linger either.

Kneeling on the bed, I prepare to straddle him again but he grasps my arms and rolls on top of me, pinning me down. The scent of his skin is heady as I bite at his neck, my nails raking down his back. His growl echoes in my ear as he spreads my leg with his knee and buries himself inside me. I wrap my arms possessively around him.

The bed squeaks and groans as Cable finds a rhythm that leaves me breathless and wanting. I rock with him, whispering in his ear, urging him on. He follows every command, every plea for him to speed up or slow down. He draws himself back, taking me to the edge of frustration them slams hard, stealing my breath away.

Raising my hands overhead, I grip the wooden bars of the bed and bury my face in my arm. Small whimpers escape my throat, fueling his thrusts. Sweat clings to my body as I wrap my legs around him, arching upward so that he sinks deep.

"Look at me," he demands.

I roll my head and stare up at him, startled to realize that I can make out the contours of his face. I release my grip on the bed and wrap my arms around his neck, drawing him close. "I see you."

The headboard beats against the wall with increasing speed. I buck my hips up into him, increasing the friction between us. His head arches back and the muscles along his neck pull taut as he thrusts one final time. Goosebumps rise along his arms. His arms strain with exertion before he collapses, nestling his head against my cheek.

I hold him, feeling a tingling warmth spreading through my body. His chest rises and falls rapidly. He gulps in breath, wrapping his arms around me.

"Thank you," I whisper as his breathing slows.

He raises his head. His skin is clammy, sensitive to the touch as I glide my fingers over his arms. He flinches as I reach his side and trail down to his waist. "For what?"

I smile and brush the matted hair back from his forehead. "For giving me what I need."

He reaches up and cups my cheek. His gaze still holds the haze of passion but there is a deeper emotion hovering just below the surface. I know that I should turn away, ignore that I see it, but he won't let me look away as he smiles. "Who said we're done?"

I arch my eyebrows as he untangles himself from my arms and crawls backward, his tongue trailing between my breasts and over my abdomen. He pauses as he comes to rest between my legs and presses a kiss against my inner thigh. As he nestles closer, I close my eyes and lose myself to the moment.

When I wake sometime later the sun seems wrong, too bright and hidden from the windows before me. I groan and rub my eyes, feeling sore and exhausted.

"You know, if you're going to have sex the least you can do is scream louder so I can enjoy it too." I bolt upright. Cable's hand falls away from my bare breast and I struggle to yank the tangled sheets out from under him to cover myself in front of Sal.

"Do you mind?"

"Not at all." He leans against the banister and stares openly.

"Cable," I hiss and smack him on the arm. He rouses and my stomach tightens at how good the tousled look is on him first thing in the morning.

"What?" He grabs the pillow and tries to tug it over his eyes.

"I need your help."

Cable tenses at the tone in my voice. He emerges to find Sal grinning down at us. His tanned skin darkens as he moves toward the edge of the bed. I quickly tuck the sheet around me. Cable doesn't seem to need it at the moment. "You have three seconds to get your ass back down that ladder before I toss you over that railing."

"Fine." Sal raises his hands in mock surrender, pausing long enough to try to get another good look at me. "I just thought you might like to know we're leaving."

"Leaving?" I tuck the sheet around my legs for good measure. "Who the hell decided that?"

Sal shoots me a wink. "Wouldn't you like to know? I'd be willing to let you in on that delicious little secret if you lower that sheet just another smidgen."

Cable growls and surges to his feet. Sal's eyes open wide, but he quickly sinks into a knowing smirk, tsking as he shakes his head. "I expected more from you, Avery. Any girl should have been screaming with that guy in bed with you."

Grabbing the front of his shirt, Cable shoves Sal back. His heels come off the floor and for a moment I'm convinced he intends to follow through on his threat.

"Cable!" His arms flex. I try not to notice the curve of his backside as he turns to look at me. The tattoo that I spied ages ago peeking through his shirt trails down from shoulder to waist. A waterfall of ink in the shape of a rugged looking cross spans the breadth of his back. The sight of it surprises me. I never took Cable as a religious man. "He's not worth it."

"Aw. Sticks and stones, love." Sal blows me a kiss. "When you get tired of him you know where to find me."

With a vicious growl, Cable shoves him off the balcony. I watch as Sal's arms pinwheel and listen as his scream is cut off with a loud whump.

"What did you do?" I yank the bed sheet off and hurry to the ladder. Alex peers questionably up at us from beneath the loft and I cower behind Cable for cover. Alex's hair is damp, his face ruddy from a recent washing. It must be later than I realized for him to have time to bring water back from the stream and boil it.

"He's fine." Cable turns and walks away. His fists clench at his sides. It's obvious just how hard it is for him to get himself under control.

Sal shouts as he fights to right himself, his fall broken by the couch. I meet Alex's gaze before I return to Cable's side. I place my hand on his arm and he flinches.

"Sorry," I whisper and draw back. I turn away from him to find my clothes but he pulls me back. He wraps his arms around me, my back pressed to his chest as he rests his head on top of mine.

"I don't want to pull away from you. Not like this. I'd planned for something a little less drama based."

I close my eyes, knowing this moment would come. I just didn't have time to prepare myself for this awkward moment when lovers become friends once more. "You don't have to. At least not too far."

He presses his lips to the back of my head and releases me. I walk away from him, attempting to put the events of the night behind me, but some things are harder to forget. Cable touched me in ways no man ever has, deeper, more intimate. Not in the physical realm, but emotional. I told myself in the early hours of the morning as he slept beside me that nothing would change. I wish I still believed that.

SEVENTEEN

I scowl at Sal as I hit the bottom rung of the ladder after dressing in silence with my back turned to Cable. My footsteps sound unnaturally loud in the quiet cabin as I pass by him to face off with Alex.

"You saw what he did?"

Alex nods and stirs his spoon around the lip of his metal coffee mug. It's filled with only hot water but I've discovered over the past few days since being here that in his mind, it's almost like having the real thing. "Saw what Cable did too."

He doesn't say an accusing word about Sal's untimely fall from the loft, or the events that led up to them. I can tell by the deep blush riding high on Victoria's cheeks behind him that my tryst with Cable before dawn didn't go unnoticed by anyone in the house.

"So that's it? Just brush it off like it's not the creepiest thing in the world to have a guy watching you while you sleep."

"While you are naked, you mean?" As he turns his gaze away and takes a sip I notice that the tips of his ears are red with embarrassment, or anger. I can't really decide which..

"That's...that's really not the issue at this point," I stammer and wrap my arms around my waist.

"The pre-dawn wake up moans say otherwise," Sal quips.

"Go fuck yourself," I snarl, turning to glare at him.

"Alright," Alex sets his mug down. "That's enough, you two. We all have to live under the same roof. Obviously we are going to have to make some...adjustments to make it all work."

My fingers dig into my sides as I shake my head, letting my hair shield me from Alex's gaze. The need to retreat, to rush out into the woods and hyperventilate over this morbid embarrassment is unbearable. "There's no need," I mutter. "It won't happen again."

Alex grabs my arm and draws me back as I try to move away from him. "What happened happened. I've got no say in that. I just want you to be careful."

"I am."

"Are you?" In the late morning light I notice that the blond hairs along his chin, jaw and cheeks have begun to fill into a beard now. I can't say that it seems all that fitting for the fly boy airline pilot but he seems more down to earth now. More likeable. I think this new life, as crazy as it sounds, suits him better.

"Cable and I have an understanding." I stare down at his hand on my arm until he releases me and steps back.

"Those have a way of being forgotten. I should know. I was the king of one night stands that ended badly."

"Who said it was a one-night stand?" I challenge.

Victoria stares hard at the counter before her. There's no food left to eat, but I'd bet she'd rather bury her face in that hunting book I found yesterday than be stuck standing here in the middle of our discussion. "I know your type, Avery. You don't settle down."

"Maybe I do. Maybe I don't. That's none of your business either, now is it?"

"Not normally." He shakes his head. "But it becomes my business when other people are involved."

I glare over my shoulder at Sal. He wiggles his fingers at me and blows another kiss. Anger simmers low in my belly but I don't show it. I don't want to add fuel to Alex's fire. "Cable and I have nothing to do with any of you."

"You're wrong." I turn back to look at Alex, surprised by the tension in his voice. "When were you going to tell me you two were followed last night?"

"Followed?" I glance toward Victoria, noting that her head has raised up a bit. "Followed by who?"

"I was hoping you could tell us. What I do know is that there were four sets of prints out there this morning when I woke. Yours, Cable's, mine and another guy. Sal pissed in the corner when he woke up so it wasn't him and Vicky here has tiny feet.

So that leaves a stranger stomping up to our doorstep while we slept. I don't know about you, but I'm not too keen on that idea."

I push back against the counter, needing the pressure of it to keep me grounded. "I saw a Moaner in the woods last night."

"So?" I blink, surprised to hear Victoria speak. It's been so long since she joined in an actual conversation I'd almost begun to wonder if she was really present at all.

"So it followed me. Or at least it watched me from a distance."

Sal snorts and pulls the lever of the recliner. He pushes it out to its full length, laying back and crossing his hands under his head. Even from this distance I regard the rash that has grown down his arm. His eyes look hazier than normal. "Little Moaner got you scared? I'd have thought a tough girl like you could take one on."

I start to snap back at him but a voice calling from above stops me. "Avery's right. There was someone in the woods last night and they didn't just pass through. They stopped and watched. That tells me that whoever it was took a bit too much interest in us for my liking." Cable's boots clunk as he leaps down the final three steps of the ladder.

His pack is slung on his back. His hat is firmly in place, tugged low enough that I can't quite make out the direction of his gaze, but I feel like it's firmly focused on me.

"What was it watching?" Alex tugs at his sleeves. The chill on the air is more prevalent this morning. Only wisps of smoke coil up from the fire now. I guess there was no need to keep it going since Alex decided to ship out.

"Me bathing." My cheeks flush red as I hop up onto the counter. The Formica is old and peeling away from the wall. Not the most stable seat in the room but it's the nearest. If I'm walking all day I might as well get the last few ounces of rest in that I can.

"Wait a second." Alex holds up his hands. He takes turns between staring in disbelief toward Cable and accusingly at me. "You're telling me that you think some Moaner stopped for a peep show last night, then followed you back here?"

"Almost impossible to believe, right Avery?" Sal chortles.

Cable adjusts his pack, buckling it around his waist to even the weight. Without food the pack caves in at the top. His boots are laced high to support his ankles on the hike. I can tell by the way he's standing that he's wrapped his ribs up nice and tight, though he didn't seem too concerned with them last night.

"Avery?"

"That's what I saw, Alex."

"Cable?" He only shrugs in response to Alex's question. I can tell by the hard set of his jaw that it's taking every ounce of restraint he possesses not to go and throttle Sal.

Alex scoffs, shaking his head. "Fine. If you two don't want to tell me the truth, that's fine. Grab your shit. I'm done with this place."

"Alex, we're not—"

"Save it." He glares openly at me. I'm taken back by his hostility. "If there's one thing I can't stand, it's liars. I should know. I'm one of the worst, but this...this is different."

I look to Cable for support but he shakes his head and turns his back. I sigh and leap down from the counter, resigned to face a really long day.

We hike through the afternoon, pausing only for small sips of water we discover seeping through the sediment at the base of a large set of stone steps naturally carved into the rock. It tastes earthy but clean. A path winds through the large boulders, making our passage easier, but we veer away when the trail begins to head back toward our previous direction.

South—it is the only direction that matters at the moment. I never really asked Cable or Alex why this was the decision. East or West seem just as good a candidate as any. I'd veto North in a heartbeat unless that whole bit about Moaners hating cold turned out to be true.

Sal marches at the head of the pack, his mouth running faster than his feet. He rambles about nothing and everything, all at the top of his voice. I've seen Alex trying to talk to him but Sal shoves him away and continues on.

I exchange worried glances with Cable but say nothing. I know he is thinking the same thing I am: if there are any survivors in the area Sal will bring them down on top of us.

The sun beats relentlessly from overhead. Beads of sweat trickle along my spine beneath the thick layers of clothes and the bulk of my pack. I had hoped once all of the food was gone that it would be an easier load to bear, but the lack of nourishment only makes the trek that much harder.

Cable remains behind me, drawing near only when we reach a steep slope. His presence is both welcoming and unnerving at the same time. Each time he grasps my arm to ease me down another boulder, a tingle begins beneath his fingers and I'm instantly swept back into the memory of sleeping in his arms.

I know he feels it too. It's obvious in the way he releases me the second he knows I'm safe, snatching his hand back as if I've burned him. He helps Victoria from time to time as well. I guess he's trying to prove that it's not favoritism or some crap like that.

"Hey, Avery." I look up to see Sal twirling atop a wet boulder. The spray of a larger waterfall has left the rock face dark and slick. "Wanna dance?"

"Alex," I shout out in warning. Though he's hardly spoken a word to me since this morning, he rushes forward to intercept Sal.

"Hey, buddy. Why don't you come down from there before you get hurt?"

Sal's face scrunches up. Spittle seeps from the corner of his lips as he shakes his head. I pause several feet below, watching Alex carefully pick his way up to meet Sal.

"What's he got that I ain't got, anyways?" Sal yells and spins once more. His footing is precarious. "Sure he's kinda good looking, got arms the size of tree but I've got experience that he can't compete with. That's gotta count for something, right?"

"Sal," Alex raises his arms. He's two rocks below Sal and not nearly close enough to avoid disaster. "I think I've got a candy bar in my pack. I'll share it with you if you come down quietly."

He seems to contemplate it for a moment, brushing his hand along the length of what little hair he has left. Victoria was right to try to get him to chop it off. That greasy mullet is repulsive.

"Listen to him, Sal." I call out.

His gaze shifts to look at me. "Not till you promise me that dance, sweetheart."

Alex jerks as Sal's foot slips, but the fool merely laughs and spins on one foot. His heavy paunch seems to balance him as he leans forward and creates the image of a fat, hairy ballerina.

"Cable?" I say. He stands beside me, his hands tucked deep into his pockets and once again I wonder if he has a weapon concealed there.

"I know. There's nothing we can do about it."

I stare hard at him. "Yes, there is."

I ease past Victoria and approach the base of the rocks. Even from here I can feel the frigid spray of the water. A small rainbow hovers in the air before me, the mists illuminated in the dappled sunlight. Clouds have begun to move in. There is a change on the air and pray that we find shelter before the next storm. They seem to come so fast these days.

"One dance, Sal, but you have to promise to keep your hands above the waist."

"That's where all of the good stuff is anyways." He spins to face me, a wide triumphant smile lighting his face. "I knew I could convince you. You're a smart girl. You just need the right leverage—"

His cry startles birds from the trees. His arms flail and the crazed look in his eye shifts as the realization that he's going to fall sinks in a moment too late. Alex reaches out for him, grappling to catch onto his foot as he teeters. "Sal!"

His boot slips off the rock and he plummets backward. Cable outstrips me as I race to climb the rocks.

"Oh, poor, poor Sal." I turn to see Victoria wringing her hands before her. "All he ever wanted was to be loved."

"Stay back," Cable warns as he inches his way around a boulder overhead. The ledge is small, barely wide enough to hold the toe of his boot. Alex approaches from above, both converging on Sal's last location.

A part of me knows that I should ignore his warning and go to Sal's aid. Another part, the more callous realist wonders what's the point. He is turning. Everyone knows it. It's only a matter of time before he becomes one of *them*.

Cable disappears from sight. The top of his back disappears behind the rock. Alex plants his hands and feet between the two rock faces and shimmies down. Several minutes pass without any sound.

"Is this when the screaming starts?"

I turn, surprised to find Victoria has managed the initial climb up to me. She looks lost and frail. Her face is drawn. Dark circles line beneath her eyes. I smile and motion for her to join me, sucking in my pride as I place my hand around her shoulder. She leans her head on me and I'm choked by the overwhelming scent of perfume. Where on earth did she uncover that crap?

"They'll be fine. We all will be."

"You always did know how to make me feel better."

I frown and pull away from her. "Vicky, are you feeling ok?"

Her brow furrows and her gaze drifts far off. "Stop fretting over me, Mom. You know I hate that."

Mom? I stare at her a moment longer and am shocked when I see her stick her thumb into her mouth. *She's regressing. Isn't that one of the symptoms too?*

I press my palm to my head, trying to think. I remember before the news reporters went off air that there was a long list of symptoms to watch out for. So many of them mirrored the common cold or flu that it left everyone sure they were next. Was this one of them?

"It will all be fine." I squeeze her shoulders and lead her toward a rock a safe distance away. "Why don't you rest here for a bit while I go help the guys?"

"You'll come back right? You promised." Her mouth puckers as she shakes her head. "You promised you'd come back but you never did. I waited for you…"

Shaken by her words and how closely they hit home with my own father, I step back and hurry away. That is all kinds of messed up right there!

"Cable?" I shout. At this point it won't really matter if anyone hears us. Either they will help or we'll fight. I doubt things could get much worse. "Cable?"

"We're here." The grunt comes from my right and I lean around the rock and see Alex and Cable struggling toward me.

Sal hangs limply between them, unconscious. Blood trails down from his head. His skin appears ashen.

I hurry forward. "Is he dead?"

"Probably should be." Alex winces as he stumbles under Sal's weight. Of the entire group, Sal's got the largest frame. Big boned, as he tried to call it. That gut is all beer and Twinkies if you ask me!

They lower him to the ground a few feet ahead of me. Leaves and dirt stick to his scalp wound as his head rolls to the side. There is an ugly cut along his hairline. The rest of him looks miraculously unharmed. I'd have expected at least a broken bone or two.

"Found him wedged between two rocks. Lucky bastard can't even kill himself right." Alex wipes at his nose. The end is pink, as are the tips of his fingers. He presses on his lower back and arches to stretch out his muscles.

"He's an idiot."

Alex nods in agreement of Cable's assessment. "In more ways than one." He turns to look at me and his expression changes. "Thanks for at least trying to help. I know you didn't want to."

"It was the right thing to do. He would have given away our location."

"Yeah, probably so." Alex turns and surveys the woods. The dark grey rock face behind us rises nearly fifty feet overhead. It curls around us in both directions. It's not a terrible spot to be in, but I would have liked to find real shelter for the night. "I guess we set up camp here."

Cable drops his pack. He sinks down low and digs through the contents to find several slightly dented plastic bottles. He holds them out to me. "Might as well fill these up while we can."

"What are you going to do?"

He points back toward the path we left less than half an hour before. "I'm going to follow that and see if we can find shelter. Judging by the look of those clouds we are in for a rough night."

"I'll come with you." Alex splashes water on his face, rubbing it through his hair. He cups his mouth under the trickle of water and drinks deep before rejoining us.

"You're leaving me with them?" The prospect of staying being with a highly perverted man and an old woman suffering from a bought of crazy mommy issues doesn't sound the least bit appealing.

"We'll be back before sundown." Alex takes an empty bottle from my hand and tosses another to Cable. "Fill up before we leave."

He splashes through the water, heading away from us. Cable stands beside me, unmoving but I can tell he wants to be nearby. "We won't go far."

"I know." The flat tone in my voice affects Cable. He stiffens and thumbs the edge of the bottle cap in his hand.

"I wouldn't go unless I felt I had to."

"It's fine. I don't need a babysitter."

"Avery—" he reaches out for me but I pull back.

"Just go. I'm fine."

He sighs and taps the bottle against his leg. "Why is it when you say you're fine, I get the feeling you mean the other thing?"

A small smile tugs at my lips, but I don't turn to let him see it. I know he doesn't want to leave me behind, but he does, because he should. It's times like this I hate being a woman. I'm not a caretaker or a nurse, but people keep trying to make me into both.

EIGHTEEN

The sun hangs heavy in the western sky. Its fading rays offer little light or warmth to the darkening woods. Victoria rocks back and forth on the ground beside me. Her mutterings incoherent, grating on my nerves.

Sal sits with his back against a tree, his hands and feet bound by strips of towel that I tore apart while he was still unconscious. I don't trust him. He is too erratic. Too unstable. Too...Sal.

I know it's the transformation progressing that causes his overbearing personality to explode. Though I've only ever seen it happen once before with Natalia, she hadn't reacted anything like this. That's the frustrating thing. There's no easy way to pin down the symptoms because they seem different for each person.

"Must be nice to have three guys hot for you," Sal says, spitting to the side. Blood tints the saliva, darkening the rocky path nearby. "Bet you love making us squirm. Though I guess Cable can stop squirming now, can't he? You already gave it up to him. Guess I'll just have to wait in line and you'll eventually get around to me after you mess with Alex's head a bit first."

"Fuck you." I hurl a stick out into the woods, wishing that I could smash his nose in. I should have gagged him but I didn't want to get close enough for him to bite me. He's infected and I won't take the risk of any of his bodily fluids touching me.

His raspy laugh sounds moist and clogged. A sudden intake of breath followed by intense coughing makes me turn back toward him. His face grows red. If his hands were free I'm sure he'd be beating on his chest, but he isn't free. I sit and watch his struggle, his face shifting through pale pinks to dark purple. His lips begin to take on a blue tint, though I guess it could be a trick of the light.

Sal's eyes begin to bulge. A vein pulses down his forehead.

"No, no, no!" Victoria rocks faster, clutching her hands to her ears. There is a steady tremor in her fingers.

Sighing, I rise and approach him. He looks at me, unseeing. I crouch before him and hesitate. It would be easy to let him go out like this, suffering, like he deserves. I could do it. Just let him choke to death, but as I glance back at Victoria I know it would unhinge her completely.

"Ain't that a bitch." I ball my hand into a fist and beat on his back. He splutters, gasping for breath. Three more pounds on his back and a glob of mucus bursts from his throat. I turn my face away, sickened by the sight and potent smell. "Don't say I never did anything for you."

I push off on his shoulder and return to my spot, actively ignoring him as he slowly recovers. The wheezing is new. I only wish I knew how many more symptoms he had to go through before the end.

"What the hell is going on here?"

I look up to see Alex appear around the bend in the path. His light blond hair picks up the final rays of twilight. Cable marches behind him, his taller frame lost to the shadows. Alex drops what looks like a large rolled garbage bag and rushes to Sal's side. He places two fingers against his neck.

"His heart rate is all over the place." He turns to glare at me. "What did you do to him?"

"Nothing."

"Liar, liar, liar," Victoria mutters. "Kill, kill, kill."

Alex's gaze hardens. "Did you try to kill him?"

Cable steps between us as I start forward. He raises his arms out to keep me at bay. "I'm sure Avery didn't do anything to harm Sal."

"Oh yeah?" Alex doesn't seem to buy it for a second and my anger multiples. Why the heck would he take the word of a crazy woman over me? "How do you figure that?"

Cable turns to look at me over his shoulder and smiles. "Because if she wanted him dead...he would be."

I nod in silent agreement, thankful that he understands just how close I came to letting it happen. Alex doesn't need to know that though.

"He started choking. I whacked him on the back a few times and he recovered. No big deal," I shrug and push Cable's arms down. I don't need to him to protect me from Alex. He's not the one I'm worried about.

Alex's hands are planted on his hips. He stares down at the mess between Sal's feet then up at Sal. I detect by the way he shifts that he's looking for some sign of bruising around his neck, probably finger impressions to prove my guilt. When he finds none he closes his eyes and sighs. "Why is he tied up?"

"I don't trust him." I say simply. I would have thought that much would be obvious.

"Did he try to hurt you?" I turn and offer Cable a smile before shaking my head no. "Good, cause if he did..." he lets that statement fall away.

Alex runs his hands through his hair. Stray bits of twigs fall from the matted strands. There are wide tears in his shirt and for the first time I notice just how disheveled both he and Cable look. I narrow my gaze on a cut along Cable's arm and reach for it.

"What the hell happened to you two?"

"We found supplies," Cable replies but I feel like there should be more to that statement.

"What, did you steal them from an angry bear?" I roll his arm over and see more cuts, some of them deep. Blood trails down his arm in jagged vines. He doesn't hiss when I press my finger near the wound but there is a tightening of pain around his eyes.

"Alex?" I turn on him, knowing Cable will try to keep the truth from me.

"We ran into some survivors. They had what we needed." His indifferent shrug doesn't fool me. He refuses to meet my gaze as he pushes past and kneels beside the garbage bag roll that he dropped upon first arriving. I follow after him, shaking Cable's grip off.

"You stole this stuff?" He nods and begins untying three rope knots that hold the bag in place. "And the survivors?"

Alex's hands fall still. His shoulders curl inward, his head bows low. "They won't be needing this anymore."

I whirl around and stare at Cable. His hand is pressed tightly to his pocket. I close the gap between us in three long strides and yank his arm away. He cries out but doesn't stop me as I shove my hand deep into his pocket. The interior is moist.

Something cold touches my fingers. I draw my hand out and open my palm. Two weapons lie in my hand: a bloodied hunting knife and a coiled bit of wire.

"Oh god," I drop the weapons and step back. Blood stains my hand. Innocent blood. "You killed them?"

"What?" Alex whirls around. "No, of course we didn't. They had turned into Withered Ones."

I glance at Cable. His expression is unreadable. "So why is there blood on these?"

Alex points to the pack on Cable's back. "That's from dinner."

Several hours later, I sit beside the small fire, watching the dancing light flicker against the trees. The smoke billows up, lost to the gray expanse of clouds overhead. Breath hangs before my lips as I warm my hands. The air has turned bitterly cold.

Cable uses his knife to slice off a charred piece of wild hog. The tusks bear signs of blood from where Cable and Alex tried to subdue the animal.

Cable hasn't said much to me since my earlier accusation. He helped me set up the six person tent in silence. It's obvious from the confidence he exuded during set up that he spent many of his summers camping. I was all thumbs trying to get the darn poles to stay up.

The tent is bright yellow, hardly what I would call good camouflage, but beggars can't be choosers. It will keep the wind off us tonight. I'm thankful for that.

Alex emerges from the tent. He looks exhausted as he wipes his hands over his face. "Vicky is sleeping. She's pretty messed up about what happened."

"And Sal?" I cast a furtive glance toward the zippered door. My protests that he should remain tied up fell on deaf ears as Alex took Sal into the tent.

"He's passed out from fever."

Cable meets my gaze then drops it again. "He shouldn't be in there with us tonight."

Alex groans as he sinks down onto a rock and takes the offered piece of meat from Cable. Juice runs down his lips and into his beard. He wipes his arms across his mouth to clean it away. "I thought we've been over this. He's part of the group. We care for our own, even when he's not the most likeable guy."

"He's dangerous." Cable tosses a bit of fat and skin onto the fire, watching it burn.

"He's in no condition to hurt anyone."

"You're wrong." Both men turn and look at me. I keep my gaze focused on the deep blue flames. "Sal knows he's turning. I saw it in his eyes earlier when he was choking. He's no fool, Alex. He remembers why you kept me in the group."

Cable lowers the leg of meat has been working on carving with his knife and turns to stare at me. "What's that supposed to mean?"

I meet his gaze head on. "They knew about my blood. That's why they kept me around. I was supposed to help Eva."

The bone snaps in Cable's hand as he rounds on Alex. "Is that true?"

Alex swallows a large piece of meat. "It was...at first. But things changed."

"What things?" Cable's voice is low and deadly. I don't know if Alex notices the way Cable's grip tightens on his knife, but I do.

"The point is," I break in, "that Sal thinks my blood can heal him, or at least prolong his fate."

Cable's hand moves back toward his lap, a visible sign of relaxing but it's just for show. If Alex makes one wrong move Cable will attack. I can't let that happen. Though I don't agree with some of the shots Alex has called recently, but there is strength in numbers.

"But your blood can't heal him." Cable takes another bite and slowly chews it. "You're not a universal donor and you're sure as heck not a cure."

Alex's back straightens as he looks toward me. "But I thought—"

"No." Cable tosses the meatless bone onto the fire and wipes his hands on his pants. "If her blood were mixed with his, he'd still die. Probably in a worse way than he already is."

"We tested her blood. Victoria said she was a universal donor."

"She wasn't completely wrong." I set my portion of meat down, my stomach no longer happy with the offering. I relay the details of my time spent in the company of the military, what we'd discovered. As I speak, I watch Alex visibly pale and wonder if he had held out hope that someday I could save his life too.

Maybe he didn't bring those men back to the farm to capture us after all. Maybe it really was a coincidence. Maybe Alex had different intentions all along.

One glance at Cable reveals that I'm not the only one thinking it.

"So what do we do? Leave him here? Let him change? "Alex rubs absently at his arms. "Victoria would never allow it. She's a tough girl, in her own right. She wouldn't leave him before."

"Then he'd probably kill her and risk mixing their blood," Cable says, staring blankly into the fire.

"There's only one choice," I whisper. My stomach twists at the thought. I don't think I could do it. Not in cold blood. If only I'd let Sal suffocate when it would have been by natural causes.

Cable remains silent. Alex's mouth slackens. His eyebrows rise in disbelief as he stares between us. "You're talking about murder."

"No." Cable presses his knees together then rises. He stares down at Alex. "That's survival."

He turns and walks away, heading into the forest. I wonder if I should go after him, but I can't leave Alex. Not until I can make him see reason.

"He's not well, Alex. You know that. It's only a matter of time before he turns."

"So then let him turn!" His nostrils flare as he kicks out his foot. A bit of dirt snuffs out the flames on the edge of the fire pit.

I draw in a breath and hold it for a moment until I'm sure I can control my frustration. "If he turns, he will be in that tent with us, or on a hiking path, or god knows where else. Do you really think Victoria can handle seeing that? She's already in some sort of shock over what happened back in St. Louis."

Slipping off my rock, I kneel beside him and place a hand on his knee. I've never intentionally touched Alex before. He swallows as his gaze settles on my hand. "Sal is part of the group. I know that, but how long will he continue to be Sal? You saw his desperation. We all did. Can you really live with yourself if he kills me or Vicky in our sleep? Can you live with yourself if you wait too long?"

Alex's skin becomes ghostly pale. His hands tremble. He sucks his lower lip between his teeth. "I never wanted people to look to me for answers."

I sink down beside him and wait as he blows out several deep breaths. His gaze grows distant, lost to the past. "I thought Devon would be a good leader. He seemed strong willed, level headed, but then he took in that man and wife. Locked them away and said it was for our own good. For Eva's."

He rubs at his chest as his eyebrows pinch in a grimace of long claimed regret. "I tried to tell myself that it was the right thing to do. To protect our group, but you were right. We were no different than those men who roamed the streets. We became the one thing we hated the most."

Reaching up, I place my hand on his forearm. His skin feels cold to the touch, despite the fire before us. "You did what you had to do to survive."

He nods slowly. "And that's what we have to do again."

He turns his gaze away from the fire to look at me. I see a haggard man, wearied and burdened by the impossible choices laid out before him. I feel the same way. I just hide it a bit better. "I can't do it."

I'd struggle to follow through with it as well. Sal and I may have an intense dislike of each other, but at the moment he's still alive, still human. Could I really look into his eyes and know that I'm the last thing he would see?

"I'll do it." I look up to see Cable has returned. The wire from his pocket is wound tightly around his hands. His feet are firmly planted, his chin held high. He has the look of a man who's set aside all emotion to get a task done, no matter how horrifying it may be.

"Cable…"

He shakes his head and I fall silent. "I won't let you have blood on your hands. We've made it this far without that."

"Someday I will have to kill."

He nods slowly. "But not today."

Alex buries his head in his hands. "I can't believe we're even talking about this. It's so...so sick."

"It's reality," I whisper, hugging my arms about myself. Has the world really sunk to this low? That innocent people are sacrificed for the greater good. I guess that happened before all of this. Kids died by the thousands each day from starvation or lack of water. Homeless died on the streets from the cold. Wars were started for financial gain.

The world hasn't become more twisted. It just, in some insane way, become more simple. You fight. You survive. Nothing else matters now.

"Not tonight." Alex says, slowly raising his head. "Vicky is in there with him right now. If we are going to do it, it has to be when she's not around."

I look to Cable and note the tension in his jaw. His grip on the wire doesn't loosen. His stance doesn't ease.

"I'll take the first watch. Make sure things stay quiet. Cable can take the second watch and Avery the final. If we make it through the night then we can deal with it tomorrow."

"And if not?" I question.

Alex opens and closes his mouth. He doesn't have the answers. None of us do.

NINETEEN

Sleep eludes me for several hours. I listen to Cable and Alex talking by the fire, focusing on the rise and fall of their tone in an attempt to will myself to sleep. Victoria rests beside me. Her frizzy hair is plastered to the side of her face, her glasses askew on her nose. Sal snores on her other side, loud and as obnoxious as usual. I should have put myself between them, to ensure Victoria's safety, but I couldn't bring myself to be near him.

The night is cold and endless. The hours trudge by as if time no longer holds any meaning. I'd like to kick old Father Time in the crotch to get him motivated again. That would show the bastard I mean business.

I lie motionless when Alex returns some time later from his shift and crashes down beside me. I don't shift away when he presses his back against mine. Instead I wait until his breathing grows deep and steady before I inch away.

Through the tent wall I watch Cable's shadow, lit by the dwindling flames. A spark flares as he leans forward and tosses another log on the fire. I'm worried about him. He needs to sleep.

More than that, I'm worried about his mental state. Offering to kill someone must mess with your head, even if you've killed before. Cable told me once that you never forget, and you never forgive. I don't want Sal's blood on his hands any more than I want it on my own.

Alex shifts in his sleep and elbows me in the ribs. I grunt in pain but have nowhere to go. A shadow falls over me and I look up to see Cable standing by the door. "I'm fine," I whisper. "Just Alex taking up too much room."

"Well shove him back over."

I smirk as he turns and heads back to the fire, giving Alex a jab in the side for good measure. He snorts in his sleep and rolls away. Tucking my arm under my head, I roll to get comfortable and freeze.

In the flickering of the firelight, two eyes stare back at me. Mangled hair and a full beard make Sal look even more fierce than I remembered. His lip is curled into a feral snarl. The bruise along the side of his face looks angry and puffy.

"Cab—" my scream cuts off as Sal launches himself at me. His hands grip my throat as he sprawls over Victoria. The woman wakes and wails like a banshee beside me, beating against Sal's side. He doesn't seem fazed by her attack. His eyes remain locked onto me.

His grip on my throat is unnaturally strong. His fingers dig into my flesh. My lips part, sucking in air that has nowhere to go.

Victoria's screams sound garbled in my ears. I claw at Sal's hands, tearing skin back from his forearms but he doesn't relent. Pure, unadulterated rage stares me in the eye and I'm terrified his face will be the last thing I see.

"Get off her!"

Sal's face distorts as a fist slams into his cheek. Blood and spittle splash my face and the grip on my neck decreases but doesn't disappear completely. I gasp for breath, taking small sips of air into my burning lungs. Heat flames in my face as blood pumps loudly in my ears.

"Alex, get him off her!"

I'm on vaguely aware of someone clawing at me. Sal's face reappears. I spot the maniacal gaze a split second before he sinks his teeth into my shoulder. I scream, arching my back.

"Shit!" Alex yells from beside me. My body shakes with each punch he lands against Sal's head. I cry out as his teeth tear at my flesh, refusing to give up his hold. "Cable, he bit her!"

"Get out of my way!"

The tent overhead shakes violently. I hear the sound of shredding fabric and a moment later Cable appears over me. A glint of silver flashes before my eyes. Sal's head rears back. My blood stains his chin. I place a trembling hand over my shoulder, wincing at the pain.

"Take care of her," Cable grunts and man handles Sal out of the tent.

I focus on Victoria's whimpers over the scuffling sounds. Alex's face is blurry as he kneels before me. I shake my head, trying to clear my thoughts but it's a losing battle.

"Just hold on," Alex says nearby. I hear rustling but give in to the pain and close my eyes.

When I wake the sun shines just above the horizon. Beautiful pastel blues, pinks and yellows dot the landscape as I ease myself upright. My shoulder twinges. I press my hand to the bandage and feel blood soak through.

"Easy." I turn to see Victoria sitting beside me. She no longer rocks, no longer looks lost to her own world. There is intelligence in her eyes for the first time in weeks. "You're gonna be sore for a few days."

I grimace at the pain. She tsks and reaches out to place a new bandage on my shoulder. The cold morning air bites at my skin and I realize that I've been stripped down to only a tank top. "How bad is it?"

"Not as bad as it feels, I'm sure."

I inhale sharply and try to look down at the wound. Victoria places a hand on my arm. "I disinfected it the best I could but...."

I understand the deeper meaning to her words. Sal was infected. It would only make sense that his bite holds the potential to spread the disease to me.

Covering my hand over my shoulder, I offer her a smile. "Thanks. "

She dips her head in acknowledgement and begins tucking the cleaning supplies back in her pack. She grabs a roll of gauze and raises my arm. I notice a quake in her hands as I grit my teeth at the pain. With my free hand I rub my throat, sure that the pale skin is a mass of bruising now. It hurts to swallow, to breathe. "And Sal?"

Her hands pause in their work, her knuckles swollen and fingers curled. Alex had mentioned that she suffers from bouts of arthritis. The cold makes it worse. The gauze she wraps around my shoulder to hold the new bandage in place falls from her fingers and she lowers her head. The chain holding her glasses swing before her chest. "Gone."

"I'm sorry," I whisper, though I know I'm not. Not sorry that he's dead. That he's no longer a part of the group. Now all I want to know is who ended it.

"Don't be." She plasters a smile back on and continues her ministrations. "He became a danger, just like you said he would."

"You...you heard all of that?"

Victoria nods. Her glasses slide down nearly to the end of her nose. She doesn't bother to push them back. "I heard a lot more than I let on."

"You were faking it?"

She offers me a pained smile. "Some. Though there were plenty of times that I would lose myself for a while. I don't blame you for thinking I was going crazy. I would have agreed with you."

"But you're back now?"

She shoves her hair back out of her face. The deep set of wrinkles and bruising along her face speaks of how hard this life has been on her. She is far too old to keep going at this pace. "For now. It comes and goes, just like before. My daughter insisted that I be checked by a specialist. That's where I was going when our flight was detoured to St. Louis."

"You flew alone?"

She nods. "Felt like a kid with those stewardesses watching over me. Might as well have stuck a little name tag on me and handed me some cookies and milk."

I grin at the imagery. "Any who, maybe that knock I took to the head last night set things right again. Guess old timer's was bound to catch up with me sooner or later. I'm no spring chicken anymore."

I laugh, a deep genuine laugh. "You're one tough broad, Victoria. You know that?"

"You may call me Vicky now, I think. The name has begun to grow on me after all this time."

Smiling, I reach out and place my hand over hers. Veins rise through papery thin flesh. "I never thought I'd say it, but I'm kinda glad you're back. Being the only girl sucked."

She seems genuinely pleased when she squeezes my hand. "I suppose you and I didn't start out on the proper foot, did we?"

"Not so much." She lifts the tape to her mouth and tears off the piece, tucking it under. I try lifting my arm and know that it's going to take a few days before the pain begins to fade. "I'm sorry about Eva."

At the sound of my friend's name, my breath catches and I fall silent. "I should have helped more, been kinder. I suppose I was afraid. Afraid of not being needed. Of being left behind. When you reach my age you'll understand what it's like."

If I reach your age, I amend silently.

Clearing my throat and making the decision to shove the past right back where it belongs, I pat my bandage. For a retired science teacher she seems fairly handy with gauze and tape. "Where are Alex and Cable?"

Vicky looks toward the woods. I follow her gaze, realizing that a massive slit has been sliced through the zippered door. "He couldn't get the zipper to work so he burst in here, knife at the ready." She turns to look at me. "That man cares for you."

"I know." And I do for him, far more than I'd like to admit.

"Well," she dusts her hands off and gingerly rises. "They should be back soon. I'd best make myself useful while I still can."

I stare after her, amazed at how easily she bounces back. Was it all just a survival technique to shut down or something else? Beginning stages of dementia? Her body's way of dealing with shock?

It could have gone the wrong way. Alex could have decided to leave her behind on the side of the road. Deemed her too big of a liability.

No. Alex may be many things, but cruel for the sake of being cruel does not seem to be one of them. He cares about his people, no matter how motley the crew may be.

Grabbing a pack nearby, I search for clothes to put on. My pack is nowhere to be seen, so I grab Cable's and dig out a long sleeve black shirt. I manage to wiggle my way inside fairly well, and with only minimal swearing but by the time I'm done I feel exhausted.

Pushing aside my weariness, I crawl out of the tent and discover a battle scene. Boot prints disturb the dirt. Blood splatters the rocky path and trees beyond. Staring at the blood, I feel weak in the knees and sink down onto a nearby rock.

"Only a little of that belongs to Cable." I look up to find Victoria watching me. I hate that my fear is so transparent. "Sal got in a few good swings before the end."

"That sounds like him." My voice is weaker than it should be. The sight of Cable's shed blood shouldn't affect me so. Heck, it shouldn't bother me at all beyond a general concern for his well-being, but it does.

At the sound of approaching footsteps, I turn to see Cable marching a few steps ahead Alex. They are covered in blood, sweat and dirt. It covers their hands and arms, soiling their shirts and caked to their pants. There is a haggardness on Alex's face that was not there yesterday. A look that only death can bring, up close and personal.

I push down on the rock and rise. A moment of dizziness nearly topples me back to the ground but I fight through it and manage to rise fully before Cable crushes me in his embrace. I want to resist the tears that swell in my eyes, but I don't. I cling to him, digging my fingers into his back as the tears come, uncaring of the blood that soaks through his shirt into mine.

"It's ok. You're safe now."

"Am I?" I choke out and bury my face in the crook of his arm. The scent of blood is less strong here. "Are any of us really safe?"

He doesn't answer me and I know why. The truth, no matter how grim, is still the reality that we face. Uncertainty. Death. A fight for survival. The trouble is that I fear this is only the beginning.

Heat radiates out from him like a warm blanket straight out of a dryer. I noticed that color sits high in his cheeks once more, but assume it's from the hike.

"I thought he was going to kill me. Maybe he already has," I whisper, hating how hoarse my voice sounds as draw back and cup my shoulder. My neck is raw, my windpipe bruised from Sal's squeezing. It will take some time to recover fully, if ever. It seems like this new life isn't interested in allowing recovery time before another disaster strikes. Each morning I wake up a little more tired, a little more sore, and with a heck of a lot less hope.

Cable presses his lips to the top of my head. "I would never let that happen. You know that, right?"

I nod and pull back, releasing my death grip on him to wipe at my nose. "I know you would try, but you won't always be around."

"Sure I will."

"No." I place my hand on his chest to stop him from hugging me again. "You won't. None of us know what will happen today, or tomorrow or a week from now. We've made it this long because we hid, but how long can we keep that up? We don't have any food. After we leave this place we'll have enough water for three days. Then what?"

He remains silent. I didn't expect him to give me some bullshit, sugarcoated answer. For all the optimism Cable tries to provide, he is at the core a realist. I think you have to be in times like these.

"We both know that towns are dangerous," I continue. "We've been lucky so far, but we won't always be. Sooner or later we are going to run into trouble."

"And I...we," he amends quickly, "will be there to help."

I lower my head. "I can't do this, Cable."

He reaches down and lifts my chin. I try to resist, knowing that if I meet his gaze I will be tempted to weaken, but he persists. "I'm not asking for anything from you, Avery. You know that, right?"

I want to say yes, to say that I know he's never officially asked me for a commitment, but it's there, in his eyes, every time he looks at me. Try as I might to ignore it, I know that I crave that look.

"One night. That's what you promised."

His hand falls away from my chin and I step back. An ache grows in my chest as I watch a shifting of emotions play across his face. He's usually very good at hiding them behind his stony exterior, but not now.

"We should go." I turn my back on him and wrap my arms around my waist, knowing that I've hurt him, hurt myself, but it's the way it has to be. For us to survive. For us to say goodbye when the time comes, because I know it is. It's inevitable.

Alex cautiously meets my glance and I nod at him. Pressing back my shoulders I move to stand beside him. "What's the plan?"

"We need supplies." I've heard that sentiment so many times it makes me want to vomit. Food, water, shelter...they are all that matter now. If I focus on that maybe, just maybe, I can make it. I've done it before. I just need to find a way to put Cable in the past.

Alex points to a map at his feet and I see that if we continue on this path, within half a day's hike, perhaps a little more we will reach a town that sits a couple miles off the main interstate heading south in Kentucky. If we can find a car we might be able to make it to the border within an hour.

Looking at the town on the map, I feel apprehension coil in my gut. It's always hard to tell just how populated that town may have once been, how many survivors may still linger. Being on the main road ups the danger. It's a risk, no matter how you look at it, but some risks I would rather leave alone.

Cable moves past me, careful not to touch me as he ducks into the tent. Alex watches me and I'm careful not to show any emotion. "You ok?"

I bite my lip and nod. "How long till tear down?"

He cocks his head to look up at the sun. "Quarter of an hour give you enough time to get yourself cleaned up?"

I grab a faded towel Victoria holds out to me. I must look pretty bad for them to already have stuff prepped for me. "Give me five minutes. That water isn't warm enough to soak in!"

TWENTY

The winds are still for the first time in weeks. A brief storm passed through during the afternoon hours, forcing us to take refuge in a small cave. We huddled together as the temperatures plummeted and the sleet came. Cable, being the largest in our group, took the outer edge, creating a makeshift wall. I huddled in the middle with Victoria. Only the chattering of our teeth could be heard. I would trade all four layers of shirts that I wear for one decent wool coat, a pair of gloves and a hat.

We continued our hike, no longer driven by the hope of reaching safety in the light of the sun, but by the need for shelter. I glance back over my shoulder at Cable and the deep seated fear that began earlier doubles.

His fever burns high once again. His face is flushed despite the freezing temperatures. The cold doesn't faze him.

His steps are unsteady. From time to time he raises a hand to bat away unseen things. We stop frequently to drink but water is not enough and we can't risk giving him too much too soon. Who knows when we will find another reliable water source?

I should have known he was feverish the instant I saw he return from the woods. Thinking back to the farmhouse when he seemed unusually warm, camping in the woods or the shack when a fire wasn't enough to warm him, but he'd improved, hadn't he? Days went by with little signs of discomfort, so much so that I'd let my fears slip away. Then I think on two nights before, sleeping beside him at the cabin, snuggling up to his radiating warmth. My hands upon his flaming skin…

He should have said something. Warned us. Surely he has known he was ill for several days. Maybe he's been ill since the night he broke us out of the military base and it's just taken this long to really settle in.

I have not noticed any other symptoms yet, but maybe he is hiding those as well. It doesn't matter now. Alex and Victoria see it but I pray that they fear only that he has fallen ill with the flu, though I doubt it. Everyone jumps to the worst conclusion these days.

Both refuse to meet my gaze so I take the lead, marching ahead with purpose. The trek through the hills is arduous. The path is steep, the crevices slick from the recently fallen sleet.

When we finally reach the edge of the forest, I halt. Ducking low, I motion for the group to do the same. Alex kneels beside me. Cable on the other side. I can feel the heat flowing in waves off him. I want to say something but I bite my tongue. Now is not the time.

There is a gully before us, no steeper than any that we have hiked today but this one gleams in the broken moonlight. The storm must have been worse here. A sheet of ice lies between us and the highway below.

On the other side of the road I spy a large building. A tall gas sign rises to the sky. Several semi-trucks sit in the parking lot. A pile up of cars betrays the panic travelers experienced in an attempt to escape a fate that was already sealed.

"I don't like this," Alex mutters. Victoria nods in agreement.

I glance toward Cable and sigh, knowing we have no choice. "Our need hasn't changed. That building looks like an old truck stop. It probably still has food, clothes, maybe even some camping supplies that we could use. That meal we had last night will only take us so far. We need to keep up our strength if we hope to keep going."

"There are probably survivors holed up inside enjoying all of those things right now." I glance at Alex but he shrugs, agreeing with Victoria's assessment.

"How far is the nearest town?" I ask, tugging the map from the side pocket of Alex's backpack. I open the worn pages carefully. They have been beaten and battered over the past two weeks. I don't know how much longer it will remain intact. Another reason why we need to risk going into that truck stop. We can find maps out of this state.

I watch his finger trail down the dimly lit page and blow out a breath of frustration. "Twenty miles at best. Maybe a little more."

From the corner of my eye I see Cable close his eyes. I know he's suffering in silence, trying not to be a burden. "I'll go," I say as I try to fold the map but finally give up when I realize it's a puzzle I'm not going to figure out in the dark.

"No!" Alex and Cable shout at the same time.

"Keep your voices down," I growl, sweeping my gaze on the road before. Abandoned cars dot the highway, some heading in a northerly direction along the road but many plunged hood first into an embankment. Several are little more than charred remains and I try not to wonder if the driver made it out or if they now wander this road with their flesh completely melted away.

I see movement among the cars, halting and labored. I point to where several Withered Ones walk repeatedly into car doors, slamming their torsos into the metal until the door finally gives way and they can continue on their path. I shudder at the sight.

As the clouds shift overhead, casting us in darkness, it illuminates the road in the distance and my throat feels parched as I stare out over the expanse.

"There are hundreds of them," Victoria whispers. She wraps her hand around Alex's arm as she kneels beside him. She is hurting. Her limp has become more pronounced. She blames it on bad hips but I think all of this traveling has just been hard on her. I've never asked her age but I'd guess she's at least in her mid-sixties. She should be bouncing grandkids on her knee instead of trekking through the woods at night.

"We should go," Alex says and starts to rise.

"No." I grab onto him. "Wait."

He turns back, shielding his face as the wind whips globs of slush from the trees. It pelts down on us. "This is insane, Avery. We need to find shelter."

"Just watch them," I whisper.

Never has there been an opportunity as great as this to just observe their behavior. From this vantage point we are safe, relatively at least. The woods are to our back and we only saw three Moaners all day.

"Can you see it?"

Alex casts a glance toward me then follows the direction I'm pointing in. In the ever shifting clouds, our window of sight narrows and expands without warning. It makes it hard to focus on any one place for long, but it's long enough. I hear the inhalation of breath from beside me.

"They are moving together," Alex says in a hushed tone.

I nod. "A herd with one apparent goal in mind."

Victoria leans out around Alex to look at me. "What goal?"

I swallow before answering. "To head south."

"Figured you would say that," Alex mutters and glances over the top of the overpass less than an eighth of a mile from us. Though that area isn't currently lit by the moon, I can still decipher movement.

"Maybe they really don't like the cold." I glance over at Cable. The dark circles under his eyes seem more prominent than before.

"We have two choices." I turn back to look at Alex. "Ride this ridge and walk parallel to those Moaners and hope we stumble across a cave or shanty to sleep in, or we head for that truck stop and find somewhere to hole up for the night. Maybe even find something to eat."

Alex glances toward Victoria. "What do you think?"

I notice that her glasses no longer perch on her nose and she's given up trying to tame her hair, instead embracing reality. Fear pinches her wrinkled features, but as she glances down at the movement on the road below, I know which she views as the lesser danger.

"I'd rather be able to see them in the light of day," is her response. I hide my smile, knowing that Cable will side with me, if for no other reason than to rest for a few moments. The tent, with its massive slit down the middle, is useless against the elements. We left it set up in the woods. Who knows, maybe it will save some poor soul's life one day?

Alex sighs heavily. "What's the good in being a leader when my vote never counts?"

I clap him on the back. "A good leader knows when to take counsel."

"Oh?" He rises beside me. "Is that what it is? And here I thought you guys just liked telling me what to do."

Alex and Victoria lead the way toward the overpass. It is the easier of the two paths, but also far more dangerous. Despite the six cars abandoned across the bridge, there will be far too much time when we are out in the open, exposed to the naked eye.

I'm not fool enough to think that the truck stop will be empty. And if it is, I'd bet the last drops of water in my bottle that it's being watched.

Grasping Cable's hand, I follow behind, my gaze steadily sweeping our surroundings. For once I would welcome the wind to help conceal the sound of our passing. Even the raspy moans below bring a bit of relief.

"This is a bad idea," Cable mutters. I feel the tension in his body, his muscles taut as he searches the shadows before us.

"I know, but we didn't have a choice."

"Of course we did." He looks down at me and I see his eyebrows pinched into a frown. "I know why you pushed for this."

"Yeah, cause I'm hungry."

He yanks on my arm. "Don't play dumb, Avery. It doesn't suit you."

Ducking down behind the first car, I crane my neck to see through the passenger side window. Alex and Victoria have reached the second car but are only twenty feet ahead.

"You should have told me." I crouch back down and search the ground, wishing I had a weapon. As if sensing my frustration, Cable hands me his knife but I push it back at him. "You know how to use it better than me."

Grabbing my wrist, he uncurls my hand and places the handle in my palm. "You need to learn."

"Trial by fire, huh?"

His gaze is intense. I don't move, even when I hear Alex and Victoria advancing, leaving us behind. He digs in his pack and pulls out a short handled ax, one of the few remaining tools we have left from the farmhouse. "How could you stand there this morning and promise that you would be with me when you knew you were infected?"

Cable grits his teeth and looks away. "Because I'm not going out like them. I'll find a way to stop it."

His sentiment is almost laughable, or at least it would be if I didn't have tears choking off my airway. "What else are you hiding from me?"

"Nothing."

"Cable—"

"Nothing." When he turns back to face me, his face is so near I could trace every curve and line on his face, feel his breath wash over me. "You explored my body pretty in depth two nights ago. You should know."

At the mention of our time spent in each other's arms, Cable tenses. "Oh shit."

"What?"

He hangs his head. "I was infected when we…when we…"

"Don't." I grip his arm. Between Cable and Sal's bite I know my chances are not so hot at the moment, but I refuse to regret spending that one night with him. "It happened and I'm glad it did."

"Really?"

I laugh at his blatant surprise. "Why do I get the feeling that you always think the worst about me?"

Reaching out his hand, he rubs his thumb across my cheek. "I could spend a lifetime figuring out how to read you and I'd still have so much to learn."

I sober at his words, knowing that a lifetime is exactly what he no longer has. "Hey," he whispers, tugging my chin so that I will look at him. "I'm not going anywhere. I promise."

"You can't keep that promise."

"Have I ever let you down before?"

I turn away, knowing that with every final breath he would fight the change. But it won't be enough. It never is.

"They're leaving us behind." I wipe at my nose and swipe my hand over my cheek to hide my tears. "We need to move."

Cable follows right behind me, his hand on my lower back. I'm not sure if he does that for his own peace of mind or simply that he needs to touch me as we weave from car to car.

By the time we hit the final vehicle we are over halfway across, but there is a large gap between us and the end of the road.

I can't see Alex or Victoria anywhere. I look long and hard, praying that they made it to one of the semis and are waiting for us. I turn and press back against the car, trying to prepare myself.

"No matter what happens, I want you to run and keep running," Cable says. His shoulder presses against me. I am drawn to his heat like a moth to flame. My fingers ache from the cold. I lost feeling in my toes quite some time ago. My ears and nose may still be a part of me. I'm not really sure any more.

"Can I trust you to do the same?"

He smiles and for a moment I almost imagine him happy and healthy again. "I guess you'll just have to find out."

"Fine. Stay on my ass and try not to fall behind."

"It will be a pleasure." I glance back to see him grinning from ear to ear as he cocks his head to openly check out my backside.

"Wow, and I thought you were a gentleman."

I don't wait to hear his response, knowing that it will only tempt me to linger. Keeping my head low, I dash out into the open. I run full out, sliding my feet like a skater over the thin layer of ice. I listen to the moans echoing up from below the overpass and the sound of Cable's boots hitting the pavement behind me.

"Over here," a hiss comes from the shadow of a semi and I veer to the left. Alex's arm reaches out for me and I slam to a stop against the truck.

"Shh," Victoria scolds as Cable slows to a halt with far more grace than I just displayed.

I toss him a 'show off' glare before ducking low and crawling beneath the rig with Alex. "See anything?"

"Not so far. No movement apart from the odd Moaner. No signs of survivors. There are patches of footprints over to the right, but there's no way to know who made them."

I search the bay of darkened windows before us. Racks of books, cheap gift items, and a cash register stand not far from the door. Beyond that I spy several aisles of shelves. The back of the shop is awash with shadow.

My breathing sounds loud in my ears. My heart thrums in my chest and I fight to lower my pulse. It won't do me any good to run in there kamikaze and get my head blown off.

"What do you think?" Alex glances over at me.

I try to shrug but there's little room to allow for that. "We made it this far without a problem."

"Yeah," he nods and looks back at the window. "That's what worries me."

I share his sentiment but refuse to express it. The chances of this place not being under surveillance are slim to none. This is a huge risk we are taking, but glancing back at Cable I know I'd choose the same thing all over again if I had to.

I start to move away, but Alex latches onto my wrist. "How bad is he?"

The temptation to lie, to blow it off as nothing, is strong, but Alex deserves the truth. "He's sick but I think it's only a fever."

"For now." His words stay with me long after I wriggle back out from under the truck. Alex leads us toward the back of the semi. He leans out around the tail end, searching the parking lot.

A middle-aged Withered One shuffles across a patch of ice, arms flailing, his tongue rolled out his mouth. It is almost comical to watch it struggle to move forward. With each step it slides back two. Alex rises and prepares to race forward when I hear a crack of the ice. I duck low and watch the Moaner slam to the ground. Blood splatters across the ice. When it raises its head I realize its nose is smashed completely, and its tongue sticks to the ice.

"That is vile," Victoria moans, clutching her stomach as she turns away. Alex places an arm around her to shield her and looks to me.

I crawl toward him. "Cable and I will go first. We'll whistle when it's clear."

"Thank you." His voice is rich with emotion as he squeezes my arm in gratitude. I glance at Victoria, at the way he holds her and realize that in some weird way he has adopted the old woman. Maybe he has mommy issues too and Victoria has become a surrogate mother.

Cable taps my arm and I move away. "On three?"

I nod and crouch low. "Three!"

Our dash across the parking lot is anything but graceful. We slip and slide, skidding into cars and toppling trash cans. I can only imagine the muttered swearing Alex is producing as we take on the obstacle course laid out before us.

Leaping onto the sidewalk, I brace for impact and slam into the side of the building. Pain ripples through my shoulder, still sore from using that semi as a stopping board. Cable stops me as I turn toward the door. He steps gingerly around me and presses his hand against the glass.

I had expected it to be broken, the interior looted for supplies but there are no signs of that. The truck stop has miraculously been left untouched by the horrors outside.

Cable presses a finger to his lips and ducks inside. I catch the door before it slams shut behind him and inch my way in behind. I turn and carefully ease the door closed, holding the small bell dangling from the handle so that it doesn't make a sound.

It is warmer inside than I had expected. Not comfortable by any means, but a far cry better than being outside.

I follow Cable's lead, ducking low as we search each aisle. Evidence of looting is more prevalent here, but it seems to have been cut short. I search the ground for any signs of struggle, of blood or other bodily fluids, but see none. When we reach the final aisle, we split up. Cable heads to the bathrooms and showers while I check behind the cash register.

Nothing.

Over there, he mouths silently. I follow him toward a hallway that leads to the rear of the store. The darkness envelops us and fear begins to trickle through me. I fight to keep it at bay but I can feel it gaining control. Cable reaches back and takes my hand, as if knowing I need him.

We search through a small waiting area. The scent of oil and rubber is prevalent in this mechanic shop. It is also completely clear of danger. Cable rises and takes a moment to shove a metal chair beneath the door handle at the back of the shop. It won't stop anyone from busting through the glass but they won't be able to just waltz right in without us hearing it.

"Come on." He tugs on my hand and leads me back to the front. Motioning for me to stay put, he heads toward the door and pokes his head out. A long, low whistle calls out into the night before he ducks back inside. "I hope they heard that over the moans."

We wait and watch from the windows, wincing at each fall Victoria makes as Alex tries to help her across the ice. I'm worried about her hips. Her body can only take so much abuse and today has been hard.

Less than five feet away from the Moaner, I see Victoria's feet slip. I cry out as she goes down. From within the small entryway I hear the crack as her head hits the ice.

"Cable!" He pauses with his hand on the handle as I shove the knife he gave me into his hand. "Just in case."

The front door slams open as he rushes out. I clutch my hand over my mouth as I watch Alex trying to revive Victoria. Cable slides to his side, tucking his hatchet into his bag and his knife into the sheath at his side and ducks low, wrapping his arms around her. Together they fight to stand. Their progress back to me is slow. Much too slow.

I scan the parking lot for any signs of movement. My breath falters as I see two sets of feet shuffling on the other side of the semi behind them. I press my nose against the glass, watching the halting steps closely, and breathe easier.

Alex slips on the ice and nearly takes the three of them down. I press my palms to the door, frustrated that I can't help, but someone has to remain as look out.

Movement from my left captures my eye. Two more Moaners emerge. The men are filthy, their clothes ragged, hair gnarled with what I think is blood. They stagger forward. Another captures my attention from the right. This man is slighter in stature, his features what some might call pretty.

I stare long and hard at him, noting the absence of tears, cuts and dangling flesh. *He must be newly turned.*

Glancing back at Cable, I'm relieved to see Alex is rising to his feet. His legs slide apart as he fights to regain his balance. Cable holds tightly to an unconscious Victoria, the solid base for while Alex grasps to.

I glance at the two Moaners approaching from behind. Something doesn't feel right but I can't quite put my finger on it. My fingers curl inward as I press against the glass, my frustration rising parallel to my alarm.

Then I see it, but it's too late.

"Cable!" I shriek and bang against the glass. He raises up at my scream but the men are upon them. I watch in horror as they break from their stagger and dive forward. Cable is thrust to the ground, tackled from behind.

Alex takes a blow to the ribs and crashes. Victoria slides, whirling around, her arm flapping erratically around her before she plummets to the ground. The two men emerging from behind the semi pause less than five feet away. I watch them draw weapons. The glint of silver in one man's hand sends me crashing through the door just before I hear the gunshot.

A scream fills my ears as I leap onto the back of the pretty man. He wails and beats at me as I dig my nails into his cheeks, tearing through his flesh. Blood soaks my fingers as I dig my feet into his sides, squeezing. He thrashes and falls. I hit hard and roll away. Blood slickens the ice between us.

Without thinking, I scramble to my feet and dive toward him, using the ice to my advantage. I slam into his side. He yells as the momentum shoves him against the curb of the sidewalk in front of the shop doors. I grab his head, curling my hands into his long hair and bash his head against the concrete. His hands flail at my face. I lean back, trying to stay out of his reach.

His hollering terrifies me. The crunching of bone sickens me, but I don't stop. I bash his head until his hands fall away and I'm slick with blood. It streaks down my face in thick, goopy trails, clings to my throat as I swallow repeatedly, tasting his blood in my mouth. My hands shake as I fall back away from his still form.

"Avery!" Strong hands grab me under my arm and haul me to my feet. I try to help, to rise and walk, but my legs feel as if all of the bones have vanished.

The glass doors burst open before me and Cable rushes me inside before turning and barring the door. I press back against the shelving system lining the first aisle. I stare vacantly at the blood on my hands. Warmth begins to soak through the seat of my pants and I slowly look to my right. A thick pool of blood surrounds me.

"Oh god!" I stare at it, unblinking and only barely aware of crying nearby. The blood fills my vision, consumes my thoughts. I can't think. Can't feel. Is it mine? Am I hurt?

"Avery." A face swims before my face as hands force my head back to the front. I try to focus, to think. "Avery, are you hurt?"

I blink rapidly. The sound of loud humming fills my ears.

My head rocks back and a stinging pain races across my cheek. The pain helps to clear my thoughts. Another slap and the clarity of my vision begins to return. "Cable?"

"Thank god!" He tugs me into his arms. A wet stickiness surrounds him and I pull back. A crimson stain coats his shirt.

"You're hurt!" I paw at his chest, searching for a wound.

"I'm fine." He clasps my hands to his lips with one hand. The other he cups my cheek. "Are you back with me now?"

"I..." I blink several more times, trying to piece together the last few moments. "I think so."

"Good, cause I'm going to need your help."

"With what?" I turn and follow his gaze, trailing beyond the pool of blood to where Alex kneels over Victoria. All color has fled from her face. Her mouth hangs open, her tongue protruding from the corner of her mouth. I stare at the whites of her eyes as Alex lifts her eyelids. "She's been stabbed."

TWENTY-ONE

My arms are slick with blood. It itches as it dries, tugging at the hairs on my arms. A stack of orange car waxing cloths lie in a stained puddle at my feet. A window sun shield lies over Victoria's body. I try not to think of her final moments, the fear I'd seen in her eyes. The way she gasped for breath as blood bubbled between her lips.

I feel numb, thinking of Alex's tears and pleading for her to hang on. Cable applied pressure to the wound, but he was wrong. She hadn't just been stabbed. She'd been gutted. When I'd arrived at her side, I had slid right into a tangle of intestines.

Alex was beside himself as he clung to Victoria, holding her head in his lap. She'd tried to speak, but words failed her. It didn't take long for the life to fade from her eyes. At least we have that to be thankful for.

I glance up at the sound of rattling and peer through the dark to see Cable working relentlessly to reinforce the doors. The chains may keep the door frame itself closed, but they will just come in through the glass. I saw it before at the hospital but say nothing now. This is what Cable needs to do so I let him.

"They're gone for now," he says as he returns. His face bears evidence of the fight. Bloodied nose. Scratches along his face and arms. Of the three of them, he fared best. He turns his gaze on Alex. A bloodied cloth is pressed to the man's shoulder where a bullet tunneled through.

"How are you feeling?" I ask Alex.

He wipes at his nose. "Better than her."

I close my eyes at the pain in his voice as he stares at Victoria. His shoulders shake with silent sobs, of regret and guilt I'm sure. He must be numb to the pain. "Don't do that to yourself. It wasn't your fault."

"Of course it was." He shouts back. "I knew I wasn't good on ice. I should have asked Cable to take her. To stop trying to be the hero and do what was right."

I slide across the floor, attempting to avoid the smeared mess dragging Victoria's body away created and grab his hand from the floor beside him, where it hangs limp. "Victoria didn't die because you weren't fast enough. She died because of those men out there."

Alex yanks his arm away and turns his back on me. I know he is angry, at himself, at the world, at fate but not at me. Not like he should be. Cable was right earlier. I did push to come here. For him.

With a heavy sigh, I push up to my feet and leave him be. He wants to be near her.

I brush my hair back out of my face, wincing at the thought of how gruesome I must look covered from head to foot in blood. Victoria's blood. Alex's. That man's.

When Cable's hand falls on my shoulder I flinch.

"Easy." I go willingly into his embrace as he envelopes his arms around me. I cling to him, ignoring the scent of blood and sweat that clings to him. "I've got you."

Closing my eyes, I allow him to lead me away from Alex, to a darkened corner where we can be alone. Where we are hidden from sight from those who linger outside. I know they are there. We are cornered, trapped within what so quickly became a coffin. How many more of us will go out the same way Victoria did? They have the advantage. It's only a matter of time before they know it.

"What are they waiting for?" I ask, despising the tremor in my voice, the way my hands shake as I cling to him. I sink down beside him and lean into him, resting my head on his chest. All thought of food, of gathering provisions no longer seem important. Not in the wake of losing Victoria.

"They are probably trying to figure out how many of us are still alive. I'm betting they weren't here for the whole show. Otherwise they wouldn't have pulled back when they did."

I stare into the dark, down the hall toward the back room. That's where Cable got the supplies to help Victoria. He blocked the door that leads to the shop and the repair center beyond. I close my eyes and try not to think about how those men could be creeping up on us right now.

Cable's chest bounces as he tries to stifle a cough. I raise my head and stare at him. He looks tired, unnaturally so. His head rests back against the wall. Perspiration dampens his hair. I watch as a bead of sweat rolls down his cheek.

Pushing back from him, I crawl away. "Where are you going?"

"I'll be right back." I count the aisles, trying to remember where I saw the first aid section. There isn't much. A few packets of pills which I stuff into my pocket. Some temporary bandages and a first aid kit. I grab the kit and tear off the packaging, tossing it aside. I rummage through it until my fingers grasp what I'm looking forward.

Tucking the thermometer between my teeth, I crawl toward a row of dark doors at the back. The scent of rotting food from the refrigerator beyond hits me as I grab a bottle and crawl back to Cable's side. "Open up."

"Does it really matter?"

"Yes." I insist and grab his chin. He relents and closes his mouth over the thermometer. A minute passes before it beeps. I glance down at the illuminated screen. "103.5"

He grunts and pushes my hand away. "I'm fine."

"You're not." I tear open two packages of pain pills and force them into his hand. "Take these."

"I don't have the flu, Avery. I doubt it will help."

I twist the cap of the bottle and the scent of soda makes my mouth water. How long has it been since I had a taste? Holding out the bottle, I grasp his hand. "I need you lucid if we are going to get out of here. Alex is messed up over Victoria, and I don't know what I'm doing."

"Yes you do." He winces at the burn of the soda as I force the bottle between his lips and tilt his head back. He swallows and pushes my hand away. "I saw what you did to that guy."

The bottle falls from my hands. Cable reaches for me, not caring that soda spills over the floor before us. "It's hard, the first time," he says with deep, knowing compassion. Cable had his first kill too, but that had been a mission on a battlefield.

Probably with a gun from a distance. He may have seen the guy drop but he didn't feel the man's blood splatter his face as he beat him senseless.

I swallow hard and draw my knees into my chest. "I don't want to talk about it."

"You need to."

"Why?"

His grip on my shoulder tightens. "Because you don't have time to internalize it. If we are going to make it out of here, you're going to have to kill again. Maybe more than once. You have to be prepared for it."

"Is that even possible?" I scoff and clamp my eyes shut against the memory. That man's blood still taints me. I can't be free of it, not without exposing myself to go into the bathroom to clean up. My palms feel clammy as a cold sweat breaks out. "It was awful," I whisper.

"I know." He strokes my hair. "But you did what you had to."

I bite down on my lower lip, giving a hesitant nod. "I guess I didn't think it would be so...so messy."

The feel of his calloused hands on my cheek pulls me back as he lifts my chin to look at him. In the dim light of the moon spilling through the windows overhead I know he can see my fear. His face is dark, but the warmth of his smile shines through as he slowly lowers his head and kisses me.

It does not hold the same passion or intensity of the last time our lips met. This is soft, a gentle unspoken promise. When he draws back he places a final kiss on my nose. "Next time will be easier."

I nuzzle into his side, for the moment content to just be. He leans his cheek against my head and after a moment his breathing slows and he leans on me for support. I hold him, allowing him a rare moment of rest. He's going to need it.

Sometime later I start at the sound of crashing glass. Cable leaps to his feet, slightly wobbly but alert. "Is that them?"

"No." He shakes his head and grabs my arm. "I don't think so."

I follow his lead back through the store, keeping low to make a smaller target. I have no idea how skilled those men are with guns. Anyone can hit a target at close range and Alex just happened to be a pretty good one earlier.

"Alex," I hiss when we discover him missing from beside Victoria. I stare at her body, wondering if she will come back. I didn't express my concerns with Cable, didn't have the heart to, but it's a legitimate question. Nothing about the Withered Ones have been textbook zombie. Not the way we thought they would be. Up until now I haven't remained near any dead bodies to see if they will rise again.

"He's down here." I look up to see that Cable has moved to the far end of the shop. He stands upright, his hands planted on his hips. I don't have to hear the disapproval in his voice to know he's not happy.

I hurry down the final three aisles and stop short when I see Alex sprawled out on the floor. "Well, I guess that accounts for the broken glass," I mutter, staring down at the collection of empty beer bottles around him.

Alex's head rolls to the side. Chip and cookie crumbles line his shirt, some sticking to the expanding stain of blood that has soaked through his bandage. "He's trashed."

"I am not," he slurs. "I'm wasted. Big difference."

I roll my eyes and glance back at the doors. No sign of movement outside but there will be soon enough. I'm sure of it. "Was this really the best time to do this?"

Kneeling down beside him, I grab one arm and Cable the other. We lift him into a seated position. The stench of alcohol on him turns my stomach. "Imminent death is the best time, in my honest opinion."

Alex burps and giggles. I stare at Cable in open amazement. There is an ugly twist of scorn on his lips. He releases his hold on Alex and crosses his arms, thrusting out his chest. "He's a damned fool."

I can't help but agree but I don't say it aloud. "Everyone deals with loss in their own way."

"You're making excuses for this sorry piece of shit?"

I place a hand on his arm. "He's hurting."

Cable grinds his teeth. I can see that he's trying to rein in his anger, but it's a battle. One that I don't entirely blame him for. Alex is a fool. If he didn't have a death wish before, he's got one signed and sealed now. He'll be lucky to make it to the back door.

"What do we do?"

Uncrossing his arms, Cable slides to the floor and rubs the back of his neck. He is silent for several moments. What once caused me frustration now brings me hope. An introspective Cable is far more reassuring than a hell bent one.

"How did you know that they were going to attack?" He shifts, tilting his body toward me. He casts a glance at Alex but the man's snores force him to look away again. "You yelled right before they struck."

I grasp my knees, feeling comfort in their pressure against my chest. I adopted this pose first as a young child every time I feel like the world is spinning out of control. That seems to happen on a near daily basis now. "I didn't see it at first. Thought they were just Moaners, but they felt...off. I watched each of them. They were good, Cable. I nearly didn't see in time. They moved in unison. They didn't blink, hardly seemed to breath. Even their appearance was near enough that they could pass for a Moaner."

He scoots closer, his knee brushing mine. "So what gave them away?"

There is a heaviness pressing on my chest as I pinch the bridge of my nose. "They weren't moving south."

Cable leans back, his arm resting atop his knee. The other is tucked beneath him, the laces of his boot soaking up the spilled alcohol. "But that's just a theory, completely unproven and invalidated."

"It worked didn't it?"

"This time," he agrees with hesitation. He turns and looks toward the front door. I stiffen at the sight of a brief movement, a foot drawn out of view at the last second. They are coming.

"Did you see—" I turn to see Cable holding out the knife to me.

"Take it. You'll need it more than me." He reaches into his back and pulls out a silver pistol. It looks like something a cowboy would use in an old Western. "I've got three rounds left but I lost the ax out there in the parking lot."

"Where'd you get that gun?"

216 | W I T H E R

He jerks his head toward the door. "I didn't go down without a fight."

"What about him?" I look to Alex. He breathes heavily, locked into a deep sleep. "Can we wake him?"

Cable reaches over and punches Alex in the shoulder, right over the entry wound. It takes two more hard hits before Alex rears up, eyes bloodshot and filled with pain. "What the hell did you do that for?"

I clamp my hand down on his mouth to still his shout. "They're back."

He falls still and I lower my hand. He trembles as he looks toward the door. I wrinkle my nose at the scent of urine and pull back. "Alex—"

"Don't," he waves me off. "I'll be embarrassed about it later."

Fear sobers him fast. I help him to his feet, keeping my hand on his head to keep him below the height of the windows. His steps are unsteady, his gaze still glazed over, but he's on his feet. That's an improvement.

Cable is gone, slipped out of sight while I take care of Alex. He rustles around in the back and I lead Alex down the dark hallway toward him.

"We should have buried her," Alex mutters, glancing at Victoria.

"You know we couldn't."

"I know." He sounds deflated, lost. He tugs back against my arm and I release him. "Alex, we have to keep moving."

"Just give me a minute. Go find Cable."

Torn with indecision, I don't move until I hear a grunt from up ahead. I rush forward, leaving Alex behind. The instant I hit the start of the windows I dive to my knees and crawl forward.

I hear Cable clearly now. He has gone through the door to the repair shop. The door remains cracked open and cold air seeps through. I press on the door and rear back as he appears, his arms loaded down with two large canisters.

"What are you doing?"

"Help me with these." I grab hold of the bottom and help ease them to the floor. He groans as the weight shifts to the floor. He sinks to his knee, breathing hard. "I can't do this alone."

"I'll help." I hear sloshing inside the can. The scent of oil burns in my nose. "Alex is in the hallway. You work back here and then grab him. I'll take the front."

"No."

I grab a canister and rise. "Now's not the time to argue over who's stronger or faster. I can do this. You need to let me."

Putting distance between us, just in case he tries to reach out and stop me, I shoot him a smile and dart away.

The canister is every bit as heavy as it looked when Cable carried it. Being forced to hunch over to avoid detection makes my arms quiver and my lower back ache.

I pass Alex in the hall, nearly clocking him in the head in the dark. I call back over my shoulder that he needs to find Cable and hope like heck that he listens. Re-adjusting my grip, I waddle down the hall, thankful to be able to stand fully upright, even if only for a minute.

The hall has never felt so long before. By the time I reach the end, I'm forced to drag the canister behind me. The screeching sound of metal against concrete is loud, certainly loud enough to be heard outside.

Peering out the front window, I see three men approaching. They walk forward with extreme caution, their knees slightly bent, their guns raised. "Shit!"

Tugging the canister, I work my way down the back aisle, past the soda and beer fridges. I pause only a second beside Victoria, remorse weighing me down. *I'm sorry.*

"Avery." I turn at the hushed call and see Cable crouching at the entrance of the hall. His gaze sweeps back and forth between me and the window. I can see the men clearly now. They are less than twenty feet from the front door. "It's too late. Dump it and run."

"Not yet," I grunt and remove the cap. I turn my face away from the potent oil scent as I dump the contents over Victoria. *Funeral by fire. It was once good enough for Kings. It's the best I can do for you.*

"Avery!" I glance up and see a man testing the front door. The chains rattle against the glass. I hold my breath as he calls back over his shoulder. More men approach, each one heavily armed. "Get your ass over here!"

The oil spreads out before me, but not nearly fast enough. It will do some damage but I want more than that. I want revenge.

I crawl forward, ignoring Cable's desperate pleas. Two aisles up ahead, I turn and lower to my belly, inching forward. It's a straight shot to the front door from here. With one swipe of a flashlight I'd be discovered.

Grabbing a couple small metal canisters off the shelves, I bite into the cap and spit it aside. I shove them to down the aisle, toward the door, listening to the fluid spill over the floor. I reach to grab another one and pause as my hand hits a long cylinder. I yank it off the shelf and hold it up before my eyes.

"I'll be damned." I tear into the packaging and release the long handled kitchen lighter. The scent of lighter fluid mingles with the oil in my nose, making me a bit lightheaded. Grabbing two more canisters, I back down the aisle. When I reach the end I see Cable crawling toward me.

"Get back!" I wave him off. He hesitates then notices the canisters in my hand.

"Avery, that's not a good idea."

"Trust me. It'll work."

A crash of glass sends one canister spiraling from my hand. Loud shouts are followed by another pane of glass exploding. I bite down on the canister and chuck it behind me. With trembling hands, I flick the lighter.

"Rapid start my ass!" I click it again and again.

"Avery," Cable hisses.

I hear the sound of glass crunching underfoot. Their movements are slow as then enter the room. "Luke, you smell something funny?"

The footsteps pause. I click the lighter again and it flares to life.

"What is that?" a man's voice echoes through the shop as I touch the lighter to the fluid. Blue flames race away from me, curling around the corner and heading straight for the front door.

"Run!" Cable motions for me to race toward him.

I push to my feet as gunfire slams into the glass overhead. I dive, curling my arms over my head as the shards slice my arms and cheeks. The scent of burnt hair is strong in my nose.

"Dammit." Cable beats at my hair, snuffing out the flames as I roll to my side, coughing over the rising smoke. "That fire won't last long."

"I know," I choke out. Blood trails down my face. There are lacerations in more places that I care to count. I hurt all over, but I ignore the pain. I shove the lighter into Cable's hand and point to Victoria. "Light her up."

He looks stricken for a second but another round of gunfire gets him moving. I crawl behind him, shredding my hands and knees on the glass. My teeth burrow into my lower lip as I fight through the pain, moving as fast as I can.

The instant I move past Cable, he flicks on the lighter and tosses it onto Victoria. The blast of heat is suffocating. I kick back with my feet, scooting across the floor as fast as I can toward the hall. The instant I'm clear, Cable grabs me around the waist and hauls me to my feet.

"Don't look back."

But I do. Half a dozen faces are illuminated in the windows. Each one staring right at us.

TWENTY-TWO

Cable's pressure around my waist increases as I hesitate, lost to the terror threatening to overwhelm me as I stare into the rabid gaze of the men waiting outside for us. I sense their rage, see the crazy in their eyes. Their companions flail near the front doors, their clothes set alight.

The store before me is a blazing inferno. Blistering heat licks at the ends of my hair. The scent of burnt hair mingles with the billowing smoke, but I feel none of it.

"Avery!" I turn away from the window in a daze. Cable's face appears before me. His shouts feel like white noise as I blink, trapped in slow motion. "Avery, snap out of it!"

"We'll never make it," I mutter.

I glance down at Victoria's body, at the sizzling flesh that was once a person. A person I knew. Maybe we didn't always get along, maybe we would have continued to butt heads in the days to come, but I will never know. I pushed to come here, to ignore the danger, to keep Cable safe and look what has happened.

I killed them.

"Yes we will." Cable's grip on my arms becomes painful and I tear my gaze away from Victoria's funeral pyre. "I'm not going to die tonight and neither are you."

With every fiber of my being I want to believe him, to have faith in some entity that maybe, just maybe, watches over me. Heck, at this point I'd even settle for dumb luck.

"Do you trust me?" Adrenaline sends a spike of energy through my body as I nod. I've already entrusted him with far more than just my life. "Then come with me."

I follow after him, knowing that I would go to the ends of the earth if he asked me to, simply because he asked, because he would be with me. I know letting myself fall for him is wrong, is setting myself up for loss. Cable is sick and I have no idea how much longer he has, but as I twine my fingers through his and run behind him, I vow to make every second count.

He pulls me to a stop at the far end of the hallway and tucks me behind him. With a flick of his thumb he ignites a lighter and chucks it onto the oil slick. "Run!"

Strong hands yank me from Cable's grasp and I crash into Alex's side. He wraps his good arm around me and pulls me toward the back door that leads to the mechanical shop. The room ignites around us. The floor warms with a searing heat that rises through the soles of my shoes, making each step painful. Covering my mouth with my shirt, I stumble forward with Alex beside me and Cable pushing from behind through the smoke.

A terrible crash comes from the front of the shop. Glass shatters and shouts rise around the crackling roar of the flames. We burst through the door and into the blissful cool of the night. My arms and cheeks feel burned. My eyebrows singed.

Alex releases me and I drop to my knees as a racking cough seizes me. "No...time," Cable chokes beside me. He wraps his arm under mine and hauls me to my feet.

Grabbing my knife from my pocket, he places it in in my palm, his hand trembling as he covers my fingers over it. "Don't think. Just do."

I try to nod, to act tough but inside I'm terrified. I don't want to fight my way out of here, to possibly suffer the same fate as Victoria. The men I saw at that window may have looked crazed but there was also intelligence still lingering in their eyes. That makes them deadly.

Cable grabs a wrench off the top of a tall red tool chest and Alex tightens his grip on a couple of flares. It is dark and cool in shop. The concrete block walls keep most of the destruction out. Flames flicker along the seam that runs at the base of the door. I step away, drawn to the cold rather than the heat.

"They will be waiting for us." I say, turning toward my two final companions. Along the way we collected and lost more people than I want to count. Staring at the men before me, I realize not all of us will make it, not to the end. To a time when maybe someone can create a cure, to reverse this mess. The odds are stacked heavily against us.

Cable reaches out and grabs my hand, squeezing it tight. Alex looks down at our embrace. "It has been an honor knowing you two."

"Cut the sentimental crap." I yank Alex into a half hug. He cries out in pain and I release him, realizing I've just grabbed his bad arm. He presses against his bullet wound but a broad smile chases away the pain.

"Isn't this how they do it in movies? The hero pauses to say a heartfelt thank you before rushing head first into a battle, which he has no earthly chance of winning but somehow lives to have the final word?"

"Yeah." Cable wipes at his face. It drips with sweat. I frown, remembering the fever raging within. "I've got nothing."

"Me either." I glance toward the two metal garage doors. I see movement beyond. Our escape path wasn't exactly a secret after we set the front on fire. "But then again...that's not really our style, is it?"

Alex grins and lifts the flares. "Cover me until I reach that semi then I'll create a diversion and meet you in the woods."

Leaning up onto my toes, I look through the garage door window to where he points. Sitting parked beneath an awning that houses six diesel pumps are three semis. I glance back at the flares in his hands. "You won't make it that far. Not in your condition."

He puffs up his chest. "I know how to hold my liquor well enough."

"I meant your arm." I jerk my head toward the blood staining through the shoulder and chest of his shirt. "You've lost blood."

Cable stares hard at Alex. The two men lock gazes and for a moment I feel forgotten, cast aside. Cable nods and pulls me toward the door. "We'll try to keep them off you."

"What? No. You know he will never make it and even if he does, if he gets one of those flares near that fuel it will blow sky high."

"He knows."

I look up at Cable and see the sorrowful resignation in his gaze. Glancing back at Alex, I see only determination, not fear. "You're both crazy."

"You're darn right," Alex grins, winking at me as he grabs the bottom of the garage door. "On three."

"Three," Cable shouts and throws up the door. I only make it half a dozen steps before Cable shoves me aside. I hear the whizz of a bullet passing far too close to my ear before I hit the ground and slide. My back slams into a stack of tires. They teeter overhead. I wrap my arms around my head and prepare to be pummeled.

"Get up." Cable yanks my arm and drags me out of the way. I kick at the tires as they spiral around me. He points to the dark, away from the mechanic shop, away from Alex. "I want you to run that way and keep going. No matter what you hear."

"No. I'm not leaving you!"

"I'll take care of Alex. Just go!" He shoves me away. My arms flap wildly as my legs begin to slip apart on the ice. My footing is precarious as I attempt to remain upright. A bullet tears through my sleeve, nicking my skin as I fall on my ass. My tailbone screams as I roll to the side and pull myself behind a dumpster. Bullets ricochet off the metal and slam into the concrete wall beside me.

I suck in shallow breaths as I look around me. I can't see Cable or Alex. There is shouting all around. It's impossible to tell who is who. Glancing overhead, I spy a brilliant glow near the roof. It won't be long before this whole place goes up in flames. The scent of burning oil stings my eyes and I'm forced to wipe them several times to clear my vision.

Ducking my head out, I try to get my bearings. The open garage door is about fifteen feet behind me. Just beyond that a long low ledge of concrete stands, its purpose to funnel cars into the bays. I see a shadow of a man leap over and crouch behind that and pray that it is Cable making his way toward Alex. I peer out again, pressing my cheek close to the dumpster. Where is Alex? I never saw him after Cable and I ran out.

Three men approach from beyond the wall. They slide more than step. Their guns are poised. My fingers ache as I grip the edge of the dumpster. I try not to breathe in the foul stench within.

In less than a minute they will converge on Cable's last known spot.

He's a soldier. He's been trained for this sort of combat, I try to remind myself as I back up to follow his last order: to run.

Fingers dig through my tangled curls from behind. I scream as I'm hauled to my feet by my hair and dragged out from behind the dumpster. "Got you."

I kick and fight against the man's grip, tossing my elbows back and wide in an attempt to wound my captor but he remains just out of reach. Blood trickles from my scalp as the fistful of hair begins to release from my scalp. Pain darkens my vision.

His thick soled boots punch through the thin layer of ice as he leads me toward the side of the building where darkness gives way to the flickering of flames. An abandoned car sits with its doors open wide. It has been stripped of parts. The tires are missing. The cloth seats ripped away. The headlights busted out and the bulbs stolen.

"Ain't you a pretty little thing?" The man whispers in my ear, leaning in close as he pushes me toward the car. His free hand winds around my waist and tugs me close to him. He presses his length against my back. "I always did have a thing for red heads."

His breath grows ragged as his hand slides down my hip and dips between my legs as we stop in front of the car. "Seems wrong to waste something so fine."

Pulling me to the side, he keeps a firm grip on my hair as he passes the driver's side door and hauls me toward the trunk. At first I think he's going to shove me inside, but he angles me away and rummages around. I hear metal clanking as he tosses things out of the trunk, items useless to his pursuit. I glance around me, forced to look from the corner of my eye. I can't see anyone. Can't hear anything beyond intermittent gunfire. Are Cable and Alex still alive?

The scent of burning rubber burns in my nose as I try to look back the way I came but the man's grip on my hair is too firm. I cry out as he grabs my arm and yanks it behind me, pinning my hand with his knee. He releases his grasp on my hair and fights to gain control of my other hand. I stretch it out before me, flapping it in an attempt to resist, but he digs his teeth into the meat of my arm and latches onto my hand when I flinch back.

"Good girl," he croons in my ear. Tears burn in my eyes as he binds my hand with what feels like a bit of rope. His fumbling fingers lash the binding.

With a hard shove, he forces me toward the front of the car and presses against my back. I'm forced to bend over the side of the hood. His hips rock against me, his hands holding me in place. His breath is rank as he bites at my ear over my back and I try to turn away.

"I like it when they struggle." He yanks on another clump of hair and I cry out. The muscles in my neck twang as I fight against the pain. "Like it when they scream a little."

Using his hips to keep me in place, wedged against the car, he fumbles with his pants. Terror seizes me as I twist and turn. "Get the hell off of me!"

My head rocks forward and slams into the hood with a blow from behind. My cheek burns as it sticks to the ice coating the hood. I taste blood in my mouth from a split lip.

The man releases my hair and grips my waist with both hands. He tugs at my pants, grunting as they slowly begin to fall. "Stop!"

"Oh, no," he chuckles as his hand slides down my waistband. I clench as rough calloused hands glide over my backside. "There will be no stopping."

"Cable!" I shriek. "Help me!"

A filthy hand covers my mouth. My eyes clamp shut as I feel him press against me. The sound of my heartbeat thrashes in my ears. My legs feel weak, my nostrils flare as terror and rage mingle.

"Don't you fucking touch me!" My shout is muffled by his hand. I try to bite him, to shift or twist out of his grasp, but he has me subdued.

"Hey!" My head rears back at the sound of a voice. My cheek burns as it peels away from the ice. "Whatcha got there?"

"I call dibs. You can have her next, Gentry." He runs his hand down my side, dipping around to pinch my breast. I buck and knock his hand away. "She's a real fighter. You'll like her."

The approaching heavy footfalls sound hollow in my ears against the rushing of my pulse. I can feel the onset of a panic attack nearing as I try to see the second man. His voice is low and gruff. When a second hand, larger than the first, wraps around my hip I thrash.

The man behind me hollers and shouts in approval. "She's a wild thing," he crows as he slaps the side of my hip.

I fall still, terrified of assisting him in his plunder. The new hand tightens on my hip. "Brian will shit bricks if he hears you took her."

"We," the man says with voice slick as oil. "You and me, Gentry. Boss man don't gotta know about it. We can do away with her after. No harm done. Just a bit of sport while they wrap up that mess back there. What do you say?"

The tension in the fingers at my hip increases. Tears spill from my chin, pattering against the hood of the car as the man named Gentry brushes his thumb along the rise of my hip. He's considering it.

"You got two minutes." The hand pulls away and I yank against the rope, knowing that I'm out of time. The fibers eat into my flesh as my captor tries to force my legs apart.

A sudden blaring of a car alarm startles my attacker. I grunt and shove back, thrusting my head. It slams into something solid and I celebrate at the sickening crunch from behind.

"Bitch!" I try to duck the swinging blow but move a hair too slow. His fist grazes off my side and slams into the hood. He hops back, howling. I turn and kick wildly, aiming for anything I can reach.

The man buckles before me. The sound of running reaches me and I know Gentry didn't go far. Probably waiting for his turn.

I wiggle against the car, desperately trying to shove my pants up. About five inches of my skin is still bare when I'm tackled to the ground. I hit the pavement hard. There is no slide this time. Glancing up, I realize the flames have come around the side of the building and are heading straight for us.

"If you don't let me go we're going to die," I rasp. My lungs feel bruised. My entire left side splintering with pain.

"Shut up." A fist slams into my side and I inhale sharply, realizing for the first time how potent the scent of gasoline is. I press my nose to the ground and sniff. The car must have had a gas leak. That's why they left it behind.

"The flames," I try again. "Look at the fire!"

For a second the man does. He falls still overhead and I allow myself a second to hope. "We are lying in a pool of gasoline. I know you can smell it."

He shifts on top of me, glancing around. He tugs at my rope bindings. "When that fire reaches that car we all burn. Am I really worth dying for?"

"Shit, no." He shoves me into the ground and rises. "I'm outta here."

"Gentry!" I turn to see my initial attacker for the first time. A thick beard covers his face, dark and overgrown. It's obvious by the length of it that his beard was already well in place before the world sank into hell. His cheeks are sunken with patches of angry red, flaking rash cover his cheeks.

"You son of a bitch! You're infected!" I hurl myself at him, yanking with all my might against the ropes as I head-butt him in the stomach. The ropes give slightly. I yank again, rearing my head back and slam my forehead down onto his chest.

My vision blurs under the impact and for a second I nearly pass out. The feel of the rope slipping over my hand brings me back. I slam my fist into the man's arms, raised to protect his face. I tremble as I beat against him, the rope dangling from my left hand with each blow.

"Never. Fucking. Touch. Me. Again." An odd numbing sensation falls over me as I land punches, hitting ribs, stomach and the side of his head. Wherever he lowers his defenses. I don't feel the skin over my knuckles split. Don't react when an enormous explosion from behind me rocks the ground and sends a fireball high into the night sky, casting its orange light across the ground.

I stare into the terrified eyes of my attacker and feel something snap. I beat him till I'm panting and drenched with sweat. His pleas fuel my rage. There is no mercy, no pity to be found within me. Only a thirst for revenge that has yet to be quenched.

Smoke hangs thick in the air. I can feel it's scorching heat and know I'm running out of time, but it doesn't matter anymore. All that matters is that I hurt this man.

An unseen blow rocks me backward as the man retaliates. My head spins and I fall to my side. The rough concrete tears at my palms. My fingers land on something cold and I retract them, before falling still. There, lying partially hidden beneath the car is a tire iron.

Without thought I grasp the iron and swing. My captor screams as I hit his raised hand. He curls in on himself as I stagger to my feet. With his feet he pushes away, slowly inching his way up the wall. Flames lick the wooden siding not far from us. The ground less than twenty feet away begins to ignite.

There is terror in the man's eyes as he watches me approach. I grip the tire iron, my hands feeling steady for the first time. "Please," he raises a hand.

Cocking my head to the side, I smile. "I like it when they scream...just a little."

I swing the tire iron with all my might. Blood splatters my face and arms. His screams rise above the crackling flames. His attempts to protect himself diminish. I swing until my shoulders grow weary and the fire nips at my heels.

The tire iron hooks on the remnants of the man's skull. I place my foot on his chest and yank it free. Thick globs of slick matter cling to my skin as I raise my arms overhead for another blow.

Something solid tackles me from the side. I scream as I slam to the ground, bucking wildly. "Shh," Cable soothes, his firm grip stilling my fight. "It's me."

"Cable?" The tire iron slips from my hands. My fingers are sticky as I reach out for his face, unable to comprehend that he is here. That he came for me.

I try to blink away the smoke stinging my eyes. Blood mats my eyelashes together. My stomach heaves as I glance down at my attacker. "Oh god."

"Don't look." Cable shields me but I know the horror that lies at my feet. I did this.

"We have to get out of here." He grunts as he hauls me to my feet. I try to skirt the edge of the flames, but my legs give way beneath me. Cable scoops me into his arms and runs full out toward the overpass. He doesn't slow to duck behind the cars or weave among them. He follows the railing and flees.

Wrapping my arms around his neck, I look behind us. What was once a single fire has become a raging inferno. Flames engulf the last section of the truck stop before we reach the other side. Cable's footing is sure on the newly melted road. The scorching heat races after us as we escape into the woods.

I cling to him as the trembling finally comes. As the realization of what I did sinks in. He carries me deep into the forest but he doesn't stop, doesn't look back. I lay my head on his shoulder and know in my heart that Alex is lost to us forever. Cable would never leave a man behind.

TWENTY-THREE

I shiver at the edge of the cave, my teeth chattering and my fingers clenched into fists in my armpits. A rain has fallen steadily for several days. The bite to the wind has shifted slightly, just enough for me to hope that spring might be on the not too distant horizon. The damp is a welcome change to the ice, though it keeps us trapped. Not that we have anywhere else to be.

Cable says I'm in shock, that it will pass. I don't feel in shock, not like the first time I killed a man. This time was different. Yes, my life was in danger. Yes, he had hurt me, but I could have walked away. Could have left him for the fire to consume, but I didn't.

I wanted to finish that monster off myself.

At Cable's cough, I turn away from the outside world and hurry back to his side. He lies near the back of the small cave we discovered not an hour's hike from the burning truck stop. Too close for comfort, but he couldn't go any farther. He was spent and I welcomed the small shelter.

The dim light escaping through the thick blanket of cloud overhead is not nearly bright enough to allow me to see well, but I don't need to. I can feel the heat pouring from him, hear the moist wheezing in his chest. Cable took a turn for the worse shortly after we arrived in the cave.

For the first two days after Cable brought us here I held on to the delusion that maybe he really did just have the flu. I was sick when he first found me and look at me now. Healthy, albeit a bit worse for wear, but I didn't turn. I survived.

He hasn't slept in nearly three nights. At first I thought he was just wanting to keep a watchful eye in case there were any survivors from the fire. Then I began to realize it was because he couldn't sleep. The light began to hurt his eyes yesterday. Now he spends most of his time curled up into a ball, shivering and moaning from random body aches, his face turned away from the light. I try to talk to him, to give him something to think about, but we both know it's a wasted effort, but we are too stubborn to admit it.

Cable's symptoms progressed fast. Maybe it's because this is the first time he's slowed down long enough to allow it to take him. Maybe he pushed himself too close to the limit. Maybe it is just his time. Either way, as I reach out and grasp his hand in mine, I know that I'm not ready to say goodbye.

He stirs, inching his way onto his side to look at me. I shift to block the light from his eyes. They are more sunken than before. His face is pale. His lips nearly colorless.

"You're freezing." He slowly lifts his hand and presses it to my cheek. I close my eyes at his chilled touch. His fever didn't break overnight. It vanished only to be replaced by an unnatural chill that he can't shake. Natalia experienced the same thing while Eric watched her slip away. I don't know if I can do that.

"I'm fine." I smile down at him with as much sincerity as I can muster.

His eyebrows rise so swiftly that I can't help but laugh. "Ok, I'm not, but you know...I'm trying to be."

"Always the martyr," he whispers. His fingers curl around my cheek. I lean into his touch, knowing soon this will be lost to me.

"That blow to your head must have knocked something loose. You're the fool who always rushes in." I brush my finger along the fading bruise that spans from his hairline down to his chin. Cable says he got that when the blast blew him backward. I can't imagine how he managed to find his feet in time to save me, but he did. Just like he promised.

It hurts to think about Alex, about all of the people we've lost along the way. Laying my hand across his forehead, I can't begin to think of what losing Cable will be like. "How are you feeling?"

Gripping his side, Cable allows me to help him into a seated position. He presses back against the wall, his chest heaving. His cheeks are rosy, his fingertips a matching hue. There is a bit of swelling to his skin, as if he's begun to retain water. Considering we've had little but handfuls of rainwater for the past few days I don't see how that's possible.

He gives me a pointed look and grins. "I'm fine."

Chuckling to myself, I sink down beside him. He slides along the wall toward me and I take the brunt of his weight as he rests his head against mine. We stare out at the darkening day. Though it is not nearly time for the sun to set, the thick layer of rain clouds overhead suck the light from the woods early.

"Are you ever going to tell me about Alex?" I hold my breath, wondering how he will take my question. I've waited for days for him to bring it up, but he hasn't. He swallows hard and reaches down for my hand.

"You might as well know." I tuck my fingers between his as Cable finally begins to spill the details of Alex's final moment. There is pride in his voice as he speaks of Alex's brave attempt to make his way to one of the semis.

"He took several bullets along the way. One to the leg and two to the arm and shoulder. Nearly dropped him right in front of me. I managed to get him hidden in one of the cars left on the side of the shop, probably waiting for an oil change or something completely random and normal."

A ghost of a smile touches his lips as he looks at the ceiling of the cave. "I knew he wasn't going to make it, but he had a good plan. All he had to do was shove a flare into a gas tank of a semi and run like hell. I figured if I was going down I was going to take them with me, so I grabbed the flares and left Alex behind."

"I took down two men before being surrounded They had guns pointed at my chest, back and head. I knew I wasn't going anywhere." His grip tightens against my fingers as he coughs. I hold on to him, waiting for the fit to pass. "Thought that was it until I heard the craziest thing. None of them could figure out where the heck the car horn was coming from."

I grin, imagining Alex beating the horn. "When those guys turned to search for that car, I grabbed the shotgun from the first guy and rammed it straight up under his throat. He went down hard. After that it was easy. They were standing so close together it only took one shot to take them out."

Cable's tale of Alex steering the hotwired car, its backend fishtailing wildly as he rammed into the gas tank, sounds like nothing more than a fable. One a father would try to pass on to his wide-eyed child as a bedtime story of amazing heroics. I never thought of Alex as a hero, but he saved my life. I know that I owe him a lot. We both do.

I turn my head and place a kiss against Cable's chin. "You saved my life, just like you promised."

Staring down at his feet, Cable doesn't react. I wait, waving my hand before his face. He doesn't blink, doesn't speak. Though his chest rises and falls, his face hangs without expression.

"Cable?" I shake him by the arm.

"Yeah." His gaze shifts slowly toward me. "Sorry. I guess I got lost for a moment…"

Lost. Is that what it feels like near the end? Confusion? A wiping of memory? Like a fog settling over your mind that you can't escape?

"It's ok." I feel shaky as I slowly release the breath I'd been holding, sure that I'd lost him completely. That is the first time I've seen him fade. How many more times will come before the end?

"What were you saying?" He rubs his forehead, as if trying to massage the memory back into place.

"It doesn't matter."

We sit in silence as the forest darkens. I listen to the pattering of rain beyond the walls of the cave. I used to like the rain. Now it makes me sad.

Exhaustion tugs at my eyelids. I try to fight back, to remain alert for Cable, but it's a losing battle. Sometime later he shifts beside me and I rouse. A cold damp has settled over our clothes, making my hair and pants feel moist to the touch. I should build a fire but there is nothing dry to use.

"I'm sorry," he whispers beside me.

My hands still as I rub my palms against my jeans to warm them. I turn toward him. His face is lost to the all-consuming shadow of night. "Sorry for what?"

"For cutting out on you early."

"Don't." My throat clenches. "Don't do this, Cable. Not now."

His hands quake as he reaches out for me. Tears slip between my eyes as I feel how cold he has become. I clasp his hands between mine and blow on them.

"You're a tough girl. I've always admired that about you. I know you'll make it."

A moan of despair escapes my lips as I turn toward him, propping my knee against his side. "I don't want to hear your goodbyes. I won't accept them."

The wheezing sounds rise and fall with his chest, a fight for each breath. "Tough."

Tears leak from the corners of my eyes as I cling to him. I don't want to lose him, to be all alone. Haven't I lost enough? Does the world really need to take this good soul from me?

"I knew from the moment I first met you that you were special," he whispers. His head lolls back against the stone. I reach out and press my palm to his cheek, easing the strain off his neck. "I could see the fire in your eyes."

"Most guys hated that about me."

His laughter turns to a cough. He doubles over. I beat on his back as he gasps for breath. Biting my lip doesn't help take away the gaping hole burrowing into my chest. Why him? Why now?

I help press him back against the wall. His shoulders slump. It breaks me to see a man of such strength reduced to this. Anger churns deep within my soul as I think of how many other good people have been stolen away.

"I'm not most guys." He spits to the side and wipes his mouth.

"No." I scoot as close as I can to hold him. "You're better. A thousand times better, Cable."

He leans his head forward, cradling it in the crook of my neck. I wrap my arms around him and clench my eyes as I feel the rattling in his lungs as my hands splay across his back. He is suffering.

I feel him rustling in his jacket and sit up. "Do you need help?"

"No." His arm moves against me. I stare into the dark, cursing it for not being able to see. "Let me have your hand."

I hold it out for him, moving it in the dark until he finds me. Something cold and heavy comes to rest on my palm. My fingers curl around it and I fall still. "A gun?"

"Your gun," he corrects and leans back.

"You're out of ammunition."

"No," he rasps. "I saved one final round."

The weight of his words falls heavily on me. "You could have used that bullet back at the truck stop, could have saved yourself."

"I was saving it..."

I bring the gun up to my chest, holding it close. "Saving it for me?"

Though I can't see his nod, I sense it. "Just in case."

I set the gun aside and push it away. "I don't want it."

Cable reaches out for me, his hand falling on my upper arm. He squeezes but there is little strength left in him. "I know, but I need it now."

"Cable, don't! Please don't do this to me. I can't—"

He tugs on my arm, shushing me. "I know that I promised you that I'd always take care of you. I tried to fight it, to survive for you and I'm sorry. I tried to hold on—"

"Shh," I whisper, pulling him toward me. "It's ok. We'll get through this."

"I'm dying, Avery, but I don't want to be like *them*. Promise me you'll take care of it before the end."

"Oh god." A whimper rises from my throat. My hands shake as I clasp them over my lips. I can't lose him. I just can't.

"There's something else. I need you to know that I've never loved anyone like I—"

I pull back and press my fingers to his lips. I know he can feel how badly they shake as I try to silence him. My shoulders quake as tears fall unheeded. My chest hitches as I begin to sob, sinking into his weakened embrace. He holds me as I cry, slowly petting my hair. He murmurs to me through my hair, pressing his lips against the crown of my head from time to time.

The moon doesn't rise this night. The dark is absolute as I cling to him, desperate for the morning's return so that I can see him again. Everything seems better in the light.

He holds me for hours, sometimes humming as we rock, other times he falls completely still and I'm forced to shake him so hard I'm terrified that I might crack his head against the wall. He always comes back to me, but it's getting harder with each slip.

I ignore the cold, the numbness in my toes and nose. I ignore the growling in my stomach or the dizziness from going too long without a drink. I refuse to leave him, even for a moment.

Finally, the east begins to brighten. "The sun is coming," I whisper.

Cable doesn't move. I bump his arm and he slides sideways across the wall. The sound of his head hitting the stone floor makes me sick. "Cable!"

I crawl to my knees, rushing to pull his head into my lap. I feel for a bump or a cut but feel nothing. Sweat no longer moistens his brow. His forehead is free of worry lines. I trace my fingers down to his lips, feeling for his slow breath.

"Cable," I pat his cheeks, using my free hand to shake his shoulders. "Dammit, Cable don't do this to me! I need you!"

I look up at the sky, willing the sun to rise faster. The curve of his shoes appear first since they lie nearest to the cave entrance. I continue to call out to him as the new day arrives. The clouds have begun to dissipate to the east. Sunlight glistens off the puddles of water all around.

The outline of his legs and hands begins to take shape. I never really stopped to notice how beautiful his hands are, how powerful the muscles that line his legs. His lean torso appears, followed by his chest. I watch as the light slowly creeps up his neck and then reveals his chin.

"Can you feel the warmth?" I ask, wiping tears from my swollen eyes. I use my sleeve to wipe at my nose, snuffing back so that I can breathe. My voice is hoarse, a croaking that sounds foreign in my ears.

I wipe my fallen tears away from his cheeks. "We never did watch a sunrise together. You always complained about me being too lazy and you were right. If only I had gone with you." I hang my head. "Just once."

Stretching my leg out, I take his weight on me, cradling him beneath my chin. "I should have not been so stubborn, admitted you were right about me all along. I should have let you hold my hand or kiss me whenever you wanted to. Held you through the night and never let you go. I should have let you in sooner, when we still had time."

I clench my eyes shut as a burning in my throat chokes off my words. I press my hand to my mouth as I sob, a deep gut wrenching cry of remorse. I taste the salt of my tears as they pool in the corner of my lip. Feel them trail down to my cheek and fall away.

My mother once told me that tears are the window to a soul. That they are only for the things you hold dearest. For once, I think she was right.

I bite back a sob and embrace the pain, for it is the pain that brings truth. No more barriers. No more lies or excuses.

Lowering my gaze, I look down into Cable's unblinking eyes. "I should have told you that I love you. With all my heart, I do, and I waited too long."

Careful not to drop his head, I inch out from beneath him and lay him down on the floor. I use the rock wall to crouch beside him, my shoulders curved to allow for the low ceiling. In the light of the new dawn, I realize that Cable has never looked more handsome, more at peace.

Though his eyes hold no emotion, nothing more than a blank glazed stare, the corners of his lips pinch just enough that his smile is frozen in place.

I kneel beside him and place a hand over his chest. His heart still beats, his lungs still move, but the man I once knew is gone, withered away into nothingness.

"You are a man I could have loved till the end of my days. I didn't deserve you, but you still wanted me." Leaning down, my hair brushes against his face as I press my lips to his, one last time.

My fingers curl around my pistol at his side. As I lean back, I draw the gun to my chest. I press it to his forehead, pausing just long enough to burn the memory of him into my memory and realize the truth that I've fought for so long. "One night with you will never be enough," I whisper and close my eyes.

Bang.

THE END

EPILOGUE

I stare at the sunrise with a longing gaze with my shoulders slumped and my posture limp against the tree. I ignore the rain that falls from above, trailing down my collar and soaking through all three of my layers. The warmer day encouraged me to shed one layer. Soon, I will be able remove more.

The landscape remains the same. Barren. Vast. Trees as far as I can see spread out before me. A road winds through those trees, like a snake slithering along the hilly earth. I have followed its path for many days. Embraced the loneliness of the nights.

I have not spoken in nearly three weeks since emerging from the cave. My hair falls unkempt about my face. Dirt tracks wash clean from my cheek as I turn my face to the rain.

Depression, the darkest I have ever felt, took me those first few weeks. I ate only when my body refused to let me walk any further. Slept when I was forced to. I gathered supplies when the skies withheld rain. Gathered ammunition and weapons for survival.

The trees were my friends, resolute and silent, though it felt as if they still managed to accuse me. At times I feel as if Cable is still with me, keeping his promise to watch over me. I hear his voice on the wind. Feel his palm against my cheek in those few seconds just before I wake. I know it is not real, but even in those briefest of moments I feel alive again.

The clouds before me are broken. Shafts of light penetrate the dark rain clouds. Wide swatches of land are illuminated, basking in radiant light. The ache in my chest has not lessened, but as I stare at the light a soft smile tugs at my lips. Cable would not want me to linger. He would tell me to get up. To fight. To be the strong women he always knew me to be.

I buried him in that cave, piled rocks high enough to seal him into a forever tomb. I couldn't bear the thought of animals getting to him. It was the best I could do.

I have watched the sunrise each morning for him. These moments I treasure. Never again will I oversleep, let creature comforts steal away the moments most precious to me. With each rise of the sun I'm reminded of just how valuable life truly is.

Turning away from the sunrise, I stare at the land before me. From this vantage point I see for miles. A veil of rain falls to the north in thick sheets. A rainbow blooms just to the south. Below me the ground is a blur of movement. Countless Withered Ones shuffle along, each one rocking in step with those surrounding them.

For a while I envied them, their lack of emotion, or ability to feel pain. Losing Cable nearly destroyed me...nearly.

I adjust the pack on my back and lean forward, pressing tightly against the tree limb as I lean over. Cable's knife presses against my thigh as I stare at the highway looming below. I keep parallel to it, watching the road signs to make sure I'm heading in the right direction. The Withered Ones move steadily south. There is no rhyme or reason to this destination that I can detect. Only single minded determination.

I must adopt that same determination if I am to make it to my own destination.

During the final hours while I held Cable that last night, he spoke of his family. Of his half-brother Lenny and his mother Teresa. Of how after Lenny's mother died, Teresa showed great compassion and took the boy into her care and raised her as her own. The sins of the father did not matter to her. A boy in need did. I wish I could have met Cable's mother, met the woman who raised such an amazing man.

The last time Cable spoke with his brother he discovered that his mother had been lost, but Cable said Lenny was a smart one. He would survive.

I owe it to Cable to try to find him. A small suburb of Nashville, Tennessee was his last known location. By best guess it would be a three or four hour drive if I managed to find a car, and a passable road to use. It would take me a month or so by foot, depending on if I got into any trouble along the way.

Trouble is exactly what I'm afraid lies between me and Nashville.

Narrowing my gaze, I chamber a round and aim my gun into the air. It is time to see if my suspicions are correct. The sounds of raspy moans and shuffling feet fills my ears as the last droplets of rain patter down on my face. I close my eyes and listen. For as long as I live I will never get used to their sound, to the potent scent that clings to their bodies. They will haunt my dreams till my final breath.

I slowly open my eyes, staring one last time at the sun before I pull the trigger. The shot ricochets through the air, echoing off the concrete embankment that rises on either side of the highway, leading to the overpass less than a quarter of a mile ahead. Birds take flight, escaping the trees around me.

The tide of rotting and tattered Withered Ones come to a complete, unified halt. Their faces tilt upward toward the sky. Silence reigns as they pause to search for the source of the sound.

Numbness settles over me as I lower my shotgun and look to the road ahead. Thousands of Moaners stand motionless for the first time ever. I fight against the sense of hopelessness and despair, knowing the path before me will be dangerous. Gangs, desperate survivors, and the lack of food were bad enough. This will be far worse.

The Withered Ones are evolving.

The Withered Ones were never a threat before…but they are evolving.

In 2015 a new enemy rises…

RESURRECT
BOOK II
THE WITHERED SERIES

3-15

DISCARD

CPSIA information can be obtained at www.ICGtesting.com
Printed in the USA
LVOW01s1444280115

424737LV00017B/1049/P

9 781502 915757